CREATED BY JULIE PLEC
based on the Vampire Diaries

the ORIGINALS

The Loss

Hodder
Children's
Books

A division of Hachette Children's Books

A Catalogue record for this book is available from the British Library

ISBN 978 1 444 92514 2

Typeset in Bembo by Avon DataSet Ltd, Bidford-on-Avon, Warwickshire

Printed and bound by Clays Ltd, St Ives plc

10 9 8 7 6 5 4 3 2 1

The paper and board used in this book are made from wood
from responsible sources.

Hodder Children's Books
an imprint of Hachette Children's Group
Carmelite House, 50 Victoria Embankment
London, EC4Y 0DZ
An Hachette UK company

www.hachette.co.uk

Dear Reader

So glad you've returned for the next instalment of Mikaelson drama. While you can tune in to see the present-day Klaus, Elijah and Rebekah, our beloved Original Vampire family, their past has about 1,000 years' worth of stories to share. You can unearth these tales, courtesy of Hodder Children's Books, in association with Alloy Entertainment, in their new trilogy of books that features part of the vast history of the Originals.

In the first book, you watched as each of the Mikaelson trio struggled with their vampire natures and their complicated heightened emotions in order to seek out love. In this book, you'll find the Mikaelsons forty years after they landed in New Orleans. They've banished the witches and werewolves, and made the city their perfect home – yet, of course, Klaus still isn't satisfied. He's lost the love of his life and he wants her back at any cost. But when a resurrection spell brings more chaos and horror than the siblings ever imagined, Rebekah and Elijah are forced to fight a never-before-seen evil.

In *The Originals: The Rise*, *The Loss* and *The Resurrection*, you'll get to see sides of the Mikaelson vampires you never knew existed. Turn the page for a book that has all the romance, murder and mayhem of the TV show, and a story that will keep you thirsting for more.

With best wishes,
Julie Plec
Creator and Executive Producer of *The Originals*

PROLOGUE

1766

*L*ily Leroux had promised herself that she wouldn't cry. Her mother would never have forgiven her for crying. Lily's job was to look strong and poised in her fitted black dress, to accept the community's condolences without seeming to need them. She was in charge of New Orleans's witches now, or whatever was left of them. She had to lead them, not lean on them.

They could certainly use some guidance. Lily's mother had done her best to hold the witches together after their hurricane had razed the city to its foundations more than forty years ago, but the loss had been catastrophic. And the guilt of having caused so much destruction . . . the guilt was even more devastating.

In the meantime, other players had stepped into the

void of power left behind by the witches. The French had recently handed New Orleans over to the Spanish, who had chosen to wholly ignore their new territory. Instead, it was the vampires who had taken the reins.

The Mikaelsons – the Originals, three of the very first vampires in existence – had made their move at an ideal time. Elijah, Rebekah and, worst of all, Klaus now ruled the city. The witches hated them with a passion, although Lily suspected that her mother nursed an odd soft spot for them. She always shut down any talk of retaliation by reminding them that the witches' own hands were responsible for their current misery. If they hadn't tried to seek reckless revenge against the werewolves for betraying their truce, they wouldn't be sequestered in the backwaters of the bayou.

But Ysabelle Dalliencourt's blind love for the vampires meant that her funeral was a sorry shadow of what Lily thought her mother deserved. Ysabelle had led her people out of the ruined city and kept their community together; she had counselled them against a destructive path of war and taught them to focus on themselves and their craft rather than on the walking abominations that sat on their former throne.

Everyone stood, and Lily rose numbly with them. Six witches lifted her mother's wooden casket on their shoulders, and she heard Marguerite sob as they carried it past. Lily rested a comforting hand on her daughter's thin shoulder, and fought the burning behind her eyes.

Her mother should have been enshrined in the heart of New Orleans, not in the little shack the witches had built in the midst of a swamp. The Original vampires were responsible for this slight, Lily knew. They could have forgiven the witches' weakness, as the witches had once looked past the brutality of the vampires. Instead, the Mikaelsons had tasted freedom and run with it, creating an army of new vampires from the humans of New Orleans and driving the witches out.

But Lily would not let a single tear escape. If she cried, it meant that the vampires had won – broken her strong spirit. Instead, Lily forced herself to see Ysabelle's passing as a sign. It was time for a new era, a changing of the guard. Lily was sick to death of subsisting under the vampires' tyranny. The Mikaelsons needed to answer for their sins, and Lily Leroux intended to make sure they paid in full.

ONE

*I*t was Klaus's kind of night. Wine and blood flowed freely, and the relaxed company and summer heat had led to an easy loosening of everyone's clothing. He could only guess what was going on upstairs, but he would leave it to his imagination for now.

There would be time enough to take it all in. That was one of the nice things about being both a king and an immortal: he could do whatever he wanted, whenever he wanted. Elijah took care of the running of the city, Rebekah took care of the running of the Mikaelsons, and Klaus was free to take care of Klaus.

Carousing vampires filled every room on the ground floor, and Klaus could hear the party continuing through the ceiling above. In the forty-odd years since they had taken possession of a dying gunrunner's modest home, the Original vampires had done a great deal of adding on and improving, but even so it was filled to capacity. To effectively rule over a city full of eager young vampires, the Mikaelsons might need to move to a larger home, but finding more land wouldn't be the problem it once had been for them. New property was easy to come by in a metropolis empty of werewolves and witches.

Most of the werewolves who managed to survive the hurricane and explosion of 1722 had drifted away, and the ones who remained kept their noses down. The witches had fared a bit better, but not much: they squatted out in the bayou, their taste for power broken. New Orleans was essentially free of vermin.

Decades after Vivianne's death, it still made Klaus's gut twist to think of what the witches and werewolves had done to her. The way the witches had offered her hand in marriage to the werewolves, as if her only value lay in her heritage as the child of both clans. After signing her life away in a peace treaty, the werewolves had demanded more of her mind and heart at every turn. She had died too young, still trying to make everything right between the factions.

He pushed those thoughts away and finished his whisky. He had been drinking liberally, trying his best to truly join in the revelry around him. Yet forty-four years later and he still expected Vivianne to walk through the door and make him whole again.

'You're so quiet tonight, Niklaus. Should I get you another drink?' A buxom young vampire fell into Klaus's lap with a giggle and interrupted the dark turn of his thoughts. Her long strawberry-blonde hair smelled like orange blossoms. *Lisette*, he reminded himself. She was part of the newest crop of recruits to their little army, but she carried herself with the ease of a vampire who had lived for centuries. She did not seem intimidated by the Originals, nor did she strain herself to impress them, and Klaus found that indifference mildly offensive.

He blew strands of her long hair away from his face. 'Would you like to still recognise yourself by the end of the night?' he asked her, an edge of danger in his voice.

'You underestimate me. I am deep and mysterious,' Lisette told him, with a mock seriousness in her wide-set grey eyes. 'Come upstairs with me, and I'll prove it to you.'

Klaus brushed her reddish hair aside and kissed her neck lingeringly. She sighed and turned a little, giving his mouth better access. 'Not tonight, love,' he murmured, travelling down to her collarbone. However grating Lisette's disingenuousness might be, he had to admit that she had a beautiful neck.

Across the room, another pair of vampires moved

together in a similar way. Watching them, Klaus continued to brush Lisette's lightly freckled skin with his lips, but it only made him feel hollow. He could go through the motions, but he couldn't be consumed by them. No matter how far he wandered down the path of debauchery, he couldn't quite get lost.

He wanted Vivianne back. That was the simple, scalding truth of the matter. He had tried to bury her and tried to mourn and tried to move on, because he knew that was how death was supposed to work. He had seen it countless times, even though no one would ever be forced to mourn the loss of *him*. His mother had been a witch, his true father had been a werewolf, and to save him from death, his mother had made him a vampire. Klaus would never die.

It was useless to compare himself to other people. Niklaus Mikaelson was never going to accept the workings of normal, mortal death. It was stupid and beneath him. If he wanted Vivianne Lescheres at his side, ruling New Orleans as his queen for eternity, why should that be an impossible demand?

Lisette shifted again, rather enjoyably, trying to bring his full attention back to her. It was no use, though. '*Ma petite* Lisette, you do not want to tangle with me tonight,' he said, sliding her back onto her feet.

'As you wish,' she said before sauntering off, glancing

over her shoulder to make sure Klaus was watching her go. He was, of course – it was a simple courtesy after rejecting her advances. And the back of her was just as easy on the eyes as the front.

He eased himself up out of his chair and slipped off in the opposite direction. A few voices called after him as he moved through the dimly lit rooms, which were full of sharp teeth, ringing laughter and sensuous limbs. He ignored them, having finally realised where he wanted to spend this night.

He climbed the ornate spiral staircase, lined with a red silk carpet that Rebekah had ordered from the Far East. As he passed by several bedrooms, he heard his name called again, but this time in softer, throatier voices. He resisted the impulse to look through the doors that had been carelessly – or deliberately – left open, making instead for a small staircase at the back of the house.

Klaus had asked his siblings to keep it private, and so Rebekah had picked a medieval tapestry to conceal the doorframe: a unicorn, with its gold-threaded mane laid gently in the lap of a lovely maiden. Rebekah had the strangest notions sometimes. He glanced behind him and then swept the curtain aside, retreating from his guests and their revelry to the safety of his attic sanctuary.

This was the one place his sister's restless hands had not touched. The attic was much larger than when they'd inherited the house, but it'd retained its original rustic look. Unpolished beams crisscrossed the high, gabled roof, and the rough floorboards creaked charmingly beneath his feet. There were a few windows set into the peaks of the gables, and during the day sunlight streamed in from all directions.

Klaus moved his easel with the sun, watching his paintings change over the course of each day. He'd sometimes climb up here at night and light a few candles, stepping back from the easel to take in the effect of all his canvases at once. He had been working feverishly and couldn't remember ever being so productive.

It was a waste, though, because every last painting was of *her*. Vivianne's left eye, black in a pale sea of skin. The outline of Vivianne running through a cobblestoned street in the middle of the night. Vivianne in his bed the first night, the last night, every night.

It wasn't work; it was torture. He could never paint anything else. Even when he started a different subject, it never failed to transform into another aspect of Vivianne.

His current painting was of her hair: as black and sleek as a raven's wings, but with a life and movement that Klaus struggled to capture. In the light of his candle, it looked flat and wrong, an entire story he was somehow failing to tell. He picked up a brush and began to work, adding texture and light in some places, while leaving others as dark as gravity.

The wailing sound of the house's protection spell went off again, as it had been all night long. Everyone else was too busy with their party to pay attention to it, but Klaus stopped, brush halfway to canvas, at the sight of a witch at the east window. She sat on the outer lintel, poised as if she were resting on a park bench.

Klaus knew her at once. No matter what Ysabelle Dalliencourt's old spell assumed, this was not exactly an unexpected intruder on their land. He could see traces of her mother's face in Lily's, in the strong, straight nose and the long planes of her cheeks. Her hair was darker, more of a russet than auburn, but her eyes were the same fathomless brown.

He crossed the room quickly, wishing that he could cover all of his canvases as he went. Vivianne and Lily might have been cousins, but Lily had no right to see her image the way Klaus portrayed it. No matter her relation, Lily was one of *them*, a descendant of the cowards and weaklings who had let Viv slip away.

He opened the window and invited her inside nonetheless. Lily was also the first witch in over forty years to respond to Klaus's overtures, and he couldn't afford to slight her.

To raise the dead was difficult, but it was more than

just that. It required dark and frightening magic that few would dare to even attempt. For decades Klaus had let it be known – quietly, without involving his siblings in something that was really none of their concern – that the price of readmission to New Orleans was Vivianne. The witches badly wanted their home back, but none had broken rank to try their hand. Ysabelle had much to do with that, he knew, but now she was dead, and her daughter had come to bargain.

'I can grant you what you desire,' Lily Leroux told him with no preamble. 'But it will cost you. One item for the spell, and another for my daughter.'

'As I have said—' Klaus began, but she waved the words off impatiently.

'I know what you are willing to offer,' she reminded him. 'Now listen to what I *want*.'

Klaus was never eager to be on the wrong side of a bargain, but if it meant that Vivianne would be returned to him, he would listen to anything the witch had to say.

TWO

*R*ebekah had to admit that Klaus knew how to throw a party. She and her two siblings had lived in relative solitude for so long that now it was as if she could never get enough of new company, and Klaus always seemed ready to provide her with plenty of friends. Lithe young vampires filled the mansion, dancing, singing, drinking and casting alluring glances at one another . . . and at her. Always at her. She was more than a celebrity among them; she was practically a goddess.

After a few glasses of champagne, Rebekah found that being worshipped suited her just fine. There were a few – well, more than a few – young male vampires who made a sport of competing for her attention, and she encouraged them shamelessly. There was a Robert and a

Rodger she constantly mixed up, and Efrain, who had extraordinary blue eyes but got tongue-tied at the mere sight of her. Tonight was about celebrating, and tomorrow night would probably be the same.

Robert (she was almost sure) refilled her glass before it was empty, and she smiled languidly at him. They were like sweet, admiring puppies, sitting at her feet and lapping up every scrap of her attention. It was impossible to take any of them seriously, but perhaps something not-so-serious was exactly what she needed.

She had been in love, and she knew how that ended. But she would live for a very long time, and it was not realistic to spend the rest of eternity running away from every sort of connection. A good fling was a fun distraction . . . and then perhaps another one after that.

A cheerful-looking vampire with reddish-gold hair strolled into the parlour where Rebekah held court, and she noticed Klaus leaving the drawing room in the opposite direction. *Sulking again*, she guessed. He was as magnetic as ever, drawing in humans and vampires alike. They flocked to the house at his suggestion, and then he hid from them like a hermit. He was going up to that draughty attic again, she just knew it.

'I'm sorry for my brother's rudeness,' she told the female vampire impulsively.

The girl's grey eyes widened in momentary surprise,

as if it'd never occurred to her to be offended by Klaus's abrupt moods. Rebekah felt foolish for having even mentioned it, but then the vampire smiled easily. Her teeth were white and even, like a good string of pearls. 'No need,' she assured Rebekah, as casually as if they were equals. 'He is who he is.'

'Wise words,' Rebekah agreed, draining her champagne and then staring pointedly at Rodger. He hurried away to find a new bottle. 'Klaus doesn't have it in him to think of others.'

The only thing to which Klaus had really applied himself over the past forty-odd years was driving Rebekah and Elijah crazy. He had won ownership of that tawdry brothel he so enjoyed in a card game and promptly lost it again. The Southern Spot had spent all of a week under the new sign reading The Slap and The Tickle before its old one had been restored. Still, Klaus spent inordinate amounts of time there, drinking and whoring as if he still were needed on hand to run the place. He had only stumbled out in the mornings to interrupt the French army's battles and feed at his pleasure, forcing Rebekah to use her powers of compulsion again and again. He delighted in tormenting the French governors until they were driven out of town, almost ruining the Originals' claim to their land when the French had signed the colony over to the Spanish after the war.

The redheaded girl sat down without waiting for an invitation. Rebekah raised an eyebrow, but she was amused, and the bold young thing didn't seem the slightest bit intimidated by her expression. 'I wouldn't expect him to think of anyone but himself,' the girl agreed easily. 'I was just trying to help him out of his mood.'

'And why would he be any less moody for you than for the rest of us? I don't even know you,' Rebekah reminded her. She was sure she had seen the girl around before, but had probably been paying too much attention to Robert/Rodger to notice. In any case, attending a few parties hardly made her a part of the Mikaelsons' inner circle.

'Oh! I'm Lisette,' the vampire chirped, extending her hand as an afterthought. She offered no other explanation or defence for her presumption, and it seemed like she was totally unaware of it. The Original mystique seemed to slide right off Lisette. After the fawning attention of Rebekah's admirers, it was like the shock of diving into a cool pool of water.

Rebekah hesitated for the briefest moment before shaking Lisette's outstretched hand. Part of her wanted to shake some appropriate reverence into the girl . . . but the rest of her actually enjoyed the novelty. A fling would be great, but a friend . . . How long had it been since

Rebekah had had a real friend? Her nature, her position and her family made it virtually impossible to make girlfriends, much less keep them. Rebekah Mikaelson was dangerous, intimidating, immortal and guarded. But Lisette didn't seem to care.

'So tell me about yourself, Lisette,' she commanded, then bit her tongue and softened her tone. 'Please?'

'Oh, me? There's really nothing to tell.' Lisette giggled, but that didn't prevent her from immediately producing a few chatty details about the other partygoers.

She went on, and Rebekah basked in the normality of it. They might have been of an age: young women navigating society together. She listened raptly, asking questions whenever Lisette needed prompting, and Lisette obliged with an astonishing wealth of information about nearly all of the Mikaelsons' guests. Most of Rebekah's pets gave up and drifted away after a while, and even shy, smitten Efrain looked around as if he might prefer to be elsewhere.

But Rebekah didn't care. Admiration was easy enough to come by these days, but Lisette was a rarer kind of pleasure. They were still talking when a commotion broke out near the sweeping main staircase, and Rebekah reluctantly decided she needed to investigate. She had put far too much work into making this house comfortable to let it go to ruin, no matter how much fun everyone was having.

When she reached the front hall, though, she realised that the newest vampires weren't the problem. Klaus had returned from his sulk, and seemed determined to spread his misery around. A few nervous-looking vampires, in various states of undress, huddled together on the staircase, cowering as Klaus pushed past them. 'If I find you've touched anything in those rooms I will slice you open from throat to ankles looking for it,' he threatened the nearest one, who could only tremble in reply.

Had something gone missing? Something of Klaus's? Whatever it was, it must be important enough that he would search for it in the middle of a party. She could not imagine what would provoke him to act so bizarrely, except that maybe he'd simply gone too long without making a scene, and couldn't help himself.

'My dear sister!' he greeted her, his voice a mockery of brotherly warmth. Then a thought seemed to occur to him. '*You* probably have it,' he told her cryptically, and climbed back up the staircase.

'I – Do you think you're going to *my* room?' Rebekah shrieked, running after him. 'Niklaus, what the hell has got into you tonight?' Skipping the party to brood in his attic sounded like a brilliant plan in comparison to this.

He didn't answer her. Instead, he threw open the door to her room and began tearing through her things. *Her* things; he couldn't even leave this one, tiny corner of the house alone.

She grabbed his arm, but he shook her hand off and upended a jewellery box onto her dressing table. Pearls and topazes spilled everywhere, and soft gold gleamed against the painted wood. 'It's nothing,' he muttered, not even bothering to lie convincingly. 'There's just a trinket I've lost, and it might have wound up here.'

He opened another box, rifling through it carelessly, dropping a ruby earring onto the carpet without even noticing. A silver chain snapped under his careless fingers, one that Eric Moquet had given Rebekah when they had both believed they could have a life together.

'Get *out*!' Rebekah cried, shoving Klaus with all of her strength. His body flew backward, crashing into the door with a satisfying splintering. 'Whatever it is, you won't find it here.'

Klaus jumped back to his feet and moved on to the next room. Within seconds, Rebekah heard another crash from down the hall. If she didn't go after her brother, she realised, the damage would escalate quickly. He hadn't even bothered to throw out the occupants of the room this time. Rebekah found him hurling clothing out of a closet while two vampires watched him from the bed, an embroidered bedspread pulled up to their chins as if the thin silk would protect them from a lunatic vampire. 'Stop this madness,' she ordered.

He waved her away dismissively and walked out to the top of the stairs, shouting that it was time for all of their guests to leave. Why was it up to Klaus to decide that the party was over? He had a special talent for ruining beautiful things.

Rebekah reached the bottom of the stairs just in time to see him disappearing into Elijah's study. She felt sure Elijah would thank her for keeping him out, and so she gritted her teeth and pushed through the crowd.

Klaus had already forced open a drawer of Elijah's desk, and Rebekah gasped. Elijah hadn't appeared yet, but the moment her brother saw what Klaus was doing, the house would not be big enough to hold the three of them.

'Don't touch that,' she shouted, throwing her weight against the drawer to slam it closed. Klaus shoved her aside and broke open the lock on another drawer. Rebekah pushed him back, and he tripped over one of the large candelabras that Elijah had along the walls. It swayed dangerously towards the window beside it, and Rebekah had just enough time to see a curl of smoke rise up from the fabric before Klaus sprang towards her.

The force of his attack knocked them both back out

into the front hall, snarling and biting. Vampires scattered, and somewhere nearby Rebekah heard the sound of breaking glass. Tangy smoke drifted out of the open door of the study, and she guessed that the curtains had caught fire. Klaus destroyed *everything*.

She couldn't live like this any more, not with Klaus the terror. He didn't appreciate anything she or Elijah did for him. He was so self-centred that he couldn't imagine that his siblings might prefer to *not* spend their lives either cleaning up his current disaster or trying to predict his next one.

As she gasped for breath in Klaus's armlock, Rebekah made up her mind: she'd find a way to destroy whatever was left of Klaus's happiness just the way he always managed to ruin hers.

THREE

*E*lijah ran an idle finger up and down Ava's bare arm, feeling perfectly at peace. Such tranquillity had not been easy, and the cost had been high, but he had persevered. He'd kept his siblings together and overcome every obstacle this city had thrown their way, and now it was time to reap the rewards.

The French had lost their grip on the region, and now Spain had seized power and established its own rule over New Orleans. But it quickly became clear that actually running the city was of no interest to King Carlos III, and the Spanish governor he'd sent over didn't find the task especially appealing, either. The French colonists were disgusted by the regime change, and Elijah had always viewed human unrest as an opportunity.

As a result of his savvy and foresight, everything of consequence in New Orleans now had to go through him. Trade, construction, legal matters . . . Elijah Mikaelson was the city's beating heart. And once he realised that the witches could no longer enforce their ban on siring new vampires, Elijah had taken particular delight in creating a new community. His family was the central core of his world, but there were benefits to building a society as well. He had everything he had wanted, and now he had Ava, who seemed determined to come up with all sorts of new things for him to desire.

She stretched across the four-poster bed, and dappled light from the fireplace painted curious patterns on her skin. Just as he reached for her again, he heard a crash and a scream coming from downstairs. He waited for a moment, hoping that it would fade back into the predictable sounds of a party, but the commotion only seemed to grow louder.

'It can't be such a disaster that you have to leave? I can barely hear a thing,' Ava protested as he rose from the bed, and the glint in her catlike eyes was almost enough to make him ignore the trouble.

'As much as I would like to keep taking in the sight of you, it seems as if my attention is required elsewhere,' Elijah said with one last quick kiss as he slid back into his discarded clothing. He had not risen to power by ignoring warning signs.

In the hallway, he could pick out both of his siblings' voices in the din. There was also a distinct crackling sound beneath everything else, and Elijah could smell smoke. Elijah resigned himself to dealing with whatever was happening below and abandoning Ava for the night.

His willingness to get involved in this kind of mess was precisely why he was in charge and the Spanish weren't, but sometimes it infuriated him to have to be the responsible one. He stormed down the curved staircase, the stench of smoke burning in his nostrils. It was coming from his study.

Elijah froze for an instant in the doorway, taking in the disaster. He had often used his study as a refuge away from his siblings' endless conflicts, but more than that he had made it into a tremendous resource in times of trouble. The Originals didn't possess magic the way their mother had, but they *were* magic. Their entire existence was framed by it, and their lives were dependent on it. Elijah had curated an impressive library of books and manuscripts on the subject, in addition to all of the ordinary paperwork his prominence in New Orleans required. Watching it all burn was an unexpected blow to his stomach, and Elijah doubled over to take in a deep breath of smoky air, his nails digging into his fists.

In addition to the curtains, two wooden bookcases on either side had gone up in flames, and many of the items looked unsalvageable. But the charred walls and books were not the only damage. His desk – a heavy piece of chestnut – stood askew, and some of the drawers that he knew had been locked were ajar. The fire had not simply been an unlucky accident; someone had been in this room, going through his things.

And Elijah could guess who that someone was. Rebekah may have provoked him – she couldn't always help herself – but the destruction in his study was Klaus's work. There was no one else in the world with such a talent for inconvenient chaos.

Even with Elijah's unnatural speed and strength, it took him a few minutes to put out the fire. In the main room, Rebekah and Klaus were locked in a pointlessly vicious struggle. Neither of them had a silver dagger or, thankfully, a white oak stake, the only two weapons that could take down an Original vampire. All they could accomplish was annoying each other and making fools of themselves. Their wounds would heal, but the embarrassment would linger.

Elijah grabbed Klaus by the collar and threw him backward, then stepped forward to rest his foot against Rebekah's chest. He heard Klaus struggling to stand, and held out a warning hand. 'Enough,' he said, his voice low. 'The two of you were content to let the house burn around you. Over what?'

They both began to argue at once, and he held his hand up again to silence them. Then, reluctantly, he pointed to Klaus. He would rather hear Rebekah's version of events first, as it was almost certainly the more accurate one. But Klaus would never sit by and let her tell it. Giving him this small concession would help re-establish peace.

'Our sister is out of control,' Klaus spat contemptuously as he stood up and flicked the dust from his coat. 'I asked for her help in finding a simple trinket, and she followed me around the house, attacking me like some kind of madwoman.'

To Elijah's shock, Klaus stormed from the room without waiting to hear another word, scattering the remaining guests as he went.

'He's lost his mind,' Rebekah argued, shoving Elijah's unresisting foot away and sitting up. 'I don't know what he's up to, but this thing he wants is no mere trinket. He wants it too badly.'

There was no doubting that she was right. Elijah couldn't imagine what Klaus was looking for, or why it had suddenly gripped his brother that he *must* have it right now, in the middle of the night. Klaus should have been enjoying the party, not tearing the house apart.

Something had set him off, and Elijah reluctantly guessed that he would need to get to the bottom of this.

Together, they followed the telltale sounds of Klaus's renewed search to Elijah's bedroom. A quick glance told Elijah that Ava had left. He felt a quick pang of frustration – Klaus's selfishness never stopped intruding on everyone else's lives.

'You're not welcome in this room, brother,' Elijah warned him, his voice cold and menacing. 'Whatever this trinket is to you, you are still a member of this family, and this sort of behaviour is unacceptable.'

He thought he heard Klaus chuckle under his breath as he opened Elijah's wardrobe and began hunting. Elijah understood why Rebekah had lost her patience and attacked him – there seemed to be no other way to get through to him in this state.

'If we knew what he wanted . . .' Rebekah whispered, her blue eyes flicking sideways to meet his own. She was right. If they could find it first, they would have some leverage to make Klaus . . . what, though? Apologise? Explain? Think? None of that was likely.

But where to even start? The house was full of powerful objects that they'd collected over the centuries, and Klaus could be after any of them. Their mother had been one of the most powerful witches in history, and they were the oldest and strongest vampires in existence.

Useful, pretty and priceless 'trinkets' were so common in their house that they never would have missed one if they had not caught Klaus searching for it.

'Tell us what you want, brother,' Elijah ordered.

To his surprise, Klaus emerged from the wardrobe, looking almost reasonable. 'I want to be left alone, *brother*,' he retorted sarcastically. His voice was light, but his blue-green eyes blazed with a passion that Elijah thought bordered on madness. Perhaps Rebekah was right: maybe their brother really was losing his wits. He had not been the same since that terrible night Vivianne Lescheres had died, but it wasn't as if they all hadn't experienced a loss during their long lives.

'You don't have the *right* to be left alone,' Elijah said. 'I have put everything into building this haven for you – for both of you.' He saw Rebekah flinch, but he didn't care. 'I have spent decades building a kingdom for us, and all you have to do is sit back and enjoy. Instead, you spend your time on this nonsense. You let our house burn while you think only of what *you* want. The same will happen with this entire city if you aren't careful.'

Klaus simply walked away. He didn't respond or complain or argue, just sauntered past them as if he had not heard a single word.

Something had shifted within his brother. They heard a door slam downstairs, then Elijah felt the hair stand up on his arms. He could hear the sound of Klaus whistling. Cheerfully.

'Good riddance,' Rebekah muttered, once the sound had faded into silence. But Elijah knew that this wasn't the last they'd hear of this. Klaus was up to no good, and whatever his plan, he was just getting started.

FOUR

*K*laus tangled his fingers through the pendant's chain. Set in silver, the large opal had belonged to his mother and held a powerful enchantment in its fire-streaked depths. He suspected that Lily knew some secret about the stone that she had kept from him, but Klaus was just thankful that someone had finally taken him up on his offer.

Long accustomed to making his own luck, Klaus had spied on every witch in New Orleans. He had sought out the renegades and rule breakers, offering ever more elaborate bribes and threats in his desperation to get Vivianne back, as his mother's curse forbade him from doing magic himself.

Eventually, his schemes had grown less frequent and

more desperate, brief flares of defiance against impossible odds. Vivianne was waiting for him on the Other Side, and he was failing her. In spite of all his power, he couldn't secure the cooperation of a single witch . . . until now. And so whatever Lily wanted, however outrageous her demands, to Klaus they were more than fair.

He knew that his siblings would not feel the same way. Elijah, in particular, would never have agreed to this sort of bargain. Rebekah had a soft spot for true love and might yield eventually, but she wouldn't have kept Klaus's secret from Elijah. They would have smashed the stone before they would let him give it to a witch.

The moment he had found the opal in the back of Elijah's wardrobe, he had resolved to say nothing to his siblings. He refused to be stopped when he was so close to getting her back.

He needed her.

Death didn't have to mean forever. Not to a vampire, and especially not to an Original. If he'd had time to give her a single drop of his blood before she'd died that night, it would have been enough. She'd have awoken the next night as a vampire with an endless second chance at life. Unfortunately, Vivianne had been killed instantly by a blast of gunpowder exploding beneath her feet, as had most of the werewolves in New Orleans.

Warm rain began to splatter against his face, and the thickness in the summer air broke as he reached the witches' cemetery. He remembered another storm all too vividly. The thunder rolling in, the werewolves surrounding the house, and Vivianne, hopeful to the last that she could somehow make everything right. She had been beautiful that night. He needed to tell her that.

The cemetery was dark. Clouds covered the moon, and the steady rain had extinguished any candles meant to light the way for the dead. Once upon a time, every space between the tombs and the trailing vines had been filled with candles, incense, flowers and charms, but after the witches moved to the bayou, it had fallen into neglect. Ivy and moss overwhelmed the graves.

Only Vivianne's tomb was as spotless as the night she had been laid to rest. The witches may have stopped honouring their dead, but Klaus had no such trouble. The white marble of the little mausoleum glowed from within, so polished were its walls. He cast a glance at the shrine as Lily emerged from behind a curtain of rain. Curiously, no water seemed to land on her.

'Do you have the pendant?' Lily asked, holding her lantern so that it cast a shadow over Vivianne Lescheres's engraved name. Her hood was thrown back, and her brown hair was pulled severely against her skull.

'No pleasantries?' Klaus remarked, dangling the opal.

'And here I thought we might become dear friends.'

'I wouldn't expect so.' The witch's tone was frosty, but she followed the gentle swing of the gem. She reached into the pocket of her wool cloak and pulled out a small glass vial. 'But along with the pendant, there *is* one other thing I'll need before I return Vivianne from her eternal sleep.'

Klaus eyed the vial, feeling his jaw set with anger – he should have expected that she'd want to raise the price when Vivianne was nearly within reach.

'And what would that be?' He hoped the words sounded undecided, but they both knew he wouldn't refuse whatever she asked.

'It's just a small matter,' she assured him. 'More of a gesture of goodwill, really. The land we live on now is stagnant and unhealthy, and my daughter has grown ill. Our arts have not been able to help her, but I believe that your blood can.'

'My blood,' Klaus repeated, his mind racing. The mix that ran in his veins was much more precious than the pendant, and dangerous in the wrong hands. It seemed possible that his blood could be used to cure a sick child, and it was just one time, one spell. A necklace and a little bit of blood; it was nothing. Not even worth mentioning to anyone else.

Klaus bit into the skin of his wrist, then stepped

forward to hold the arm where her vial would catch his blood. The vial filled to the top, and Lily pressed a soft wax stopper into it. 'That's everything,' he told her firmly. 'Begin.'

Lily snatched the opal from his hand, and lost no time in marking out a curious design in the wet earth in front of Vivianne's grave.

'Stand at this corner here,' she ordered, pointing with one long finger. 'You're the anchor for the spell.' When Klaus hesitated, she shoved a lock of hair from her face and sighed impatiently. 'She's coming back to *you*,' the witch explained, as if to a child.

Klaus's mind filled with questions he knew he should ask. Did that mean Vivianne's new life would be tied to his? Would she be mortal, this second time around? Would she truly be her former self? But he'd proceed no matter the answers, so he would rather not know. Klaus had always subscribed to the notion that it was easier to ask forgiveness than permission . . . if he had to choose between the two at all.

He stepped onto the spot Lily indicated and focused on the only thing that mattered: Vivianne coming back to him. That very night, he would hold her again. He could see her already, just as she had been in that last moment. Before the earth had exploded beneath her feet, she'd looked up at him through the window. Her black

eyes had flashed in her pale, perfect face; her dark hair
had shone in the moonlight. Her defiant, strong-willed
spirit had made itself known in the angle of her pointed
chin, and her blood-red lips had seemed to be calling
to him.

Lily began to chant, and in his head, Klaus heard
Viv's laughter rippling below the incomprehensible
words. He concentrated on it, holding fast to the idea of
her, trying to pull her back from beyond the grave.
He let himself become consumed with thoughts of
Vivianne until they drowned out everything else, even
the words of the spell that would bring her home again.

Klaus felt the tingling of magic, not around him but
rather all through him. It pushed and tugged, nagging at
him until he had no choice but to notice what the witch
was doing. The spell was wrong somehow.

Lily unstoppered the vial of his blood and carefully
tipped out a few precious drops onto the gleaming
white opal. They faded into the stone as if it had
swallowed them. Then she hung the chain around her
neck, chanting something that was not the spell to raise
his beloved from the dead.

But he was afraid to stop her . . . A mistake in this
would cost him everything. No matter how sure he was
that something was wrong, Vivianne might still step out
from the tomb before him and erase all of his doubts.

Instead, Lily stopped, breathing heavily, as if she had been running. The tingle of magic flared through Klaus, and then it ended.

'What was that spell?' Klaus demanded. He tried to shake off the spell, but he could feel it holding fast, weaving itself into his blood. What had she done to him? 'Speak now, before I tear out your throat.'

'I wouldn't do that if I were you,' Lily warned him with a smile. She produced a small blade from her cloak and sliced it across her arm. Klaus felt a stinging on his own skin, and looked down in surprise to see a thin line of blood rising up through his sleeve. It perfectly matched Lily's wound. 'I have linked us together, Niklaus. Whatever happens to me now will happen to you as well.'

The words enraged him. He'd assumed that he would at least be able to kill her if she betrayed him, but now he was trapped. He couldn't hurt her without hurting himself . . . at least, not directly.

'You have people,' he reminded her, his voice icy with fury. 'I don't have to touch you to hurt you. I'll suck the life from everyone you love until you sever the link between us. I'll let you cure your daughter, and then I'll take her away from you again.' He stepped across her line in the dirt, bringing his face so close to hers that she couldn't mistake the truth in his eyes. 'I will make you *want* me to kill you.'

Lily blanched a little, but she did not step away. 'You won't,' she disagreed, her voice trembling in spite of the certainty in her words. 'I have not yet brought back Vivianne Lescheres for you, but I still intend to do so. It's in your interest to keep peace with me, vampire, until I've done what I've promised.'

Klaus fought the urge to strike her. The satisfaction of the smack almost seemed worth the answering pain it would cause him. 'If you really could bring her back,' he sneered, shoving the tiny glimmer of hope down into the depths of his disappointed heart, 'then why not just do it? If you had that kind of knowledge, you wouldn't waste your time with these games.'

'I had to protect myself,' Lily argued. 'I serve a purpose to you until Vivianne is alive again. As soon as that's done I'll be expendable to you, and then this link is what will keep me safe. You can't hurt me, and your kind will leave me in peace, even after they learn what I have done for you. What I *will* do for you,' she reminded him, resting a courageous hand on his sleeve, 'as soon as I can arrange the spell.'

'Arrange what?' Klaus asked, in spite of himself. His tone remained rough, but he wanted to be convinced, and what choice did he have but to keep hope alive? He had given up his blood and the pendant, and now he was linked to this treacherous witch. Having already gambled, he might as well let the wager ride.

'I'll need some help from my clan,' she informed him, confident that she had brought him back into the fold. 'The full moon is the best time for this spell, and that's not until tomorrow night. And, of course, we will need Vivianne's remains.'

Klaus pointed to the small white tomb. 'She lies there,' he reminded Lily. After the great hurricane, he had buried Vivianne himself on a knoll where she could see a little curve of the river. He realised suddenly that the rain had stopped, and a few stars struggled to pierce through the hovering clouds. It was a lovely spot, perfect for Viv.

'She *did*,' Lily corrected. 'Did you really think we would let her lie in a vampire's tomb, where you knew exactly how to find her? You've been sniffing around my kind for decades looking for a way to resurrect her. We would have been fools to leave the body where it was. The day my aunt Sofia died, we removed her daughter's bones and brought them somewhere . . . safer. Our bargain is still intact, Klaus,' she added, watching his face carefully. 'Continue to keep your end, and I assure you that I will keep mine.' With that, Lily disappeared back the way she had come, and Klaus was left to grapple with what had just happened.

She was coming back.

The knowledge paralysed him, burning into his brain like a toxin that shut down every other response. Suddenly, a fear crept in among his hope. What if it wasn't the same as before? What if Vivianne didn't love him any more? What if she was at peace and didn't want to come back? Klaus forced himself to push those thoughts away. What was done was done, and whatever Vivianne's resurrection brought with it would just have to be outweighed by his love.

FIVE

*R*ebekah surveyed the aftermath of the party with her upper lip curled in distaste. It was possible that some of the damage was the result of their guests, but to her eye it was all Klaus's fault. Every stain and splinter, every crack and crease, was somehow the result of his selfish ransacking. With each new ruin she accounted for, her desire to punish Klaus sank deeper into her chest. He couldn't just ruin everything because he felt like it.

She still had no idea what he'd been looking for — what he had found. But Klaus never needed much of a reason to turn their lives upside down and their house inside out. He didn't care about the effort his siblings had put into building a life for themselves in New Orleans. He only cared about himself.

She straightened the gilded frame of an oil painting, turning her head so that the light moved across the brush marks of its surface. The painting itself looked unharmed, and so she moved on to a silk-covered divan, which had not been so lucky. The bloodstains in the champagne-coloured fabric were dire, but the slit at its edge put the thing beyond repair. It looked like the work of a knife, and Rebekah had no trouble imagining Klaus slashing up the upholstery while searching for his precious object.

She pushed the edges back together anyway, then let them go again in disgust. 'I saw Ava Duquesne catch her ring on that,' a voice observed, and Rebekah spun round. Lisette stood in the doorway, looking totally unfazed by both the sorry state of the mansion and the fact that all the other guests had left. The soft candlelight washed her hair into a deeper red than Rebekah remembered. 'She thought no one would notice, which is obviously ridiculous.'

'What are you still doing here?' Rebekah asked ungraciously. 'I thought all of you scattered when Klaus went on his little rampage.'

If Lisette recognised the hint that she *should* have left, she didn't acknowledge it. 'I had brothers growing up,' she said, and picked up the feet of a dead human, jerking her chin towards Rebekah to indicate that she should lift his arms. To her own surprise, Rebekah complied, and the two of them carried the corpse towards the door while Lisette continued. 'I was raised on a farm up near Saint Louis, where my brothers taught me to ride and to shoot,' she explained cheerfully, stepping through the doorway as if she carried bodies out of the house all the time. 'They taught me to clean a deer and a rifle, to tell a joke that could make a blacksmith blush and never, ever to be intimidated by anyone's family but your own.'

Rebekah laughed so unexpectedly that she nearly dropped the arms of the man they carried. She found herself liking Lisette all over again, in spite of her own foul mood and the girl's unreasonable lack of deference. Still, it would set a bad precedent to encourage that kind of familiarity, so she rearranged her face in a stern expression before replying. 'We *are* your family now,' she reminded Lisette. 'We keep the bodies over there, a little way into the woods.'

While the Mikaelsons mostly preferred to do their hunting in the twisting streets and alleyways of New Orleans, it was only polite to provide in-house refreshment for their guests. After a dozen or so of their parties, the corpses had really started to pile up. A little hollow in the forest downwind of the house had been repurposed as a mass grave, with leaves and underbrush piled on top of it in a half-hearted attempt at concealment.

'I noticed a few more in the drawing room, and one

under that odd sculpture near the stairs,' Lisette suggested, unconcerned with Rebekah's reproof. 'It might be better to take two at a time.'

'Indeed,' Rebekah agreed. They could each easily carry a human by themselves, but it was pleasant to have company. Even odd, chatty company was an improvement over dwelling on the infuriating mystery of Klaus's outburst. 'My brother is trying to drive me mad,' she blurted out, and then looked away from the expression of pity that she knew must be on her newfound friend's face.

'They do that,' Lisette agreed amiably, falling into step beside Rebekah as they turned towards the mansion and the brightening sky. 'I'd heard that he's been a bit wild since the hurricane when his fiancée died,' she added, as if it were meant to be reassuring. As if Klaus acting out for over forty years were just a phase.

'She was never his fiancée,' Rebekah snapped, 'and he was "wild" well before then.' And they had both lost someone that night, although to hear Klaus tell it no one in the world had ever experienced the kind of pain he did when the perfect, extraordinary, peerless Vivianne Lescheres had run out and got herself killed.

At least, he had told it that way at first. Before too long, he had stopped speaking of it entirely. Now that Lisette brought it up, he *was* a bit worse than usual.

Perhaps he was still clinging to his doomed love affair with the half witch, half werewolf that had nearly drowned the entire city.

If so, it was well past time for him to get over it. New Orleans was full of far more appropriate candidates for Klaus's affection now that the witches were no longer able to enforce the old treaty that had barred the Mikaelsons from making new vampires. In this new, livelier city Rebekah had managed to move on from her loss, filling her life with enjoyable distractions. It was absurd to imagine that Klaus might still be stuck on the same girl. The one thing that Rebekah had learned as a vampire was that people die and you had to move on.

On their fourth trip back from the makeshift burial ground in the woods, Rebekah noticed that the front door had been closed. She felt sure they had left it open. Elijah was still brooding in his scorched study, and that left only one possibility.

'Are you nervous?' Lisette asked, nodding her strawberry-blonde head towards the closed door. 'I know plenty of vampires who would hide from Klaus, but just as many would hide from you as well.'

Rebekah remembered the icy-cold feel of a silver stake piercing her heart, followed by a moment of blankness that had spanned years. Klaus wasn't better, stronger or smarter than she was, but he still somehow managed to be more dangerous. His selfishness made him unpredictable, and his distrust of his own siblings only made things worse. 'I am not intimidated by him,' she retorted, although she wasn't entirely sure it was true. 'Our family is simply more complicated than the rest of you can understand.'

Lisette shrugged. 'Elijah's the one I wouldn't want to cross,' she observed. 'But I would also trust him to give a fair hearing. For every weakness, a strength.'

It struck Rebekah that she would have reversed those two, but at the same time she realised that the sky over the bayou had grown decidedly pink. The daylight ring on her index finger protected her against the sun's blistering rays, but Lisette had no such magic. She had already stayed too long.

'Go home for the day,' Rebekah told the girl brusquely. 'I'm not afraid of Klaus, and I'll deal with him. Thank you,' she added, feeling warmth towards the young vampire. 'I appreciate your help tonight, but you've done enough.'

'I'd imagine you could use all the help you can get,' Lisette suggested, although her impish grin took a little of the sting out of the words, 'with a brother like yours.' She hugged Rebekah, who was too surprised to object, then spun on one heel and ran towards the heart of the city. With a final reddish-gold twinkle she was gone, and

Rebekah inhaled a deep breath before stepping up onto the veranda and shoving the front door open.

'Niklaus?' she called, not wanting to delay their confrontation. 'Niklaus, I know you're home.'

She expected him to descend the spiral staircase – lately he seemed to spend all of his spare time in that dusty, draughty attic he refused to let her renovate. But instead, he emerged from the shadows of the billiard room, holding a crystal goblet loosely in one hand. There was a layer of dried blood on his sleeve.

'Dear sister,' he greeted her gamely, but the smile that twisted his lips didn't reach his eyes. 'Welcome home.'

'That's all?' she demanded, taking a step closer to his infuriatingly smug face. 'You have nothing else to say about your behaviour tonight?'

Klaus frowned. 'I think not,' he decided after a moment. 'And you?'

It was almost unbearable. The idea that *she* had something to answer for, that *she* had somehow wronged *him* . . . It was all she could do not to just fly at his throat right then and there. In spite of Lisette's help and Rebekah's own diligent efforts, the mansion was still in shambles. And there stood Klaus, using their one unbroken crystal glass and acting as if he had done nothing wrong.

'You *attacked* me,' she snarled, unable to keep her

anger in check. 'You turned the house inside out, and then you attacked me, and then you just *left*.'

Klaus's brow furrowed, and his turquoise eyes shadowed for a moment. 'That's not how I remember it.' He shrugged. 'Rebekah, I'm not responsible for every scuffed floor and bad mood of yours.'

'I don't *care* about the floors!' she insisted, although the floors were one more mark against him. But that minor concern was far outweighed by her distress at being flat-out lied to by her own brother. At being shut out, yet again, because he never really felt that they were on the same side. 'I care that you won't just *talk* to me!'

Klaus had begun to walk away, but at that he rounded on her. For a moment, she thought he might tell her everything, not because he trusted her, but because she had finally made him angry enough. 'You don't want to hear what I have to say,' he spat. 'You couldn't possibly know how I feel, what I am going through. You can't understand what my life has become now.'

'Not if you don't explain!' Rebekah was so frustrated she was practically shouting, but she didn't care. The sight of Eric's broken silver chain flashed before her eyes, blocking out Klaus's furious face. Elijah could break up yet another fight between them if it came to that. Klaus always listened to him, if reluctantly. He would sneak around behind their backs, but when it came down to a confrontation, he respected Elijah's opinion in a way he had never respected hers.

'I don't have to explain myself to you, sister,' Klaus retorted, driving home the unfairness of it all. She *could* understand. Better than anyone, probably, since she had known him and looked up to him her entire life. And she might even be able to help, if Klaus didn't always dismiss her and keep her at arm's length. But he didn't even see a point in letting her in. He was so self-absorbed that the only pain he could see was his own.

Suddenly, she felt the fight drain out of her. He wasn't going to listen, no matter what she said. He would just carry on with his own secretive plans, acting like his own family was nothing but an obstacle in his way. 'No, you never do,' she agreed. 'You just keep barging around, ruining everything without bothering to talk to *anyone*.'

Rebekah could have reached the foot of the staircase without touching him, but she chose to push past him instead, shoving one shoulder hard against his. She thought she saw him smirk out of the corner of her eye, and she fumed all the more at the possibility that he was laughing at her.

He thought he could just do whatever he wanted, pursue his own goals, never consult with her or respect her opinion. Maybe she had been going about their fractious relationship all wrong, she considered, as she slammed the ruined door of her room behind her. Her jewellery boxes lay in chaos, their contents spilled across her dressing table and onto the floor. Maybe her sympathy and concern had been the problem all along.

Klaus didn't *want* to be understood, and perhaps he didn't need it, either. Perhaps the best thing she could do was treat him with the same coldness and lack of consideration that he treated her. She was now more determined than ever to ruin *his* fun, and see how he liked it. It might bring him down a notch, make him humbler and more willing to turn towards his family in times of need. At the very least, it might make it more tolerable to be stuck in a house with him.

Rebekah pulled a ruby earring out of the soft pile of the carpet, setting it carefully beside its mate in one of her lacquered boxes. She removed the gems she was wearing one at a time and added them to the collection, admiring the soft glint of each one before she closed the box's lid. Elijah had power, Rebekah had beauty and Klaus had trouble. They had each created lives that suited them, but Klaus's was a constant threat to the other two. That was his nature.

She traded her gown for a loose silk robe, and sat on a tapestried stool to brush out her long golden hair. Watching her dim reflection in the glass above the dressing table, she looked for some sign that she could be as ruthless and self-serving as her half-brother. She could, she decided. She had watched Klaus be a brute for centuries; she certainly knew how it was done.

When Klaus least suspected it, he would learn how wrong he had been to constantly discount his siblings. She would show him what it truly meant to have no one looking out for him, no one watching his back. He always claimed he had no one to rely on but himself, and she had tolerated those insults for far too long. She would find a way to wound him, just a little. Just enough. He would learn to appreciate what he had in his siblings, or she would continue to make him pay.

SIX

*T*he shouting was getting louder, and Elijah wanted nothing to do with it.

He tore the scorched remnants of the curtains away from the windows and heaped them in a charred pile in the middle of his study. Dozens of his books were unsalvageable, and traces of smoke lingered in every corner of the room. The damage was too extensive to fix on his own, but if nothing else, it would keep him away from his siblings. He didn't particularly want to see them at the moment. As long as no one got staked, Elijah had better things to do.

Hours passed and night fell. Something nagged at Elijah as he leafed through each spell book, checking to make sure the writings could still be deciphered. What was wrong? Was it that he hadn't heard a sound from Rebekah or Klaus in hours? No, something else was tugging at his conscience.

Flashes of a vision came to him, bits of Spanish moss and cattails. He could feel danger all around him, except it wasn't around him at all. It was around *her*. If he concentrated, he could almost see her, although he couldn't sense whatever it was she fled from.

All he knew for sure was that Ava, the vampire he had made, the woman who had shared his bed just hours ago, needed him. Elijah shoved away from his desk and charged through the house, slamming the door behind him as he raced towards the bayou.

He found her trail quickly, as he knew her habits. She hunted in these marshes, catching lost travellers and stray bandits, and now and then he had hunted there with her. The marks of her passage were almost invisible, nothing but a broken reed here and a footprint-size puddle there. Fortunately, Elijah knew what he was looking for, and his eyes were sharp. He followed one clue to the next, working his way through the sucking mud and waist-high grasses. He did not want to think about what it meant that he had to track Ava like a deer, that he couldn't sense her through the bond they had once shared.

He almost stumbled over her prone body before he saw it. Ava Duquesne lay on her back in the swamp, with her long legs at a strange angle and her hands clutched like claws at something just out of her reach. But all he could look at was the ragged hole where her heart had been torn out of her chest.

He brushed the tangle of chestnut hair away from her face to see her green eyes open and staring, fixed on whatever monster had hunted her down and murdered her. For a moment, he remembered her again as she had been, as she should have been, stretched languidly across his bedsheets with a knowing smile on her pink lips.

And then he was jolted back to the brutal sight of her now: limp and broken, with a bloody hole in her chest the size of a fist. Her skin was covered with scrapes and fine scratches, as if she had run instead of standing her ground. Elijah couldn't imagine what type of creature a vampire would be afraid of. He hadn't known her well – their connection had always been more physical than conversational – but she had never struck him as fearful.

He looked for her heart, hoping it would be a clue, but it was nowhere to be found.

Elijah's mind grasped at possibilities. This wasn't the work of witches or werewolves, the most obvious natural enemies they had. Something had chased Ava down and mutilated her, and Elijah couldn't even begin to imagine what it might be.

He couldn't even rule out the possibility that it might

be personal. He hadn't made a big show of his liaison with Ava, but he hadn't thought to hide it, either. Could someone have been trying to send a message to him through her, or get revenge on him for some forgotten slight? If this gruesome work was meant to hurt him, he wouldn't stop until he had torn that person to shreds. It was the least he could do for Ava, and perhaps all he could do for her any more.

Elijah half lifted Ava's body, cradling her against him even though the smell of her drying blood was almost overwhelming. Every tiny sound that came from the bayou sounded close and suspicious. He felt watched, seen from every direction by some menacing, unknown monster. He had no idea where the danger was, only that the very air around them was suffused with it.

Without warning, the creature hurtled into him from the side, throwing him back with such force that he lost hold of Ava. A woman hovered over him, but she was no ordinary woman. She held him down with nothing but her own incredible strength. He could feel the intense coiling of her muscles as he struggled against her, and he knew that she wasn't using magic. She had pinned him to the muddy earth because she was stronger than he was, and no one was stronger than he was.

His disbelief was so total that it was a full second before he felt a warm wetness spreading from where her left hand pressed against his shoulder. He risked a glance away from his attacker's eerily calm face to see Ava's heart in her hand. Looking back into the creature's dead eyes, Elijah understood that murdering his lover hadn't been a message after all. To her, Ava was just prey.

'Who are you?' Elijah demanded, and the strange woman smiled horribly.

She lifted the heart to her lips and took a delicate bite. Blood dripped down her chin and splashed onto his shirt, but from the expression on her face the woman might have been eating a ripe plum.

'Who are you?' he asked again, as curious as he was repulsed.

'Wait your turn,' she rasped between bites of the heart, her voice sounding rusty and unused. 'You will have your turn.'

For a bizarre moment, he thought she was offering to share her gruesome feast, but then her more likely meaning dawned on him. She looked like any other human woman: lank, light-brown hair framing an ordinary enough face. But her strength, her odd, creaking voice, and most of all the heart in her hand . . . There was nothing ordinary or human about her. Whatever she was, she had chosen him as her next victim.

Elijah had lived for centuries, and had survived wounds that would have killed another vampire hundreds of times over. Even the loss of his heart would not end him, but he didn't want it ripped from his chest if he could help it. As he watched the madwoman lick her lips clean of Ava's blood and lower her face to take another bite, he did not intend to lie there and find out what she was capable of.

The hand that held him was like a steel vice around his shoulder, but she was distracted by the heart in her other hand. He drove his body upward and sideways, knocking her off balance and creating just enough space to leap to his feet.

She rolled to a crouch, her blue eyes watching him with something that looked like amusement. Every movement she made gave Elijah chills, her bones creaking as she rose to her full height. She was *wrong* somehow. People liked to call his kind 'unnatural' and even 'abominations', but what he was facing truly did not belong in the world.

'We're coming for you,' she croaked. Her voice sounded as if it came from a corpse. 'Witches have returned to this land, and there is no escape.' She smiled, and he could see blood on her teeth. Elijah grimaced at the sinew that came away from the heart as she took another bite. 'You are afraid, and you should be. But fear won't save you now.'

Elijah had never heard of a witch who devoured

hearts. And she had said 'we'. Elijah could sense more of them now, perhaps a dozen creatures like her, lurking in the woods. They were closing in on him, and in spite of his better instincts, he flicked his eyes away from the witch's for the briefest of seconds, and in that second she struck.

The blow knocked him sideways, and his legs tangled in Ava's. He fell across her body and then rolled before the witch could pin him again. But she was as fast as she was strong, and she nearly caught him again. Her fingernails raked at his face and arms, seeking the centre of his chest while she still held Ava's heart in her other hand.

He lashed out with a vicious kick as they separated, catching her squarely in the stomach. She bent at the force of his attack, almost doubling over but not quite winded. She lunged for him again, and he heard the rattling of indrawn breath behind him. He ducked her hand and grabbed her by the wrist, spinning her into another witch who had crept up on them.

The two creatures backed away from each other and snarled, but another pair of impossibly strong hands caught Elijah from behind. As he struggled, more creatures slunk out from the shadows. Where were they coming from? And why?

He managed to shake off the witch who held him – a

short man with a disturbingly cheerful smile on his face – and smashed his fist into the skull of another, wincing at the sickening crunch of the thin bone around her temple. But she didn't even flinch, just continued to come at him with half of her skull caved in. Elijah was so shocked that her hand plunged through his flesh and brushed his ribs before he managed to get out of her range.

Holding a hand over the wound in his chest, he feinted one way and then another, trying to divide the dozen of them enough to fight his way out, but to his surprise none of them seemed to be that interested in him any more. The short witch was smiling again, although not at Elijah. He was turned towards Elijah's first attacker, who still held Ava's half-eaten heart. Elijah realised that *all* the witches were staring at the pulpy mess.

Elijah stood perfectly still, sensing that this was not the moment to strike. He forced himself to watch, although he had a sick feeling about what he was about to witness. The creatures closed their circle around his first attacker, their attention rapt and hungry on the heart. Like a pack of wild beasts, they were turning on their own kind to get at her prize.

She gave a low protective hiss and clutched the heart closer to her chest, prepared to fight for the last scrap of meat. Her flat eyes found Elijah's again, and her thin lips pulled apart into a ghastly smile. 'Soon enough,' she reminded him in her dead, rasping voice, and then the witches struck. They threw themselves at her all at once, like a bursting dam of bared teeth and sharp nails.

Elijah heard the tearing of skin and the crunching of bones from somewhere within the writhing mass of hungry monsters, and he hoped that some of them wouldn't live through the brawl. But he could still picture the woman who had lunged at him with her skull caved in, and he suspected he couldn't rely on the resilient beasts to thin their own ranks.

Although Elijah hated to leave a fight, he knew that the smartest move would be to take this opportunity and run. His feet flew over the swamp, startling a flock of birds out of the weeds. He made for home, for the safety of the protection spell and the army that was his family. He needed to figure out what these creatures were before they became an unstoppable threat, and he hoped that the answer was in whatever was left of his study. Even with some of his books lost to last night's stupid, wasteful fighting, the sources he had collected over the centuries were his best chance of understanding what evil now lurked in the bayou.

At the edge of his land he finally glanced behind him, half expecting to see the crowd at his heels. But there was only rustling grasses and tree branches that waved gently

in the night breeze. Yet he knew that he would see the
bloodthirsty creatures again.

SEVEN

*I*t had been forty-four years since Niklaus Mikaelson had felt so alive. His impatience was like a drug that sharpened all of his senses while time seemed to stretch and blur. He stood at the edge of the bayou, watching the moon slide up over the horizon. It was as red as blood when it first rose, then turned gold as it climbed. Its reflection echoed in the river, growing smaller and smaller until it was just the moon, pale white and perfectly round.

Another moon was vivid in his memory: the one that had risen the night Vivianne had embraced her dual heritage and triggered her werewolf side. At the time Klaus had felt betrayed, even disgusted by her choice. Now, though – now that Vivianne had been dead for decades and he had nearly lost hope of seeing her again – none of the petty issues that had once divided them felt like they mattered.

He just needed *her*. The witch, the werewolf, his lover, his loss. Whatever she wanted to be, it was fine as long as she was his.

He had been told she would rise with the moon, and that Vivianne would find him. So Klaus waited at the edge of the bayou, trusting that Lily hadn't betrayed him a second time.

He was torn between the two impossibilities, trapped where he stood by the warring forces within his own heart. He hoped that Vivianne would come and suspected that Lily had lied. They balanced against each other, needing only one tiny nudge to consume him.

There was a flash of white, just barely visible through the tangled and matted undergrowth. It might have been the lifted tail of a deer or the moonlight glancing off a pool of stagnant water, or it might have been the love of his life. Perhaps it was her ghost, come to punish him for failing to save her.

But it moved like her . . . That little scrap of brightness across the swamp could mean something true and profound. It could be an arm; it could be a hem. And then, unbelievably, the indistinct flash of white stepped out into the open, and it was Vivianne Lescheres.

She wore a loose white gown that shifted and twisted around her as she walked. It stirred the mist that rose off the water, which swirled in her wake. It seemed to Klaus that she wore the night itself, the stars and moon moving with her as she made her way towards him. Finally, finally towards him.

He almost couldn't understand that it was really her. There had been too many disappointments, too many dead ends and dashed hopes. Klaus had never given up and he never would have, but at the same time it was hard to keep his faith alive.

And yet there was Vivianne, walking towards him through the mist. The full moon shone on her raven hair and her bare arms. Could she feel the night air pressing against her skin? Was she now warm for the first time in years? She was graceful and lithe in her bare feet. Had her people entombed her that way? Or had she simply slipped off her shoes along the way, eager to feel the solid earth beneath her feet again?

She came closer, her black eyes never leaving his face, an unreadable smile on her warm, solid red lips. He could see a hint of her sardonic humour in the face that tilted up towards his. He could feel the heat radiating from her fair skin, and over the hum of the bayou he could hear her heart beating, clear and steady. Her chest rose and fell, and her eyes . . . He could see her living soul flaring through those marvellous eyes.

'My love,' he gasped, and he couldn't wait any longer. With one step he closed the space between them and took her into his arms. She melted against his body, moulding every curve of hers into its proper place. It was as if they had never been apart.

'You found me,' she whispered, and her voice sounded hoarse from disuse. 'I was so lost for so long.'

'I found you,' Klaus agreed, brushing her dark hair back from her forehead to kiss it. 'I brought you back.' It was as if the moon were growing brighter, as if the whole world were glowing with the joy that caught hold of him. After forty-four years, he could finally feel *this* again: this almost painfully exquisite thrill of contact with the woman he loved.

She rested her head on his collarbone, exactly where it belonged. Her hair smelled very faintly of lilacs. He remembered every second they had ever spent together in vivid detail: the initial, testing conversations; the secret meetings; the passionate letters; that first, amazing night in the hotel that had blown down in the hurricane just a few short weeks later. He remembered her smile, her skin, her laugh, and the pale half-moons at the base of each of her fingernails. Holding her in his arms again, he could recall every single thing about her at once.

Then she lifted her head and kissed him, and every

other thought fled from his mind. He wrapped one arm around her waist to keep her close and tangled his other hand in her loose black hair, wanting to freeze time so that their kiss would never end. He wanted this forever.

'Marry me, Viv,' he demanded when she finally broke away, their breath coming fast and ragged. He threw himself to one knee, feeling dampness from the bayou soak through his breeches. 'Say that you will. I can't live without you, and I won't do it again.'

She smiled. He searched her face for any sign of her former state, but there was no trace of death on her. He had assumed that she would be fragile, even traumatised when he managed to bring her back to life. It was a gift beyond price to have her back at all, but that she was so unflawed, so present, so whole, was more than he could have asked for.

'Don't you even want to know what I've been up to?' she asked teasingly, and his head spun with the strangeness of it all. 'You don't look a day older, my love, but I know I spent longer than that on the Other Side.'

Klaus hesitated, flustered by her frank manner. She seemed so at ease with the subject of death that she might as well be discussing the latest fashions at a dinner party. He had expected her to be haunted or at least shaken. But Vivianne was so natural that he could almost forget she had ever been gone. 'Do you remember it?' he asked curiously. 'You can tell me, or not – whatever you wish.'

She smiled again, and this time it reached her eyes. 'I'll tell you that I will marry you, Niklaus,' she told him reprovingly. She took his hands and lifted him back to his feet, one quirked eyebrow indicating that she thought the question had been unnecessary to begin with. 'Of course I will. I've spent my afterlife thinking of you and wishing that I could be with you again, and now you have made that impossible wish come true. We will marry when and where you like – now, even.'

He gathered her against his chest again, feeling the miracle of her heartbeat. She had been gone so long, and she had missed so much. Vivianne had died at nineteen years old. She had been full of dreams and plans, and then she had simply ended. He had vowed to himself that when he brought her back, she would have everything she had lost, everything she had not yet had a chance to experience. Vivianne would have a wedding fit for a queen. She would never have another regret, or another squandered moment.

'I will give you the wedding of your dreams,' he promised, running his fingertips along her spine. She shivered and snuggled closer into his chest. A wolf howled in the distance, and Klaus started, holding Vivianne away from him at arm's length to study her.

'You are here in your own form,' he marvelled, 'even though it is a full moon.'

Vivianne looked down at her own body as if she were surprised to see it. 'The Other Side cleansed me of that terrible mistake I made.' She smiled. 'I am as I was born, not as I became during my first life. We truly have a fresh start, thanks to you.'

And thanks to Lily, but he pushed the thought from his mind.

The only two things that had ever come between him and the love of his endless life – Vivianne's changing ceremony and her death – had been erased. Whatever else came their way they could face together. Now that she was back they had all the time in the world, together as husband and wife. He bent down to kiss her lips once more, whispering, 'Vivianne . . . Vivianne Mikaelson, my wife.'

EIGHT

*R*ebekah had just finished a light meal of chambermaid when Klaus wandered in. The protection spell had warned her that he was not alone, but she felt like she was in a dream when she saw who trailed into the house behind him.

'Elijah,' Rebekah whispered, staring at the girl who looked exactly like Vivianne Lescheres. When she repeated it, it came out as a scream. 'Elijah!'

He was with them in a heartbeat, and Rebekah noticed that he looked as if he had been thrashed by a vampire twice his size. Deep scratches crisscrossed his face, and a bruise on his cheek wasn't healing quite fast enough to hide its vicious purple-green colour. Rebekah wanted to ask him about it, but the problem on Klaus's arm was far more pressing. 'What is the meaning of this?' Elijah demanded, his voice low and dangerous. 'Klaus, what have you done?'

Vivianne hung back, her eyes flicking back and forth between the three vampires. Rebekah wondered if dying once had made death seem more or less frightening for her.

'Can't you see what he's done?' Rebekah asked, waving a hand towards Klaus. 'Is it really so hard to believe that Niklaus would endanger us by playing with magic and generally being a reckless fool? The proof is standing right here.' Her brother's expression was so smug that she fought the urge to slap him.

'Rebekah,' Vivianne said suddenly, her eyes locking on her future sister-in-law. Rebekah felt a chill, as if death itself had sneaked up to breathe down the back of her neck. 'I'm sorry this is such a shock. I'm so thankful to be back, but I didn't realise that Klaus had acted on his own. I wish you were happier to see me again.'

Elijah's face reddened, and he looked as if he might spring on Klaus at any moment. 'Have you lost your mind?' he demanded. 'Niklaus, explain yourself.'

'Congratulate me, dear siblings,' Klaus suggested with every scrap of arrogant boldness he possessed. 'Mademoiselle Lescheres and I are engaged.'

The colossal upheaval in Rebekah's mind drowned

out even Elijah's scathing reply. Not only had Klaus resurrected a dead woman, he had *proposed* to her. It was insane and yet typical. Rebekah studied Vivianne closely, ignoring the rising shouts of her two brothers. The girl looked well enough, not weak or scarred by her time in the grave. Maybe it was only the surprise of seeing her that unsettled Rebekah. Maybe Klaus's lunatic plan had somehow, impossibly, worked. Of course the lucky bastard had got the love of his life back.

Not that magic ever gave anything away for free. Surely, Klaus had paid a hefty price for his prize. But he owed his sister as well. For everything he had put her through, for the disrespect, the self-indulgence and for dismissing her loss while obsessing over his own.

As shocked as she was that he had raised his bride from the dead, Rebekah realised that Klaus had just presented her with an opportunity to collect on his debt to her. 'Congratulations,' she blurted, and an expectant silence fell over the hall as all eyes turned towards her. 'Sister,' she added for good measure, striding towards Vivianne to embrace her warmly. Vivianne felt solid and real, although Rebekah's skin still crawled slightly at their contact. She didn't show it, though. She had far more to gain by appearing to accept this perversion of natural laws.

Elijah hesitated, and then decided to follow Rebekah's lead. 'Engaged,' he echoed, as if he had not quite heard

Klaus say the word before. 'I cannot say I approve of your methods, brother, but you certainly couldn't have chosen a worthier bride.' He bowed his head politely towards Vivianne, and she gave Elijah a forgiving smile.

The scratches on Elijah's face were fading, but Rebekah detected some stiffness when he moved. It was just one more mark against Klaus: his problems always had to eclipse everyone else's. He didn't even seem to notice his brother was hurt.

'I truly am sorry to surprise you both,' Vivianne offered, and Rebekah hushed her gently.

'It's hardly your fault,' she pointed out. 'Please forgive us for our hasty reactions. When do you two plan to wed? Or have you not had time to discuss that yet?'

Elijah glared at her, but Rebekah ignored him. Elijah had forced diplomacy and caution on his siblings so often that he had no grounds to complain about whatever his sister had learned from him.

'Soon,' Klaus replied, his voice intense and earnest. The tightened muscles in his jaw betrayed his impatience. Rebekah could use that eagerness to her own advantage. Klaus could be so single-minded when something he wanted was within his reach. As focused as he was on marrying his dead bride, he would never see Rebekah's little act of revenge coming. Even now, he didn't seem to realise that there was anything suspicious about her sudden interest in his nuptials. 'As soon as possible, but we would like something . . . festive.'

He met her eyes then, and Rebekah realised that in his own grudging way, Klaus was asking for help. *Her* help. Of course, he could never possibly plan a wedding without her. It was almost too easy. 'We will throw the most dazzling wedding this city has ever seen,' she assured him. 'I know how long you have waited for this moment, and we'll make sure it doesn't disappoint.'

'I'm afraid I won't be able to help,' Elijah disagreed, his tone bordering on ungracious. Klaus's lips tightened, and Rebekah stifled a smirk. Even Elijah was unwittingly helping her cause, making her Klaus's only real ally, the sibling he could rely on. 'I encountered something in the bayou tonight that I have never heard of before, and I will need to devote my time to—' He broke off suddenly and stared at Vivianne as if he were seeing her for the first time. 'Did any other witches return with you?' he asked urgently. 'Were there more on the Other Side who came back?'

Vivianne frowned. 'I woke up alone in my coffin,' she said. 'I saw the witches who performed the spell, and they only seemed concerned with raising me. Have you seen others who were – who should be . . . ?' She bit her cherry-red bottom lip.

'They weren't like you,' Elijah admitted. 'They were

single-minded and barely able to speak, but they called themselves witches. All of them were unnaturally strong. I crushed the skull of one, and she kept right on fighting as if she didn't even notice it. They ate the heart of . . . of a vampire I knew.'

Klaus looked as stunned as Rebekah. He finally took in Elijah's wounds and scratches, speechless.

But Rebekah was more interested in Vivianne's reaction. The young woman's expression was strange, tense and hungry like a feral animal that had gone for days without eating. What exactly had she seen on the Other Side?

'I have never heard of a witch like that,' Vivianne apologised, and whatever look Rebekah had seen was gone. Vivianne's face looked just as it always had, and she sounded entirely sincere. Rebekah shivered a little, trying to shake off the fleeting impression that there had been something *else* where Vivianne now stood. 'The witches who brought me back were just like the ones I have always known.' She frowned, her black eyebrows drawing together in concentration. 'One said we were kin. But then she told me that I had no more business with our kind, and that I should go to Klaus and not return. I don't think I have any real family left to ask about creatures like the ones you describe.'

Klaus wrapped an arm around her waist and kissed her

forehead. 'I will be all the family you need,' he promised, and Vivianne laid her head against his shoulder.

They were well matched, even Rebekah had to admit. 'Learn what you can about this new threat, Elijah,' she urged her brother. 'I will take care of everything else, and we will hope that this new evil can be stopped. These two deserve a wedding that will be remembered for centuries, and I'll make sure they get it.'

'Robert!' Rebekah shouted, growing more impatient by the second. He appeared in an instant, hat in hand, and she realised it was Rodger she'd meant. 'No, not you, Robert. Go and fetch Rodger.' She was going to have to pin tags on their clothing or something, but at least neither of her admirers seemed to mind being called by the wrong name. 'And is our coach ready *yet*?' she called after him.

'Yes, miss. The horses are waiting in the courtyard,' he turned to say as he went off to find his counterpart.

If there were any more delays, Klaus might find a reason to convince Vivianne not to go into town at all. He had been absurdly protective over her since her return, and it had been almost impossible for Rebekah to get even a few minutes alone with her. It was understandable that he would worry, especially with Elijah's mysterious un-witches roaming around, but that didn't make it any less annoying.

Rebekah was putting together an extraordinary event in record time, and now and then she needed to consult with the bride. Even more important, she needed to lull Klaus into trusting her, into believing that she thought of Vivianne as the sister she had never had. If he saw Rebekah as an ally, he would never suspect that she was behind the little prank that would be the highlight of his wedding.

It was only going to be a minor inconvenience, not dangerous at all. Just embarrassing and easy to blame on some rogue werewolf.

All she needed was to get *going*. Vivianne needed a wedding gown, and Rebekah needed a vial of werewolf venom. Neither of Vivianne's two families had shown any interest in embracing her upon her return, and so her wedding guests would be exclusively vampires. A little poison in the food would create the right amount of chaos . . . and Klaus would have to dole out his own blood to heal the vampires stricken by the venom. Only a hybrid's blood could stop the wolf poison from killing a vampire – but it's not like the prank would even go that far.

Between sampling hors d'oeuvres and comparing place settings, Rebekah had even been turning new vampires, just so that there would be more of them to cure. The more blood Klaus had to shed, the happier she would be. She reached for Eric's silver chain in the pocket of her skirt, wrapping it around her fingers. She'd begun to carry the broken silver chain everywhere, letting it be a physical reminder of the grudge she nursed.

'Viv, dear!' she called through the foyer as the coach pulled up to the door. 'The coach is here!' Vivianne finally drifted down the broad, curving staircase.

'It will be nice to see the city again,' the girl remarked, although Rebekah knew Vivianne would never think to blame Klaus for keeping her so isolated. She'd been infatuated with him even before he had rescued her from the Other Side, and now they were virtually inseparable. Rebekah had always thought of Vivianne as an intelligent and perceptive young woman, but she had rather unfortunate taste in men. The werewolf fiancé had been dull, but he would never have put her through a fraction of the heartbreak Klaus had caused.

Then again, Rebekah had followed her own heart to disaster a time or fifty, so she wasn't one to judge.

Rebekah gave Rodger the barest of nods as he helped her into the open-topped coach, and he looked as if he had just been pardoned from certain death. She enjoyed his flattering attention too much to kill him over something so minor, but there was no upside to letting him know that. 'Madame Pavin's shop,' she ordered, 'and we're in a bit of a hurry.'

The horse violently shied away from the sound of her voice, nearly kicking Vivianne as she got inside. Rodger got it back under control quickly, but it still stamped and snorted, its eyes rolling wildly white in their sockets. Horses had never cared for Rebekah, but the reaction seemed excessive even to her. It settled a bit as Vivianne arranged herself inside the carriage and Rodger climbed up to take the reins.

The coach flew over the cobblestoned streets. It was too noisy to talk, especially when pedestrians and waggoners shouted at Rodger's aggressive driving. Rebekah felt a secret relief at that – it was always hard to know exactly what to say to Vivianne. She seemed happy, healthy and downright normal. Which *wasn't* normal, as far as Rebekah was concerned. No one who had endured the Other Side could emerge unscathed. But that was Klaus's problem, Rebekah reminded herself, not hers.

Once they reached the shop, Rodger helped them out of the coach, keeping his eyes on the cobblestones at their feet. As Vivianne stepped into Madame Pavin's, Rebekah hung back and took Rodger by the arm. 'We'll be here at least an hour,' she whispered, glancing at the open shop door to make sure no one was close enough to hear. 'There's a package waiting for me at the Southern Spot, but I can't be seen there myself. Go, and ask for

Thomas. *Discreetly.*' Rebekah's voice hovered just on the edge of compulsion. 'Buy some time with one of the girls so that no one notices you, and do not speak of this to anyone.'

'My lady,' he murmured, taking her hand and pressing it to his lips. 'It will be done just as you require.'

The dressmaker was thrilled to see them, and even sent her apprentice out for a bottle of champagne. They sipped their drinks while she brought out one bolt of silk after another. Madame Pavin was known for receiving goods from Paris before any other tailor, and the quality of her merchandise was famous. Vivianne's pale cheeks flushed, as much from excitement as from the champagne. She stroked each bolt of silk, as if not quite believing that she would be dressed in such finery.

'You've always looked good in white,' Rebekah suggested, leaning back in her chair and swirling the bubbly liquid in her glass. Planning this spectacle took a great deal of work, but it was also more enjoyable than she had assumed it would be. Vivianne was agreeable, and Klaus's only input was to repeat, 'The best of everything,' in response to every dilemma, and now there was champagne. She refilled her glass.

'I think that Klaus would suggest the gold,' Vivianne murmured, running one hand over each of the silks in question. 'But it's never flattered me nearly as well.'

'He'll marry you if you wear a flour sack,' Rebekah said dismissively. 'You have to think of yourself and your audience.'

'My *guests*, you mean,' Vivianne corrected, giggling a bit. 'Will I even have met half of them?'

Madame Pavin emerged from her storeroom with an armful of peach-coloured silks, then retreated.

'The world is full of people now I've never met,' Vivianne went on, holding the pink fabric up near her face in the mirror. 'This washes me out. I look dead.'

It was as if the champagne had increased Rebekah's intuition by gently blurring her other senses. For the first time, she realised that this *wasn't* exactly the Vivianne she had once known. She had been so busy marvelling at what was there — at the girl's cool poise — that she hadn't really noticed before what was missing. Vivianne's spark had been muted somehow. She was still clever and witty, but now her jokes were drier and more self-deprecating.

'Do you remember it?' Rebekah blurted out. Vivianne met Rebekah's eyes in the mirror, but she didn't speak. 'What did you see on the Other Side?'

'It was . . . dark,' Vivianne answered at last, setting aside the silk and returning to a bolt of heavy Indian cotton printed with flowers. 'I don't remember much at all. Except that I was there for what felt like forever, and

I longed for your brother the entire time. Every moment, every second, I wished to see him again.'

Rebekah was silent. She wondered what afterlife Eric Moquet had found. Unlike Vivianne, he had no supernatural heritage, and so he could not have gone to the Other Side. She hoped that he had reunited with his deceased wife and didn't miss Rebekah at all.

No matter how much she had loved him, she could never do what Klaus had done. She was even surer of that now that she could see the mark it had left on Vivianne.

'I'm so excited for the wedding,' Vivianne went on after a long pause, but her smile didn't reach her eyes. Rebekah could see the scars now, the pain that had been branded onto her very soul. The wound had healed over, but Vivianne would never be exactly the same.

Well, forty-four years on the Other Side would do that to a girl, Rebekah supposed. Perhaps time would heal even this, especially if Niklaus got his head out of the clouds and managed to notice that his bride wasn't quite as perfectly herself as he wanted to believe.

She refilled her glass from the dwindling bottle of champagne, and as if on cue Madame Pavin appeared with a new one. Through the window she saw Rodger return to the coach and pat the skittish horse on its muzzle. He glanced inside and nodded at Rebekah, confirming that he had the vial. Vivianne would get her husband, and at the same time Rebekah would get her payback. She couldn't say that everything was 'perfect', exactly, but things were heading in that direction.

NINE

*E*lijah slammed another book closed. Somewhere down the hall, the pounding of a hammer shifted the noise level from annoying to intolerable. Rebekah's incessant wedding preparations were worse than a nuisance – they were a constant reminder of the black magic Klaus had harnessed in order to get his way.

Klaus knew that all magic comes at a price, and a resurrection spell requires a heavy fee. Elijah wasn't quite sure what it was yet, but he suspected that the grisly murders over the last few days were only its beginning. The city was starting to devolve into a panicked state after a handful of humans had been found dead and with their hearts ripped out. The *morts-vivants*, as the locals were beginning to call them in terrified whispers, had not faded back into the bayou. Elijah had imposed a curfew on the entire city, and not even the rashest of citizens had been foolish enough to break it.

He pushed his chair back and stalked through the house, determined to get answers one way or another. None of his books – not even his mother's grimoire – had anything to say about witches who devoured hearts, which made Klaus's close-lipped stubbornness even more unacceptable than usual. Elijah *needed* to know what was happening in his city, and he was absolutely sure that his brother knew more than he was telling.

Klaus was prowling the front room like a lion in a cage, obviously distracted and irritated by Vivianne's absence. He could hardly stand to be away from her for ten minutes at a time, and Elijah had no idea how Rebekah had convinced him to let her take his fiancée out for the entire morning. Klaus had positioned himself so that he would be the first to see them return.

'It's time you tell me about that spell,' Elijah said, and for good measure he moved between his brother and the big bay window, blocking his view of the courtyard.

'It's done, and it worked,' Klaus snapped. 'That's all I have to tell.' Elijah wasn't sure what had made him so touchy about the subject, but he was beginning to guess that it was something he very much needed to know.

'It did what you wanted it to,' Elijah agreed, crossing

his arms over his chest. 'I need to know what else it might have done.'

Klaus stopped trying to see past him through the window and grew dangerously still. 'What else *might* it have done, dear brother?' he asked in a tone Elijah knew all too well. This line of questioning made Klaus see him as an enemy, but it was too important to just let drop.

Elijah had become convinced that the so-called *morts-vivants* must be returned from the dead. There was no other explanation, really. Elijah understood the ache of hunger he had seen that night in the bayou, as if the sight and smell of the heart had consumed them. They *needed* that heart in order to live, and to Elijah that meant they had to have been resurrected somehow.

And everywhere he turned, there was Vivianne, a witch who had been revived on the very same night. That could hardly be a coincidence, and yet she was completely different from the mob that had attacked him in the swamp. She seemed a bit subdued compared to her former vivacious self, but Vivianne was still thoughtful and articulate, and above all she had no interest in eating living flesh. She was nothing like the ravenous monsters he had encountered.

Elijah understood why Klaus resented the implication that there might be some kind of connection between them. For all his faults, Elijah knew that Klaus's love for

Vivianne was absolute. That was what made it so dangerous.

'I don't see why it matters, Elijah,' Klaus sneered as he turned to leave the room. In a leap, Elijah pinned Klaus to the far wall with his forearm pressed against his brother's throat – his patience evaporated.

'The *morts-vivants* could be a threat to *her*, you idiot!' he snapped, and although he had expected Klaus to fight back, those words finally seemed to penetrate his impossibly thick skull. 'If you really cared so much about protecting Vivianne, you'd tell me everything you know about who raised her and what they wanted in return. Unless you're more worried about protecting yourself?'

Klaus's lips pulled back in a feral snarl, but he raised his hands in a lacklustre approximation of surrender. 'I asked a witch,' he admitted, and Elijah relaxed the pressure of his forearm just a little bit. 'Her daughter was sick, and she wanted my help. I told her I wanted Vivianne in exchange, and she was willing.'

'Give me a name,' Elijah growled. He knew that Klaus wasn't telling the whole truth.

'It doesn't matter,' Klaus argued. 'All she wanted was a little of my blood for her brat. She did the spell and we were done. If witches did something to create your monsters out there in the bayou, it has nothing to do with me. Or Viv.'

'We don't know that!' Elijah snapped, shaking his brother for good measure. Klaus shoved Elijah hard enough to push them apart, and made a show of straightening his coat. Elijah backed off a step, but he didn't take his eyes off Klaus.

'There's something you don't know, brother?' Klaus mocked. 'I thought nothing in this city escaped your notice.'

That may have once been true, but hearing it out loud only made Elijah miss Ysabelle Dalliencourt even more. For forty-four years she had been not only his friend, but also his discreet window into the witches' councils. There could never have been a surprise like the *morts-vivants* while she had been alive, but witches didn't live forever. Although, if recent events were any indication, perhaps they didn't die forever, either.

'Who has your blood?' Elijah asked again, refusing to be drawn out by his brother's feint. 'Did you see her use it to heal her child?'

Klaus looked uncertain. It was unbearably stupid to hand out blood like it was nothing, and Klaus knew it.

'If you're so worried, ask to see her daughter yourself,' Klaus suggested, using bravado to hide the fact that he was conceding to Elijah's argument. 'It was your friend's daughter who took the blood. Lily something . . .'

Lily Leroux.

Elijah left the mansion and headed out for the swamplands.

Since the hurricane, the witches of New Orleans had been quite secretive about their location. It was common knowledge that they had made a home for themselves somewhere in the bayou, but no one seemed ever to have seen it for themselves. Not even Ysabelle would say where it was, but she had continued to visit with Elijah until the year she died. Through those meetings he had formed a pretty strong guess as to where the rest of her kind were hiding.

He crossed into the large clearing where she used to materialise. But even with his unnaturally sharp senses, all that lay before him was empty swampland. A bird trilled somewhere, and dragonflies chased each other through the lush undergrowth. Elijah knew better than to trust appearances over logic. He took a single step forward, and suddenly he could see everything.

There was an entire town where there had been nothing before – wooden houses, gravel streets and all of the witches who had deserted New Orleans – surrounded by a high wall.

Several people stared as he emerged through their magical barrier, but they didn't look particularly threatening. Some carried pails of water, and one had a basket of bread from which he was selling loaves to passers-by. He could hear the ring of a hammer on a blacksmith's anvil, and a flock of chickens ran loose across the muddy gravel. It looked ordinary, like any town he might have stumbled across.

'I need to see Lily Leroux,' Elijah announced to none of them in particular. He remembered Ysabelle's daughter as a chubby-legged little girl, but she now had a child of her own, and Elijah realised that he should have kept a better eye on this coven.

An older woman finished paying for a loaf of bread, then gestured for Elijah to follow her. She led him to the centre of the compound, where the thatched roof of a large meeting house rose above all the other buildings. Indicating that he was to go inside, the white-haired woman left without speaking a word.

He recognised Lily at once; although her colouring was darker than her mother's, her aristocratic nose and her brown eyes were immediately familiar. Elijah could see a little of her father, Abelard's, softness blurring the edges of her features, but otherwise Ysabelle's face had bred true in her only daughter.

She held court at one end of the meeting hall, surrounded by young witches and the remnants of what looked like a powerful spell. The entire floor was taken up with a massive pentagram, and the earthen ground looked as if it had melted. Not for the first time, Elijah wondered what kind of magic it had taken to pull Vivianne from her grave.

Lily did not rise to greet him. She watched his approach with an amused smile playing on her lips.

'I require an explanation,' Elijah told her when he reached the end of the hall. 'Monsters from beyond the grave are terrorising the city, and my brother tells me you were raising the dead on the night they first appeared.'

Lily looked around at her companions, as if sharing a private joke. 'Someone is being terrorised?' she asked curiously. 'You may have noticed that we are no longer part of the city's inner circle. Gossip takes some time to filter out our way.'

'It's hardly gossip,' Elijah countered. 'I've seen them with my own eyes, and I have no doubt you know the creatures I mean. They tear the hearts out of men's chests to eat, and they call themselves witches.'

Lily rocked back in her chair as if he had struck her, mocking surprise. 'You know our kind better than most, Elijah,' she scolded. 'You know we don't eat from humans.' *Not like you do* lingered unspoken between them.

'I know what I witnessed,' Elijah said. 'Aren't you at all curious about these things that stalk the bayou, committing brutal murders in your name?'

'My name is my own business,' Lily said. 'What others

do with it is theirs. I know nothing about this, and I cannot help you.' She leaned forward to rise to her feet, and as she did the shawl wrapped across her shoulders shifted just a bit. Just enough. 'I think it's best that you go. I'm sure you're extremely busy.'

'I am,' Elijah agreed, but instead of turning to go he bounded forward, pulling the corner of her shawl aside to reveal a silver chain that ended in his mother's opal. Klaus hadn't mentioned *that*. Elijah could think of a hundred reasons why he would have lied about it, and none of them were good. 'But I think we have a bit more business here, first.'

To his surprise, Lily didn't flinch. 'I now understand why it took so long for your brother to find someone to cast his spell,' she sighed, brushing his hands away from her collar. 'This kind of trouble always seems to follow you vampires.'

Elijah stepped back, surprised by her brazenness. She was by all accounts a powerful witch, but to show such contempt to his face was truly impressive.

'What was the true bargain you struck with Niklaus? He gave you his blood and my mother's opal?' Elijah demanded an answer. 'I suspect that curing some ailment of your daughter's was just a cover. Tell me the truth, before I show *you* what it feels like to have your heart torn out.'

Lily laughed, chuckling in the face of death, and Elijah realised that she must be quite mad. 'You can't hurt me, vampire,' she warned him, a teasing note in her voice. 'Don't you know what my pretty new necklace does?'

Esther had owned countless baubles and charms, but most of their secrets had died with her. Elijah honestly had no idea what the large opal could do. Reading his silence, Lily relaxed back into her chair, resting her hands on its carved armrests. 'This pendant links me to your brother,' she told him. 'He can't be killed, so nor can I. In the meantime, though, everything you do to me will happen to Niklaus. I can't be touched, Elijah. Not by someone who values family as much as you do.'

Elijah considered the merits of torturing his brother, but Lily was right. She was safe for now.

Trust Klaus to strike a bargain with such a devious, untrustworthy witch. Elijah felt positive that Lily's spell had something to do with the undead witches, but thanks to Klaus, his questioning had reached a stalemate.

'I understand that you have a wedding to prepare,' Lily said to him. 'I'm afraid I won't be able to attend, but I hope you'll give the happy couple my compliments.'

'I'll do that,' he assured her, venom dripping from his voice.

The *morts-vivants* would come out when darkness fell, and Elijah still didn't know what they were or how to stop them. Lily had been another dead end in a series of failures.

He had no choice but to turn and leave the hall. A slight brown-eyed girl shrank back from the doorway as he passed, and in the strong planes of her face Elijah recognised Ysabelle's features again, one more generation removed. Even if he managed to get rid of Lily, there was another Leroux – a perfectly healthy one, he couldn't help but notice – just waiting to take her place. It was exhausting.

Witches would continue to rise and fall, but his real problem was Klaus. Gravel crunched under Elijah's feet as he approached the palisade gate, and in his bleak mood it sounded like the grinding of bones.

TEN

*K*laus feathered paint onto the canvas with his brush, spreading little arrows of shadow into Vivianne's throat. Painting her from life was nothing whatsoever like the desperate work he had done before. It was as if she poured herself into the images, giving them a movement that he had never managed to capture while she had been gone.

It was soothing, too, which was a pleasant change from his encounter with Elijah. Klaus was sick of all the suspicious, accusatory looks, and that afternoon Elijah had taken the accusations too far. His implications had been offensive and insulting, and Klaus was ready to enjoy an evening alone with his bride-to-be.

'Can I see it *yet*?' Vivianne begged, laughing. Her

black hair tumbled unbound over her shoulders, and one slim leg had slipped out from the filmy fabric of her shift. Every time Klaus looked up from his work he longed to hold her, to drink from her, to make love to her, to possess her entirely.

There would be time for all of that, though – to enjoy each other in every possible way again and again. After everything Vivianne had endured, what he wanted most of all was for her to feel safe again, comfortable with him. He could wait for the rest until she was ready.

Vivianne raised her wine glass to her lips, which were as red and luscious as the liquid. 'Don't move so much,' he chided, and she giggled and waved her arms above her head. 'I mean it!' he insisted. 'I'll start over. You'll have to wait for this masterpiece as long as it takes.'

Vivianne watched him from beneath lowered eyelids. 'I think I've had enough of waiting for a while.'

Klaus cursed his choice of words. It seemed he was always doing that, relaxing into a happy moment and then ending it with a careless reminder of Vivianne's absence. 'I can paint you from memory, love,' he replied. 'There's no need to stay still any longer.'

They had barely spoken about what she had experienced during the long, dark years she had been gone. He couldn't bear the way her light dimmed, the way her sharp gaze softened and drifted away. Most of the time he could almost believe that Vivianne was untouched by the years she had passed in her tomb, but now and then he could see the memory of them filling her like a storm cloud. It was obvious that it pained her, and Klaus tried his best to spare her by steering clear of the subject . . . which was proving nearly impossible.

Klaus turned the canvas towards Vivianne without a word, letting her see the portrait that was unfolding. She gasped, and jumped up from her chaise to look more closely at it. 'It's beautiful,' she whispered, tracing its lines with a finger that hovered over the surface of the wet paint. 'Is that how you see me?'

'That's how you *are*,' Klaus told her, watching her face absorb the image.

She smiled, and it almost reached her eyes. 'Maybe on the outside.'

'I have lived centuries with only two siblings who distrust me, and two more I've had to keep daggered in their coffins,' he said to Vivianne, pulling her close. 'Believe me when I tell you that you're special. I have never met anyone else like you in all of my existence.'

'I just feel like I've failed everyone.' Vivianne sighed, surprising him. 'I went about things all wrong. I should have just told my family about us, and trusted them to understand I could never marry Armand once I had met you. Perhaps if I had, that ugly night would never have happened. My heart is still wracked with guilt.'

'Vivianne, you can't blame yourself for failing to keep the peace when all we've ever done is go to war against one another. Their deaths are not your fault.'

'I wish I could make up for it somehow, even if both sides of my family have renounced their ties to me . . .' She trailed off and put her head against his shoulder.

Klaus supposed that Viv wouldn't be herself without her overwhelming sense of responsibility, but he wished she could see how inevitable the war had been. As he looked down at her, he could discern the outline of dark circles beneath her eyes. 'It's just that . . . once, they all thought I would be the one to unite them under one banner of peace. I wish that I could now give them everything they were meant to enjoy.'

Klaus considered how unappealing that sounded. New Orleans was better off under Elijah's rule, and the Mikaelsons had no reason to miss the days when they had fought for any scrap of power. They were flourishing now, with no restrictions and no one to answer to.

'Once you are my wife, you'll be able to help the witches and the werewolves if you so desire,' he improvised. He couldn't imagine wanting to do such a thing himself, but if it was important to Vivianne he supposed he could look the other way. 'You'll be the queen of New Orleans. They may never quite forget their grudge, but they will respect you, and in time they *will* come to love you. Just as I do.'

He pulled them onto the chaise, so that she was sitting sideways across his lap. Holding her hands between his, he felt that her skin was soft but cool, not quite as warm as he had expected it to be. Touching her, he felt keenly aware of her otherness.

'You have always been my champion,' Vivianne remembered dreamily. 'If I had simply listened to you from the start and broken off my engagement when you asked, none of this misery would have happened.'

She hadn't been ready when he had first asked, though. They might have lived happily ever after, but they were stronger now. To have lost her and got her back made Klaus treasure Vivianne all the more.

A log crackled in the fireplace, warming the room. He caressed her bare arm, and saw goose bumps rise on her cool skin. 'You're here now,' he told her. 'That's all that matters. All we can do is look forward, and soon enough we will be wed.'

'I don't want to wait that long,' Vivianne whispered, turning her face up towards his. He could see the glistening of unshed tears in her eyelashes, and without thinking he bent to kiss them away.

She leaned back so that his lips met hers instead of her

tears, and suddenly every memory of every night they had spent together was as fresh in his mind as if they had happened only moments before. He had not wanted to rush her, unsure of what she might be feeling after so many years apart. But this kiss . . . It spoke of the same passion he felt, the same longing he had endured for decades of seemingly endless separation.

'I don't want to wait,' she repeated, then kissed him again. He lifted a hand to cup her jaw, and she shifted so that her legs draped around his waist. 'I missed you so much.'

He lifted her easily and carried her to the canopied bed beside the glowing fireplace. Her eyes gleamed, and he pretend not to see the hint of sadness that still lingered in their dark depths. He could chase it away; he could make her forget her pain.

He laid her gently on the silk bedspread, and she pulled him down onto the bed after her. He could feel heat beginning to suffuse her skin now, radiating out to wrap around him like a pair of inviting arms. He could get lost in it, drunk on it. She was different, there was no denying it. But she was also the same. His Vivianne, his heart.

She reached up to touch his face, stroking along the stubble that lined his jaw with an expression almost of wonderment on her face. He caught her fingers with his mouth, kissing them, keeping them, unwilling to let the smallest part of her go unclaimed. She sighed, although she didn't quite smile.

He wanted to forget where she had been, but he owed it to her to help her forget it first. She had spent forty-four years in the darkness because he hadn't been able to bring her back sooner, and every moment of her pain was his burden to lift. He longed to make her bright and joyful again, and over the years Klaus had learned a number of ways to produce that effect in women.

She tried to pull his mouth down to hers, but Klaus resisted, instead turning her hand to brush his lips across her palm. He moved to the sensitive skin on the underside of her wrist, then continued up along her arm, improvising with his touch the way he liked to do with the strokes of his paintbrush.

He feathered his mouth along her collarbone, her throat, remembering that she had once vowed he would never drink from her. Perhaps this second chance at life would change her mind about that, but the salty, sweet taste of her skin was enough for him for now.

He slipped down the shoulders of her shift, caressing each new inch of skin that was exposed. She twisted under his touch, the unshed tears still sparkling like topazes in the light. When her undergarments finally revealed the place her legs parted, he bent his head again, pressing his mouth to just the spot he knew would make her moan.

Her back arched, and her fingers caught in his hair, but he remained where he was, attending to his masterpiece. Her sounds of pleasure grew louder, and without seeming to realise it she pushed her hips up towards him.

Finally, taking advantage of his unnatural speed, he rolled, pulling her suddenly on top of him and undressing himself as he did. She laughed to find herself astride his naked form, and then she leaned back, her body gleaming in the light of the fire, and found a rhythm they could share.

The fire was nothing but embers by the time they finished and lay, still naked, above the bedspread, with their bodies twined together so closely that Klaus couldn't tell where his ended and hers began.

ELEVEN

*T*he ceremony took place at midnight, just on the cusp between one day and the next. The musicians found their places on the emerald lawn, testing their instruments for pitch while the guests chose their seats. Klaus stood motionless before the fountain, now half covered in moonflower vines bearing white blossoms drinking in the New Orleans air.

Rebekah's loving attention to every detail showed, and even the weather had submitted to her will. The night was sultry, and the sky above the Mikaelsons' mansion was an endless canopy of stars. Cicadas sang outside the ring of light cast by the thousands of candelabras, and laughter echoed off the house. The guests were in a lively mood, lulled by champagne, blood and the anticipation of the momentous event to come.

When things went wrong, it would be because Rebekah had planned it.

Elijah emerged from one of the side doors, immaculate in his formal black coat, with a heavy jewelled goblet held loosely in one hand. Rebekah had barely seen him between his endless research and his forays out into the countryside in search of his *morts-vivants*. He was obsessed, but Rebekah had yet to see them with her own eyes. Part of her wondered if they were even *real*.

Her brother went to stand beside the front door, and Rebekah took her place by Klaus's side. Klaus's eyes never left the doorway as the first strains of an old, familiar tune began to take shape and the last stragglers hurried to their places. The moment caught Rebekah's breath in her throat, no matter how cynical she had been before. Her brother was getting *married*, she realised. How strange, after all these centuries they had journeyed together.

Vivianne appeared, framed by the house and haloed by the light that spilled through the open doorway. Her dress was an extraordinary confection of white and red silk that clung and billowed and moved like a living sculpture around her slim body. Her black hair was piled high on the crown of her head, then tumbled down in thick, shining curls over her bare left shoulder. She carried an armful of red and white roses, and in the moonlight her pale complexion and flushed, excited cheeks seemed to mirror their colour.

Klaus looked like he might faint.

Rebekah steadied him with one hand on his elbow. She could see his muscles relax ever so slightly, and she knew he was glad that she was there.

Vivianne began to descend the steps of the porch, her gown spreading around her to float down to the lawn. When she reached the grass, Elijah bowed and offered her his arm, and together they walked to meet Klaus and Rebekah at the fountain. Elijah stepped back, and Klaus took both of Vivianne's hands in his own.

In other times they might have asked a witch to preside over a ceremony such as this one, but the couple had simply written vows, trusting in their own authority to seal the pact. Klaus was to speak first, but Rebekah had to elbow him, gently at first and then rather more sharply, before he seemed able to begin.

'Vivianne,' he said, the play of water in the fountain lifting and carrying his voice across the lawn. His voice was rough with emotion, almost hoarse at first. But as he went on, it grew stronger and clearer, and Rebekah could hear the clarity of his emotion in every word. 'I have lived a very long time, and seen more of the world than most people ever will. In all that time I never thought I would meet a woman as extraordinary as you. Your intelligence, your kindness, your beauty and your pride speak to me and touch me in a way I had never experienced in all my life. I told you once that meeting you ruined me, and it's true. I cannot be whole unless I'm with you. But my feelings mean nothing without your consent, your love. So this is my pledge to you, Vivianne: I will be yours for the rest of my days. I will cherish you, protect you and honour every request you make of me. Whatever your happiness requires, I will find a way to provide it. I will never give you a reason to regret your faith in me, even for a moment. I will be your family and your home, and I will spend the rest of my life showing you what it means to me that you have chosen to be mine.'

Rebekah dabbed her eyes discreetly with the handkerchief she had hidden in the pink folds of her gown. Standing like this, Klaus and Viv could have been any human couple, exchanging vows while their loved ones looked on. But they were so much more, and had been through so much more together. In spite of Rebekah's concerns about Vivianne, her rage at Klaus's hubris, and the accumulation of more than a thousand years of grievances and slights and unforgivable offences, Rebekah found herself moved by the depth of their love.

'Niklaus,' Vivianne replied, her voice quivering with tears. 'From the moment I met you, I knew that our connection was something rare. I was afraid to admit it at first, scared that I would be swept away by you and lose myself in the process. I had always intended to meet the world on my own terms, and the force of you – your chaos, your power – seemed overwhelming to me. When I let down my guard and began to learn about your heart, your true nobility, your loyalty and your fierce, passionate spirit, I realised that you didn't want to divert me from my true destiny. Instead, you were its instrument, showing me an entirely new path I would never have dreamed of on my own. I trust you, and I believe in you. I want to spend the rest of my life with you, and any others I may have after this one. I pledge to give you all of my love, to bring you every joy. I vow to be yours, Klaus, forever.'

They kissed then, so fervently that Rebekah could not have said which of them moved towards the other first. The crowd of vampires erupted in cheers and whistles, drowning out every other sound in the midnight air. The kiss lingered, and she exchanged a rueful smile with Elijah. It had taken a few centuries for their stubborn, difficult brother to grow up and find his true love, and it looked like he was planning to enjoy every second of married life now that he had his bride in his arms at last.

Elijah took Rebekah's hand and led her towards the house. 'Please join us inside for a meal to celebrate the union of this happy couple,' Rebekah called as they walked between the guests. She assumed that Klaus and Vivianne would simply join them when they were ready, which might not be for a few more minutes given their current state.

Now that the moving, emotional portion of the evening was over, it was time to put her sentimentality aside and attend to the more entertaining part of her plan. Klaus could be happy with Vivianne for the rest of eternity if he didn't find a way to cheat himself out of it, but he owed Rebekah one night of small, satisfying revenge. She couldn't let this chance for a bit of fun pass her by. A little dose of humility would be good for Klaus, and the harmless prank would fortify her against the next time his antics became almost unbearable.

Rebekah hurried to the kitchen, pretending to sample dishes and inspect garnishes while one hand worked the stopper loose from the little blue vial she had concealed among the rose-coloured folds of her skirt. A large pot of thick potato soup rested on one side counter. Rebekah leaned over as if she only wanted to smell the curls of delicious steam. Then, with a quick glance around to make sure no one was watching, she tipped the werewolf venom into the pale, creamy liquid.

'It will be ready in minutes, mademoiselle,' a cook assured her, appearing so suddenly beside her elbow that

Rebekah started in shock. The vial slipped out of her hand, and she didn't dare attract more attention by grabbing for it. It rolled away into a gap between the two pots, invisible but definitely, damningly there. 'We will pair it with the Riesling and the Romanian virgins' blood for the first course. Would you like to sample some?'

Rebekah eyed the pot and then the cook. The venom had seeped into the soup quickly, and he didn't look as though he suspected anything. But tasting the soup now would make her sick – not as ill as it would make a common vampire, but enough to notice. There could be questions, and the whole plan might unravel. She couldn't risk it; she couldn't even try to recover the empty vial. 'I'm sure it's fine,' she told the man. 'I look forward to tasting it along with the rest of our guests.'

He nodded, and with one last glance at the soup, Rebekah had no choice but to leave. The banquet hall seemed almost like a dream after the bustling of the kitchens. She had draped the walls with honeysuckle vines, and the warmth of the candelabras carried the subtle, sweet smell throughout the room. Waiters were beginning to pour the wine, moving silently as shadows among the cheerful, lively vampires they served.

Rebekah took her seat beside Elijah and tried to appear nonchalant. He looked preoccupied, his brown eyes focused on something far beyond the walls of the mansion.

'I'm sure the good people of New Orleans can manage without you for a night,' she said a bit more tartly than she intended to thanks to her own anxious nerves.

'Not all of them,' he replied grimly. 'The *morts-vivants* take new hearts every night, and no one has yet found a way to stop them.'

'Can you think of a single night since we arrived where no one has died in New Orleans?' she asked, tipping some wine into her mouth. Another servant set a goblet of blood beside her right hand, and she could already imagine the refined flavours mingling on her palate. 'The darkness has always been full of monsters.'

'This is different,' her brother insisted, glowering at his own goblet as it arrived. 'These are monsters with a purpose. They're connected to us somehow.'

'To *her*, you mean,' Rebekah said. Vivianne's flashes of darkness still troubled her – those sudden moments that Rebekah couldn't quite put her finger on. Sometimes, when she looked at her new sister-in-law, she would have sworn she was looking at someone else entirely.

Or perhaps Elijah wasn't the only one who needed a crisis in order to be content. Maybe Rebekah was looking for trouble. She had got so used to Klaus's endless drama over the years that it might just feel unnatural *not* to assume the worst about his actions. She found herself hoping that, once the dust from her little joke had settled, she would be in a better frame of mind to receive Vivianne into their family without jumping to fantastical conclusions.

The soup course arrived, and Rebekah tasted hers delicately, letting just a tiny bit of it spread across her tongue, alert for any hint of something amiss. The venom was tasteless, and she couldn't detect the faintest trace.

She forced herself to swallow another, larger spoonful, knowing that she needed to fall ill along with the rest of the crowd in order to avoid suspicion. It wouldn't be nearly as bad for her as for the rest – she would heal on her own, without having to rely on Klaus to cure her – but it still felt wrong to knowingly poison herself.

Elijah ate his portion with none of her reserve, seeming to barely taste it. 'Lily Leroux did the spell for Klaus,' he told her between mouthfuls, 'and they both lied to me about whatever arrangement they made. She used an opal pendant of our mother's to link herself to him for protection, which he didn't even bother to tell us.'

'Then she has something worth hiding,' Rebekah considered. She thought she heard a moan from one of the tables at the far end of the room, but she couldn't see what – if anything – was happening. 'And you think it's something to do with those things you're chasing around the bayou every night.'

'I do,' Elijah confirmed. Then he frowned and turned

his head, following the sound of another groan that was more distinct this time.

Rebekah was sure that the venom was beginning to do its work on the guests, because she could feel it herself. The entire room was growing hazy. The smell of the thousands of flowers became an overripe perfume, just on the verge of rot. Things moved at the corners of her vision, shadows that may or may not have been real. Around her, conversation flagged and faltered, and beneath the cheerful strains of music she could hear more and more pained cries.

'Why would a witch want to kill random humans?' she asked, trying to hold on to the thread of the conversation with all her might.

Elijah's eyes squinted and unfocused, as if he were listening to music she couldn't hear. 'She wouldn't,' he said.

A vampire fled from the hall, and another rose to her feet only to collapse. The first scream rose up from the diners, a high-pitched, strangled sound. 'Sabotage,' Rebekah heard, and then, 'Werewolves.'

It was working perfectly. She saw Klaus push his chair back so hard it fell over, his face a mask of rage. He first checked to make sure Vivianne was unharmed – the poison wouldn't affect her – and then he caught the nearest server by the collar. Although Rebekah couldn't hear what question he asked she could see the raw power of compulsion in his eyes. The girl answered without hesitation, but Rebekah knew she couldn't possibly tell him anything of use. Klaus snarled in frustration and snapped the server's neck. Poor thing.

'Werewolf poison,' she heard someone say again, and that finally spurred Klaus into action. His blood, that unique hybrid mix of vampire and latent werewolf, was the only known antidote. That always surprised Rebekah, coming as it did in the body of someone who was normally so destructive by nature.

Klaus worked his way around the room, systematically offering his blood-smeared arms to one vampire after another. Vivianne trailed after him to make sure each guest was on the mend. Vivianne was Rebekah's one source of minor regret. No bride would want the memory of her wedding feast marred by this kind of unpleasantness, and it was a shame that she had to suffer for Klaus's sins.

Klaus didn't bother healing Rebekah or Elijah, passing them without so much as a glance. Rebekah was free to simply watch, savouring the bedlam she had created during this elegant, happy occasion.

Rebekah found that her gaze kept travelling back to Vivianne, her gown standing out like blood on snow. To Rebekah's surprise, Vivianne didn't look angry or even afraid. She looked pale, almost sick. She paused to lean on a chair, clutching its carved back as if it were the only thing keeping her on her feet.

The werewolf venom shouldn't have affected her, *couldn't* have affected her. She was part werewolf, just like Klaus. And yet the longer Rebekah watched her, the worse she looked. Had Rebekah miscalculated some part of the poison? Klaus would never forgive her if that was the case.

Suddenly, Vivianne's hand shot out, snatching a goblet off the table and downing its contents in one long swallow. She spilled some of the thick, viscous liquid down her chin in her haste, and it ran out of the corner of her mouth. A few drops of Romanian virgins' blood splattered on the bodice of Vivianne's dress, blending in so neatly that if Rebekah hadn't seen it happen she might have thought it was part of the silk's pattern.

Vivianne straightened and wiped her lips self-consciously, looking around to see if anyone had noticed. Her hands shook at her sides, and she gripped her dress to keep them from trembling.

'Elijah! Elijah, did you see that?' Rebekah tried to whisper, but her mouth wasn't quite working.

'*Hmm?*' Her brother couldn't even turn his head towards her, and had missed the moment. He closed his eyes in pain and wiped the sweat from his forehead.

Rebekah was the only one who had seen Vivianne

drink blood, and now she couldn't stop seeing the scene over and over again.

Rebekah had known that Vivianne might be changed by the Other Side, but this went further than that. This wasn't trauma. What Rebekah had witnessed was the price of some terrible curse: the need for blood.

Just like Elijah's undead witches in the woods, she realised. They were eating hearts in order to stay alive, the same way vampires drank blood. And now Vivianne had joined them, another dead thing borrowing life from elsewhere.

She hadn't simply been given a second chance, the way Klaus insisted and his siblings had hoped. She had been altered somehow, and there had to be consequences – there always were. Rebekah had felt it since she'd first set eyes on Vivianne. Of course, her brothers had missed it. They were always looking for truth in the wrong places.

Vivianne must somehow be connected to the ghastly *morts-vivants*. She wasn't ripping hearts from chests – at least not yet – but there was darkness in Vivianne that was burning like a fuse towards gunpowder, and when it exploded there was no telling what might happen.

Rebekah's prank might have been juvenile and maybe even a little mean. But it had revealed a truth: Vivianne was dangerous. Even Klaus would have to admit that once Rebekah told him what she had seen. He had gambled to get Vivianne back, but he had got something evil in her place.

As if to drive that reality home, Rebekah heard the unearthly wailing sound of the house's protection spell. Someone had trespassed. The sound grew, and Rebekah cursed the awful timing of her 'harmless prank'. It had rendered the vampires weak and disoriented just when it looked like they would be needed most.

It had been foolish to think the wedding might ever go so smoothly that she would need to sabotage it, anyway. She turned to Elijah, who still looked a little glassy-eyed from the poison, although he had straightened in his chair at the sound of the alarm. He was shaking off the venom's effects far faster than the others, but still wasn't back to normal. 'Look alive, brother,' Rebekah urged him. 'I think tonight's surprises are just beginning.'

TWELVE

*E*lijah felt like he was emerging from a bank of clouds, stepping out of a haze into some kind of hell. Bodies writhed in pain all around him. Klaus was bleeding from both arms and his neck, and Rebekah was grimly separating the healthiest vampires from those who were still incapacitated by the werewolf venom. The chaos seemed nearly total until the chilling sound of the protection spell keened yet again, reminding Elijah that things could always get worse.

He stumbled to the nearest window. There was no way to miss what had set off the spell: they were everywhere. He even recognised one or two faces from the mob that had attacked him in the bayou. The *morts-vivants* had come in force.

'Close the doors!' Elijah bellowed, and even over the commotion in the hall he could see some vampires staggering to obey. Many of them didn't even seem to have heard his shout, or perhaps they thought he was just another hallucination brought on by the poison. 'We're under attack; lock everything!'

Elijah motioned to Klaus to keep feeding his blood to the last of the poisoned vampires. None of their army was at full strength yet, and their foes couldn't be killed. It was going to be a bloodbath.

He could hear the sound of doors and windows slamming shut all around the house, but it couldn't block out the sound of the dead things' grating voices. The noise was like a screw being turned in his ear, drilling slowly but inexorably towards his brain.

'We're sitting ducks in here,' a redheaded girl warned him, slamming wooden shutters across a pair of French doors. 'We need to take the fight to them.' She must have been poisoned along with the rest of them, but she had probably been among the first to drink Klaus's blood. Her freckled cheeks were flushed with excitement, but her grey eyes were sharp and focused.

She was half right, and her instincts for battle were sharp. The *morts-vivants* couldn't get inside, thanks to the protection spell that Ysabelle had worked on the house. More than forty years later, it still held, and if the monsters outside really were witches, they wouldn't be able to enter without an invitation. But Elijah couldn't just stand by while the vile things stalked his city, and he wasn't about to hide behind magicked walls when an enemy showed up on his doorstep.

'And who might you be, with such wise advice?' Elijah asked the redhead.

'Oh, I'm Lisette. Pleased to be at your service.' She extended her hand to be kissed, as if they weren't in the middle of preparing for a battle.

'Lisette,' Elijah replied, bending to lightly kiss the top of her hand. Her named rolled in his mouth. 'How long did it take you to heal, Lisette?' Elijah asked her. 'How soon do you think the rest will be ready?'

The girl evaluated the hall with shrewd eyes. More vampires were beginning to stagger back to their feet, but most of them still looked sick. 'We're not that easy to kill, you know,' she reminded him, deliberately sidestepping his questions with a sardonic smile. 'Not even if the werewolves warm us up for our enemies first.'

The connection was so obvious Elijah was surprised he hadn't seen it first. The arrival of the *morts-vivants* so close on the heels of the poisoning was no coincidence. The witches and the werewolves must be working together somehow, and for the werewolves to take such a risk they must have been sure the witches could finish off every last vampire.

Hugo Rey's tunnels had collapsed in the explosion forty-four years before, but Rebekah hadn't forgotten their value when she had improved the house. The original dirt passageways had been replaced with a network of wood-braced tunnels that ran to the very edges of the property. Those doors were points of weakness that the Mikaelsons had taken great pains to conceal and reinforce. The benefit of having such tunnels, of being able to outflank anyone who dared to approach the house uninvited, far outweighed the risk of leaving a tiny opening in the protection spell.

'There's a way we can attack them from behind,' Elijah suggested, blocking out the image of Ava's lifeless body over and over. He had lived far too long to be afraid of a fight, but that didn't mean he was enthusiastic about a battle against a horde of brutal, unkillable heart-eaters. Vampires would be killed, but it had to be done.

'I'll lead a group through the tunnel to the east,' Klaus announced, appearing at Elijah's side with a savage grin on his face. The disastrous end of his wedding feast had enraged him, and then enemies had appeared practically wrapped in a bow. Klaus's shirt was covered in blood, Elijah saw, and his self-inflicted wounds had barely started to heal.

'You'll sit this one out,' Elijah countered. Klaus opened his mouth to protest, but Elijah raised a hand to cut him off. 'Stay with your bride,' he ordered. 'She can't be in this fight, and no one will protect her as well as you will, as much as I would like you to join us, brother.'

He decided not to tell Klaus how important it really was that Vivianne survive this battle. It was about far more than sentiment: Lily Leroux was hiding something important, and Elijah felt sure it was related to the monsters at his door. Vivianne might well be the key to unravelling whatever Lily was plotting, and he wasn't about to let her die a second time before he was able to figure it out.

Klaus hesitated, torn between his vows to his new wife and his lifelong passion for battle, but with a muttered curse he ran to Vivianne's side, gesturing towards the great curving staircase and explaining something Elijah couldn't hear. They left the hall together, and that was one less thing for Elijah to worry about.

'Rebekah, take a group through the tunnel to the south. I'll take west, and' – Elijah's eyes fell on the redheaded vampire who still lingered nearby – 'Lisette, good. You'll take north.' The girl nodded, standing at attention like a soldier awaiting orders. She'd do well enough, he could see. 'Choose one more vampire you trust to replace Klaus in the east. The sickest will just have to follow us as they can. I've never seen one of these creatures die, and I don't know if they can, so whatever you do to them don't expect them to stay down for long.'

'If we can't slaughter them, we'll at least drive them off,' Lisette agreed, and he could see that she would execute her part of the plan just as well as his own brother would have. Perhaps even better, without Klaus's trademark unpredictability.

'Go,' he ordered, and she flashed him a startlingly winning smile before spinning to make her way through the crowd. He could hear her calling orders as she went, and the disorganised clumps of vampires realigning into something resembling an army.

Elijah worked his way around the room in the opposite direction, picking the most stable of the vampires and directing them towards the barricaded door in the cellar. Rebekah met him there with a sizeable band of her own.

Together, they unbarred the door, working quickly to unblock the heavy slab of stone and move it aside. Lisette arrived, along with another vampire that Elijah recognised as one of Rebekah's smitten admirers, each with several dozen others at their backs.

'We're under siege by monsters who don't stay dead,' Elijah announced, opting for brevity over detail. 'Break them up and get them away from the house however you can, and the first of you to figure out how to kill one gets the honour of killing a hundred more.'

'Stirring speech.' Rebekah grinned, and he noticed a smile on Lisette's face as well. The two women turned towards their opposite tunnels, Elijah and the other leader – Efrain, he remembered at last – hurried in their own directions, leading what Elijah hoped would be a coordinated attack.

A *mort-vivant* jumped on him as soon as Elijah leaped up through the concealed door in the grass. The witch's face was a rictus of hunger and fury, and the battle was joined before Elijah could so much as blink. They were just as strong as he remembered, and perhaps even faster. It lunged again, arms outstretched towards Elijah's chest, and as he ducked aside he found himself face-to-face with three more.

He wondered for a moment if this was what it was like for a human to be hunted by a vampire, to know that the powerful creature bearing down on him saw him only as a meal. Luckily, Elijah was a great deal more than human. He grabbed one of the monsters by her arm and ducked his shoulder to roll her across his back, throwing her hard to the ground. He twisted the head of another all the way round, hearing her neck shatter as he did. The third got close enough to sink his teeth around Elijah's collarbone, ripping into the flesh and viciously holding on until another vampire arrived to pull him off. The *mort-vivant*, an undistinguished-looking man in a wool coat who might have been about thirty, shoved his arm into the vampire's chest and tore her heart free of her battered ribcage.

Just like before, the other witches seemed to sense the heart. A few of them turned on the one who held it, and the fight grew hopelessly complicated as they all battled for the same thing. Elijah focused on protecting the vampires, freeing those who got cornered and engaging their attackers until his troops could regroup and fight again.

He knew that his side was losing. One vampire after another fell to the *morts-vivants*, and although a slow trickle of fresh soldiers still came up through the tunnels, he knew those reinforcements would soon run out. Sooner or later the house would be empty except for Klaus and Vivianne – how was that for a wedding night?

Elijah heard a strangled scream to his left, and spun to see a vampire impaled on the arm of a grinning *mort-vivant*. He sprinted towards them, but Lisette got there first. She had ripped her gown above her knees for freedom of motion, and what was left was so covered in gore that its original yellow colour was barely discernible. Her face was grim and focused, and she didn't hesitate before plunging her own arm through the chest of the dead witch. 'How do *you* like it?' she demanded, twisting her hand and withdrawing the organ. She clutched the *mort-vivant*'s slimy red heart in her hand, and held it up spitefully in front of his face.

His grin faltered. He lost his grip on the vampire, who staggered away as fast as she could. Her injuries were grave, but they would heal; her attacker wouldn't be so lucky. The *mort-vivant* crumpled like burning paper as Elijah watched. He collapsed on the grass with a final, spasmodic twitch, and then lay still.

Lisette studied him for a moment to make sure he wouldn't rise again, then lifted her head to shout. Her voice was like a hunting horn, cutting smoothly through the noise and chaos of the battle. 'Take their hearts!' she cried. 'They die without their hearts!'

Elijah could feel the shift among his kind as the cry was taken up again and again, spreading to every corner of the battle. Every vampire who heard the words attacked with renewed energy.

They had taken on many losses, and if the vampires hadn't been outnumbered at the start of the battle they surely were now. But the monsters now had a mortal weakness, and that was all Elijah's army needed to know.

'Die, bloodsucker,' a voice rasped beside him, and Elijah didn't blink. He shot out his arm; skin and muscles tore under the force of his blow, and his fingers closed around the monster's wildly racing heart. Elijah crushed it in his hand as he tore it out, savouring the faint gasp of shock that would be the last sound that ever escaped the *mort-vivant*'s lips.

Finally, he was able to exact some measure of vengeance for Ava's untimely death. All of the anger and outrage he had been forced to contain since that night came bursting out of him, and he attacked the *morts-vivants* with merciless savagery.

The re-dead witches started to pile up, and Elijah could now hear cheers among the screams of pain. The *morts-vivants* fought hungrily, but there was no doubt that the tide of the battle was turning.

By the time the sun rose, forcing both sides to retreat, the lawns were covered with corpses. Dozens of vampires were lost, but by Elijah's estimate they had taken at least a hundred of the undead witches with them. The rest of the *morts-vivants* – three hundred or fewer, he guessed – fled from the lightening sky to the east, melting back into the woods.

The vampires made their way back the mansion, some limping and others carrying wounded comrades. Elijah saw Lisette again, supporting a friend who had lost one of his legs and whispering encouragement to him as they hobbled along. She seemed to feel Elijah's eyes on her, turning for a moment to smile at him as if all the carnage had been nothing more serious than a picnic on the lawn.

Elijah watched her for a moment longer than he could really explain, then lifted a groaning vampire nearby and started back across the bloody grass. In spite of the long and trying night, he felt energised. The next time the *morts-vivants* dared to come out into the open, Elijah and his vampires would slaughter them all. With one last satisfied look at the mutilated corpses, Elijah strolled inside the house to rejoin his family.

THIRTEEN

*T*he battle wasn't going well. Klaus could tell that even from the shelter of the attic where he had taken Vivianne. He prowled from one window to the next, his sharp eyes picking out one fight after another. The *morts-vivants* just kept coming, no matter how badly they were crushed, slashed or disfigured.

Klaus understood that his presence outside wouldn't make much difference, and that protecting his new wife was more important. But he still longed to fight, to tear, to rip.

The ring of fighters seemed to contract a little every time he looked, getting closer to the walls of the mansion. He saw vampires he had made with his own blood fall while even the most horribly injured witches kept fighting.

It had to be Vivianne they wanted. They had only started harassing the city after she returned. She was the key: they had come to pull out her beating heart and drag her back to their cold graves with them.

'We can't stay here,' Klaus said, his voice falling flat in the still, empty air of the attic.

'The protection spell will hold,' Vivianne assured him. 'If it survived the hurricane, it will survive this.'

Vivianne had never flinched away from fear for her own life, but she could be moved by fear for others. She *should* be afraid. For the first time in a long time, he was.

'No, Vivianne . . . I think the dead witches have come here for you,' he said, letting the worry show in his eyes. 'They will keep attacking as long as you are here.'

Magic might have a price, but that didn't mean Klaus intended to pay it. He might not be able to defeat the army that was trying to steal back his wife, but he could outrun them. He had managed to steer clear of Mikael for centuries – this would be no different.

She twisted her hands together, absorbing that news. 'I'm endangering the vampires by being here, you mean.' Her black eyes darted. 'The only people who were willing to welcome me back, to celebrate our wedding, to accept us, are out there dying for *me*?'

Put that way, it sounded even worse than he had

meant it to. 'If we leave, though, they'll have no more reason to attack. They'll break off, and morning is getting close. We can be halfway across the world by the time they're ready to try to pick up our trail. If we get away now, they may not be able to find us again at all.'

He had no way of knowing how the witches had followed Vivianne in the first place, actually. It was likely that they had secured the help of the werewolves, who had weakened the vampires in advance of the attack. The wolves might be prepared to follow them during the day, trading off stages of the hunt. Even worse, maybe more *morts-vivants* would rise from their graves wherever Vivianne went.

He would fight off however many came for her, and they would stay on the move as often as they needed to. All that mattered was that they were together now. Vivianne had *died* and that hadn't ended their love – they could work around any other problem that the world threw their way.

Another scream rose from the garden, and Vivianne jerked forward, almost running towards the stairs. 'We are already packed,' she said, as if reminding herself.

'We're just leaving for our honeymoon a bit early,' he assured her as he followed. 'We'll stay away until Elijah learns the secret to sending these creatures back where they belong' – *they*, not *her* – 'and then we will return to help my siblings destroy them.'

The heavy trunks they had intended to take on their honeymoon would be far too bulky to bring along, but there were also a few smaller packs that Klaus could carry with ease. All were waiting beside the kitchen door, ready for a servant to port to Klaus's stagecoach. He picked through the pile of luggage quickly.

Vivianne occupied herself with finding some food, ignoring the remnants of the tainted wedding feast. As she pushed aside a platter of beautifully pink peeled shrimp, something caught Klaus's eye. It was a blue glass vial, lying half concealed by a giant soup pot. He had seen that vial before, or at least several dozen others just like it, during his brief reign as owner of the Southern Spot.

The whores always needed special teas and mixtures, and a good portion of the clientele also dabbled in laudanum and other substances. The suppliers of more common articles such as whisky, soap and fruits all had side businesses to meet those needs discreetly, and Klaus knew exactly which one used blue vials.

He snatched up the vial from the counter and gingerly tasted the inside of the rim. The stinging sensation was immediate and familiar. This was no medicine, nor was it some drug. This vial held werewolf venom. No werewolf would have needed to trade for a vial of their own toxin. But a vampire would have.

Klaus was used to betrayals by now, and he knew that his own family wasn't exempt from the practice. But this was worse, somehow. Elijah and Rebekah must have conspired to let their enemies win by poisoning their own. His dear siblings had fully intended to let the horrifying creatures reach Vivianne, and they had tried to shift the blame away from themselves, making convenient scapegoats of the werewolves.

There was only one possible explanation for such treachery. Elijah must have taken Rebekah into his confidence. Through his endless research, Elijah *knew* that the witches were coming for Vivianne.

And Rebekah herself was unbelievable. She hadn't wanted to help with the wedding at all. She had never wanted to welcome Vivianne as a sister; she only wanted to help put her back in the ground. His own brother and sister had plotted the death of his wife to save themselves. He would never forgive them.

They would have their honeymoon, but they wouldn't ever return. The whole city could sink into this cesspool of deceit for all he cared. The *morts-vivants* could pull out the hearts of every single inhabitant of this vile swamp in search of Vivianne's, but they would never get another chance at her. There was no one Klaus could trust to keep her safe except for himself, and that was exactly who he would rely on from this moment forward.

'Come on,' he told Vivianne, hating the rough, angry sound of his own voice. It was ridiculous that this would still get to him after a thousand years of being let down by his family.

'What's wrong?' she asked, laying a cool hand on his forearm.

He almost laughed at the absurdity of the question. What *wasn't* wrong?

'Nothing as long as you're with me, my love,' he told her, and kissed her forehead. 'But we can't stay any longer.'

'Then let us go,' Vivianne agreed, shouldering one of the lighter packs. It was an odd combination with the trailing silk wedding gown she still wore, but the defiant angle of her chin made her look brave and even a little rakish.

Vivianne squeezed his hand, and he smiled down at her. The entire world was ahead of them, where they could spend forever in each other's arms. Finally, after decades of disappointments, they were free.

FOURTEEN

*R*ebekah watched the injured being carried back into her home for what felt like forever. Her voice sounded numb in her own ears, but as much as she would have liked to retreat into her own room and stay silent, she had forfeited that luxury. 'Take her to the green bedroom in the south wing,' she ordered, resting a cool hand on a mauled vampire. 'Keep talking to her until you see her starting to heal. Her name is Amelie.' There were dozens of them, all with names and memories and gaping, gruesome wounds.

Rebekah was filled with conflicting emotions, and if there was one thing she hated, it was feeling uncertain of herself.

She had been wrong to play her silly little prank at the

wedding. Just when the vampires had most needed to stand together, Rebekah had divided them, letting her resentment against Klaus get the better of her common sense. She had no way of knowing how many of her kind might have survived if they had all been at their full strength. Their blood was on her hands.

Blood on her hands, though, was still less troubling than blood in Vivianne's mouth. Something was terribly wrong with her new sister-in-law, and Rebekah was the only one who knew it. Klaus wouldn't see – he didn't want to see. And Elijah had been so busy trying to discover the origin of the *morts-vivants* that he had missed the vital clue right under their very noses.

Rebekah needed to investigate Vivianne's strange behaviour at the wedding, and she needed to apologise to Klaus (preferably without explaining exactly what she was apologising for).

But the newlyweds were nowhere to be found. Rebekah's search took her from the attic all the way down to the kitchen, where she noticed that some of their luggage was missing from the pile beside the servants' door.

Klaus had fled with his bride, leaving his siblings behind to clean up his mess. It was just like him, and Rebekah would have been outraged if she didn't bear so much of the blame.

At least his sudden departure afforded Rebekah the opportunity to dispose of the evidence of what she had done. She ran to the counter where the potato soup had rested, but although the large pot was still there, she could find no trace of her little glass vial. She checked the tile floor, and then, with mounting anxiety, all of the other counters nearby.

Anything might have happened to it. A cook might have unwittingly reused it for some other substance, or perhaps it had broken and the pieces already cleared away. But in her heart, Rebekah knew better. Klaus had been here to collect his packs, he had found the vial and he knew that the traitor was someone in his own house. He had left to find safety with Vivianne – the least safe person he could possibly have chosen – because of Rebekah.

She ran back upstairs to find Elijah, who was deep in conversation with Lisette. They seemed to be reminiscing about the moment when Lisette had killed the first *mortvivant*, and Elijah's face was animated.

'I need to speak with you,' she interrupted, nodding an apology to Lisette. She stepped away and left the siblings alone.

'What is it?' he asked, and she could see the energy of the battle still written all over his face.

'Niklaus is gone,' Rebekah told him, rushing on. 'I'm

sorry, Elijah, but my temper got the best of me, and I meant to just play a harmless joke, to take him down a notch or two.'

'The—' Elijah frowned, then his brown eyes held her own, and she knew he had figured it out. 'The venom.' The playful excitement Rebekah had seen when he was speaking with Lisette was entirely gone. He was furious. 'How could you be so stupid? I expect this kind of thing from Klaus, but I didn't think I'd see you stoop to his level.'

If she'd felt stung before, that hurt a hundred times worse. 'I know,' she snapped. 'I need to find Niklaus and apologise to him, but I wanted to tell you first. You were right about the *morts-vivants* all along, and I was too angry at Niklaus to see it. But, Elijah, they aren't the only danger, and my apology isn't the only reason I need to find Niklaus.'

Then everything she had seen over the last few weeks tumbled out of her at once. Rebekah related every false note Vivianne had struck until the moment she had drained the goblet of blood. It wasn't until she had finished, nearly breathless, that she dared to glance at Elijah's face, to see if he believed her.

'I think Lily Leroux used Niklaus,' he mused. 'She brought Vivianne back, but I believe she also conjured the *morts-vivants*, or communicates with them somehow.

I think she *needed* the bargain with our brother, in order to further her true agenda.'

'So you see why I need to find the newlyweds,' Rebekah said. 'I plan to leave immediately'

Elijah hesitated, as if he were considering her previous mistakes. But instead he kissed her once on each cheek in the French style. 'Go,' he agreed. 'We both have work to do.'

An entire army of vampires had disturbed the packed earth of the tunnels, but only one exit had footprints leading *away* from the house. Rebekah following their trail east towards the ocean and realised that she already knew the way and had travelled these same roads forty-four years before. Rebekah had told Vivianne about a cabin by the sea where she had spent an unforgettable few days with Eric Moquet, and the young woman had been so charmed by Rebekah's description that she had convinced Klaus that they should retreat there for their honeymoon.

When she reached the cottage there was still some daylight left. She couldn't just barge up to the door and knock, and she wanted to understand more of what was happening to Vivianne first. Rebekah had known some humans and a few witches who had been resurrected from the dead, and none of them had ever sickened for want of blood. It wasn't normal, and it wasn't right. Vampires were the only creatures who were supposed to possess such hunger, and Vivianne certainly wasn't a vampire.

And so instead of marching to the door and making things right with her brother, Rebekah hid. Even on their honeymoon, surely Klaus couldn't spend *every* second with his new wife. Sooner or later one of them would have to leave the cabin alone.

So she waited, listening to the ceaseless lullaby of the waves sliding up the sandy beach. The rest of the day passed without even a glimpse of the happy couple, although Rebekah knew they were inside. Candles glowed to life in the small windows of the cottage as night fell, and eventually they were put out again. A cool breeze began to blow in across the water, carrying a familiar tang of salt with it. Rebekah dozed at intervals, bored beyond belief, and every time she was startled awake she expected to see Eric Moquet striding across the sand, the moonlight glinting off the dusting of silver hair at his temples. No one had ever claimed that atonement was easy.

A scream jolted her awake, and Rebekah leaped to her feet, instantly alert. The door of the cabin hung open, the darkness behind it gaping like a missing tooth. The sound had come from the beach, where she could just see a figure running for her life. But nothing was chasing her.

Vivianne screamed again, and the noise spurred Rebekah into action. Klaus was a heavy enough sleeper, but it wouldn't be long before he realised that his beloved was no longer slumbering by his side.

Rebekah raced along the beach, overtaking Vivianne within moments. She caught the distraught girl's arm, but Vivianne screamed again and lashed out, striking Rebekah hard across the face. 'It's *me*,' Rebekah whispered urgently, but Vivianne fought even harder against her grip.

'Let me *go*!' she shrieked, her voice entirely unhinged. Her sharp fingernails raked across Rebekah's cheek, and Vivianne froze at the sight of the blood that welled up in their wake. Then she lunged forward, her lips curled back in a feral snarl, and Rebekah felt the other woman's teeth sink into the skin her nails had broken. She was *drinking*, trying to drain Rebekah's blood while her hands searched for a better hold.

Rebekah shoved her away in horror, and Vivianne ran into the shallow, lapping waves like a woman possessed. Deciding that the time for delicacy was past, Rebekah tackled her around her slim waist, driving her down into the muddy sand and soaking them both in shockingly cold salt water.

Vivianne rolled with an unusual strength, almost overpowering her for a moment before Rebekah managed to catch her by her shoulders and hold her beneath an oncoming wave. Vivianne sputtered and coughed, lunging back for the shore, but Rebekah had the upper hand now and she wasn't about to lose it. She pushed Vivianne's head below the water again, reminding herself as she did that it was for the girl's own good.

'Stop fighting,' she warned, but Vivianne kept thrashing like a mad thing.

She gulped in a breath of night air before moaning, 'Just kill me.' They were both drenched in seawater, but Rebekah felt sure she could also see tears coursing down Vivianne's face in the moonlight. 'Please,' Vivianne whispered, so softly now that her voice seemed to fade into the crashing waves. 'You have to just let me go back.'

'You want to . . . die? Again?' Rebekah sat back in the sand, ignoring the waves.

'Something is wrong with me,' Vivianne gasped, pushing back wet strands of black hair. 'I can feel it inside, and it wants to get out.'

It was exactly what Rebekah had suspected, and yet hearing it out loud was different. For all the strange moments she had noticed, there had been hundreds more when Vivianne seemed perfectly normal.

'It's not easy to live again after dying,' Rebekah told her gently, helping her to her feet and holding her up against the pounding surf as they made their way towards the shore. The girl was docile in her arms, seeming to rely entirely on Rebekah's strength as if her own were suddenly gone. 'I know, Viv. But that doesn't mean—'

'Klaus!' Vivianne screamed at the top of her lungs, stunning Rebekah into silence. Another wave broke against their knees, and Rebekah lost her grip on the girl's arm. 'Klaus, help! Your sister is trying to kill me!'

Vivianne sprinted for the shore while Rebekah floundered in the water, cursing her own stupidity. Vivianne had *told* her what was wrong, and she hadn't been willing to listen. She had forgotten what she had known for over a thousand years: no one had a stronger desire to live than someone who had already died.

Vivianne's pain was real, and Rebekah believed that there was a part of her that was horrified by whatever darkness was creeping up on her. But that glimpse beneath the surface had been buried before Rebekah had wrapped her mind around it.

Vivianne's white shift glowed in the moonlight as she ran up the beach, and Rebekah caught her halfway back to the cabin. The two women fell together, striking the sand so hard that it knocked the breath out of their lungs.

'Klaus, help me!' Vivianne cried again, and Rebekah clapped a hand over her mouth.

'I'm trying to *help* you!' she hissed. 'Shut your mouth for a minute and let me!'

Vivianne bit her instead, clamping down hard on Rebekah's left arm and holding on as if her life depended on it. Rebekah felt her blood coursing hotly along her skin, and at least a little of it made its way into Vivianne's waiting mouth.

Rebekah was repulsed, just as horrified as the real Vivianne would have been. This *wasn't* the real Vivianne, she understood now. It walked and talked like her, but it was something else that wore her skin and even her personality like a mask. And it was eating away at the inside of that mask, thinning it out until little glimpses of its true nature showed through.

She ripped her arm away and slapped Vivianne's face so hard that her head whipped sideways.

Then Rebekah felt herself jerked up and backward by a powerful force. Her time was up. She wouldn't get a chance to find out what was wrong with Vivianne that night, and maybe not ever.

Klaus had finally woken up, and he was in no mood to talk.

FIFTEEN

*E*lijah's curfew had worked. Every door in New Orleans was locked against the night, all the shutters tightly latched. The cobblestoned streets glistened from the summer rain, and there was no other sound except for the vampires' footfalls echoing off the stone walls.

There weren't as many vampires as there had been at the wedding the night before, but they had healed, and most importantly of all they knew how to kill their opponents.

Tonight was going to be their night.

Klaus had fled and Rebekah had gone off after him, trying to atone for her horrid lack of judgement. Their inability to keep their emotions in check had cost Elijah two of his strongest warriors, and he resented being the only Mikaelson who was truly dedicated to his family's well-being. But the rest of Elijah's army was at his back, and they were more than ready for a good fight.

There was no sign of them until the vampire army reached the town square. There were dozens – maybe even hundreds – of torches approaching the square from the opposite side.

No humans would have dared to venture out so late, not even en masse. This was an entirely different kind of uprising. Elijah signalled to his vampires to spread out, and to capitalise on the keen vision that made torches unnecessary for them. They could see the witches coming, but the flames would blind them. They were walking into a trap.

Small bands of vampires hid behind buildings, fountains. They waited while the witches marched straight for the centre of the square, with its rather unfortunate statue of King Carlos III.

Through the light of the torches Elijah searched for their leader. Her straight nose and high cheekbones were just like her mother's, and the torches warmed her brown hair almost to the same auburn glow. Lily Leroux marched at the head of an army of witches, both living and undead, and the light reflected in her brown eyes was pure madness.

'I see you've stopped hiding behind your minions,' he

called, and each side took in their enemy. The addition of the living witches to the *morts-vivants* had swelled their ranks considerably, and Elijah could see that they were well outnumbered. There had been hundreds of witches the night before, and now there might have been nearly a thousand.

'Your time is over,' she called back, her voice pitched chillingly low. 'New Orleans has always belonged to the faction with the strongest army, and that advantage is no longer yours.'

He could hear the bitterness in her words, filled with the memory of her people's fall from grace. They had never been quite as powerful as the werewolves, but the witches had occupied a place of pride since the city had first begun to emerge out of a shabby fishing village stuck at the edge of the bayou.

It had been their own fault they had lost all of that, but obviously Lily didn't see things quite that way. She had raised the dead. She was responsible for human and vampire deaths, she was responsible for Ava. She had used Klaus and Vivianne to further her own quest for power, and in doing so she had struck at the very heart of the Mikaelson family.

No one could be allowed to attack Elijah's people and then simply walk away. 'Strike!' he shouted to his forces.

'None of them leave this square!'

The vampires surged forward, and the witches leaped to meet them. Grunts and screams rose into the still night air. Elijah pulled the hot, slimy heart from the first *mort-vivant* he could reach and held it up, hearing a cheer rise from the vampires around them.

There was an intense flash of light and something knocked him sideways. He pulled himself free and jumped back to his feet, noticing a huge scorched patch beneath his feet. He spun round and saw Lisette rising from the ground as well, brushing her clothing off without any sign she was hurt.

Lily let another fireball grow between her hands as she whispered her spell. She aimed the second bolt directly at the tall redheaded girl, who was too distracted by a knot of three other witches to see it.

Elijah dived to pull Lisette to the ground, and the spell sailed over their heads, crashing into a pack of witches. All three burst into flame, so burnt to a crisp that it was clear no ordinary fire consumed them. Lily was throwing something far more powerful and dangerous.

'We need to take her out,' Lisette grunted, rolling up to a crouch.

Another vampire – a blue-eyed waif Elijah dimly remembered being smitten with his sister – took one of the fireballs to his chest, and his scream pierced the noise of the melee around them. It went on for what seemed like minutes as the unnatural fire consumed him, burning away his flesh and then even his bones. In moments there was nothing left of him at all . . . and Lily was already brewing another ball of her potent magic between her hands.

Elijah drove forward, trying to reach Lily before her next assault could be launched, but the fighting seemed thickest around her. Every step he took brought him up against more *morts-vivants*, and more stake- and spell-wielding witches. He struck and hacked, but he couldn't seem to make any real forward progress.

Lethal spells sizzled through the air, and Elijah could tell that Lily's aim was wild and out of control. Her fire burned through his fighters and hers alike, destroying witches, vampires and a considerable number of manicured hedges.

An especially far-flung spell struck a stable near the edge of the square, and it went up like a torch in the darkness. Flaming timbers splintered and fell, and out of the corner of his eye Elijah saw the town house beside it start to smoulder. Lily would burn down the city if she wasn't careful . . . and she showed no signs of growing cautious.

A tavern across the way caught fire, and the two patches of brightness began to move towards each other, encircling the square in flames.

'Your mother would be ashamed of you!' Elijah

roared, and Lily finally turned his way. She was enjoying this, revelling in the death and destruction she was raining down. She shot a spell off quickly, almost flippantly, immolating two vampires along with an undead witch.

'My mother died in the swamp,' Lily spit back, and he could hear her over the din of the battle around them as if they stood alone in the empty town square. 'I've learned all she had to teach and more, and I have no desire to emulate her example.'

She launched fire at him and he sprang clear, using her distraction in the moment she released the magic to get closer. Only a few defenders separated them now.

A *mort-vivant* clutched at his back, catching hold of his shirt and attempting to slide her arm around his throat. Then she twitched and jerked, releasing him as quickly as she had caught him. 'Go,' snarled Lisette, her arm covered in the dead thing's blood, its hot, red heart in her hand. 'We'll keep them off you.'

In spite of the generous 'we', she was the only vampire in the vicinity. Apparently, though, she was enough. He felled two more witches who stood between him and Lily.

'I'll give you one more chance,' he growled when he reached her. He couldn't kill her, not with the spell still connecting her to Klaus. But he could distract her and create an opening to knock her unconscious. Klaus would be outraged, but he'd have to understand. 'Think about your honour, Lily, the honour of all of your kind. Your mother's memory deserves better than this evil.' Elijah could feel waves of heat emanating from her hands, but she didn't bring them together. Lily knew she was safe, even if her army was dying around her.

'I don't care about *honour*,' she hissed. 'I care about taking this city back, and that's exactly what I intend to do. Whatever it takes, whatever it costs.'

'Half of *your* new city is burning, then,' he said. 'Haven't you ever noticed that it's only when we're fighting that there doesn't seem to be enough of New Orleans to go around?'

She laughed bitterly. 'As long as we're content being under your boot or the werewolves', you mean, everything is just fine. I don't think so.'

'Every time you try to take power, look what happens,' he pointed out. He needed to defeat her, but the fact was that he *wanted* to reach her. He couldn't look at Lily without seeing her mother's face, and her mother had been Elijah's friend. 'You can't rule this city without razing it to the ground.'

'Better gone than yours.' She shrugged, and then smiled. Elijah leaped forward, but it was too late. With a sudden pressure in the air around them, Lily vanished.

As if some signal had been passed between them, the

morts-vivants began to drift away down the cobblestoned streets, disappearing among the flaming buildings. Over the fire's roar, Elijah could hear the clatter of hooves and the sound of shouting voices, and he realised that the humans had arrived to stop the fire.

As Elijah turned to follow his vampires back to the house, he nearly tripped over a prone body that lay half in, half out of the fountain. Her hair shone reddish-gold in the glow of the flames, and Elijah cursed his carelessness.

Lisette had certainly held her own and more, but from the look of things she had fought off over a dozen witches while he had traded threats with Lily Leroux. She stirred as he lifted her, lashing out blindly even though her heartbeat was so weak he could barely hear it.

'The fighting's done for now,' he told her, gently restraining her hands until her grey eyes were able to focus on his face. The news that Lily had got away could wait. Lisette had gone above and beyond to make it possible for Elijah to take out the power-crazed witch, and he could only imagine what she would have to say when she learned that he hadn't managed to do it. He looked forward to seeing Lisette back on her own two feet while she dressed him down for his failure.

It was time to leave. The plaza was littered with bodies, and there was nothing to be done about that. He called to the nearest vampires and signalled a retreat.

He needed a new plan, and his options were running out. His forces were badly weakened, yet the witches only seemed to be growing stronger every time they clashed. Elijah needed reinforcements, and there was only one place left to turn.

There was no love lost between the Original vampires and the werewolves. But the werewolf Pack had never much cared for the witches, either. The uneasy truce between those clans had been plagued by setbacks and betrayals even before the witches' hurricane had destroyed the werewolves' home and sealed their exile.

Now that Rebekah had admitted that she had been behind the poison, it seemed that the werewolves still hadn't chosen a side in Lily's war. But everyone wanted something, and Elijah had a lot to offer to new allies.

He turned, with Lisette still in his arms and her head lolled against his chest. She would be better in no time, he knew, but for now he carried her, stepping carefully.

Elijah had never had the slightest intention of ever doing the werewolves a single kindness again, and he knew what Klaus would say about the idea. But containing Lily and her kind was of the utmost importance. If he had to make friends of old enemies in order to save the city from her madness, then that was exactly what he would do.

SIXTEEN

*F*or decades, Klaus only had one recurring nightmare. He would roll towards Vivianne in bed, reaching for her, and find nothing but the cold, crumpled sheets behind him. He was always seeking her, and she was always just out of reach.

For a moment he thought he was dreaming again – the empty bed was just another nightmare he would wake from if he just kept reaching. His hands slid blindly across the cold bedsheet, trying to find the warm curve of her body. The screaming was a new addition, though, and the longer it lasted the more wide awake Klaus felt.

The screaming was real, he realised, and Vivianne was nowhere to be seen. It wasn't just the bed; the entire cottage felt cold and empty without her. And someone was screaming.

He bolted out onto the darkened beach, and he saw them immediately. The two women who struggled together on the sand were so familiar to him that for a moment Klaus thought he might be dreaming after all. His sister had never appeared in this dream, but in all of these nightmares, everything imaginable stood between him and Vivianne. Rebekah slapped her so hard that her head snapped backward, and Klaus could see blood on his wife's fragile skin. The mismatched fight offended him to his very soul: Rebekah's invulnerable immortality stacked up against a woman who had been dead longer than she had been alive. It was unfair, and worse than that, it was *mean*. Klaus had always been able to fall in and out of hate with his siblings, but he couldn't remember ever feeling such contempt for his sister.

He crossed the wet sand between them in the blink of an eye and threw Rebekah back, putting as much distance between her and Vivianne as he could. Vivianne looked unharmed, but she was crying hysterically and clung to him.

'What the hell have you done?' Klaus demanded as he rounded on Rebekah.

She sat frozen in an awkward half-crouch, but looked ready to spring at him. It was bad enough that she had conspired with Elijah to ruin his wedding, but *then* she had chased him down to ruin his honeymoon, too? That seemed low, even for her.

'That's not Vivianne,' Rebekah growled, but she stayed where she was. 'It's something else, something unnatural.'

'We're *all* "something unnatural",' Klaus scoffed. He positioned himself between the two women, with Vivianne behind him. The hairs on the back of his neck stood up, and he cursed Rebekah for trying to plant doubts in his mind. 'I know what you and Elijah did, dear sister, and you won't have to worry about seeing me and my "unnatural" bride back in the city anytime soon. I won't abide traitors.'

'Elijah?' Rebekah straightened slightly, brushing wet sand from her skirts. 'Elijah had nothing to do with this. You're so paranoid, Klaus – it was a *prank*. A stupid prank that got out of hand, and I regret that. But after it was done, I saw—'

'A *prank*?' Klaus had thought he was jaded to the depths of Rebekah's bad judgement, but she constantly managed to surprise him. 'You meant it to be *funny* to poison us at our own wedding?'

'I didn't poison either of you,' she pointed out, twisting her loose golden hair into a wet knot at the nape of her neck. Vivianne shifted a little, and Klaus wished he could keep his eyes squarely on them both without putting Viv in harm's way. Why had she left the cabin at all, and why couldn't he make that uneasy prickling sensation stop? 'And I came here at least partly to apologise. But—'

'But nothing,' Klaus interrupted.

'She didn't seem to want to apologise when she attacked me,' Vivianne murmured, and the soft, wounded sound of her voice made him even more furious. She had trusted Rebekah. She had thought she was gaining a new family to replace the ones that had turned their backs on her. And instead Rebekah had used her to make a point, to get back at Klaus over whatever petty gripes she imagined she had against him. Her betrayal of Vivianne was even worse than of him, because at least he should have known Rebekah well enough by now to see it coming.

'She ran out of the cabin screaming,' Rebekah told him, low and urgent, as if she could tell the tide was turning against her. 'She drank blood at the wedding when no one was looking, and she just begged me to kill her.'

Did Rebekah really believe that Vivianne wanted to die again? They had gone into the water for some reason before continuing their fight back up on the beach. Had his sister tried to drown the love of his life while he slept just a few hundred yards away?

'She keeps saying those things,' Vivianne whispered. 'I don't understand what she's talking about.'

Rebekah seemed to almost explode in anger. She sprang, knocking Klaus aside to grab Vivianne by her thin, trembling shoulders. 'Tell him!' she shouted, and Vivianne cringed into herself. 'Tell him what you did, what you said!'

'Please,' Vivianne whispered, and then Klaus smashed his fist into Rebekah's temple. She reeled away, but she didn't retreat.

'How long have you known me, Niklaus?' Rebekah's pretty face was a tragic mask of disappointment and despair. She had some nerve, trying to trade on their long history together as if it had all been happy family memories. 'I would never betray you like this. I'm trying to *help* you.'

Vivianne sobbed beside Klaus, her pale arms wrapped around her body as if they could protect her from the next attack. But they wouldn't need to — that's what she had him for. 'You expect to trade in on some bond we never really shared, to convince me that my wife isn't who I think she is? The only one who has betrayed anyone lately is you, Rebekah, lest you forget.'

'The prank was stupid,' she agreed, her chin set stubbornly. 'And I am sorry, but I can't regret it entirely,

Niklaus, because while everyone was poisoned I finally saw Vivianne's true nature.'

'Enough,' he snapped. It was too ridiculous. Drinking blood and begging to die and circular reasoning that somehow justified Rebekah's appalling actions – it was as if she honestly believed she had somehow saved them all with her childish pranks.

To be fair, he'd had questions of his own at times: whether Vivianne was as whole and as strong as she wanted him to believe. But that was only natural, not the alarming disaster Rebekah was making it out to be.

Vivianne shivered in the cool breeze that blew off the waves. The tide was coming back in, and the cabin looked like it was miles away.

Rebekah had nearly reached Vivianne by the time he saw her coming at all, and before he could grab her she was gone again, dragging his bride towards the pounding surf. Vivianne screamed, but Rebekah didn't falter.

'Tell him,' she ordered again, ducking Vivianne's head below the waves. She came up gasping for air, and Rebekah pushed her under again. 'I know you remember. Tell him what you told me!'

Klaus felt blind rage overtake him as he waded into the sea.

'I don't know,' Vivianne sputtered, spitting out seawater, her hands trying to push off the water. 'I don't know!'

Unbelievably, Rebekah still wasn't satisfied, but Klaus had seen more than enough. He reached them at last, catching Rebekah by her knot of hair, stiff with salt water, and dragged her head back. He bit her exposed throat, his fangs tearing through skin to leave a bloody hole in the centre of her windpipe.

It wouldn't kill her, but for the moment she lay limp on her back, bobbing on the waves like driftwood. He only needed time to get Vivianne away, to go somewhere his lunatic sister wouldn't think to look for them. It had been foolish to come to the cabin at all, but he wouldn't make the same mistake twice.

He carried Vivianne gently, cradling her against his chest. She stared up at him, her black eyes as deep as the sea itself.

They were less than halfway to the cabin when he heard the pattern of the crashing waves change, some disturbance in their rhythm that alerted him just in time. Klaus set Vivianne down carefully on her feet and turned to meet his sister's renewed attack. Her throat was still a bloody mess, and she couldn't speak. Her dark-blue eyes were riveted on Vivianne, as if her only purpose in life were to destroy what he loved most.

As if she had a chance in hell of reaching his wife.

SEVENTEEN

Rebekah choked up salt water. She was floating, face-up and buffeted by each passing wave. She could taste her own blood mingled with the briny liquid. Klaus could be on the move already. Spiriting Vivianne away to some new hiding place. She couldn't let them get away.

With some effort, her feet found the swirling sand beneath the water, and she forced herself to run.

Klaus turned when Rebekah was only steps away from Vivianne, and she saw the flash of his fangs just before she felt them tear into her. He aimed for her throat, trying to reopen her wound. She shifted and spun so that his fangs sank harmlessly into her upper arm. She continued her rotation, landing a solid kick that would have liquefied his internal organs if he had been human.

As it was he staggered back, taking a piece of her arm with him as he did. Vivianne shrieked like the damsel in distress she was pretending to be, and Rebekah could feel that her throat had healed enough for her to find her own voice again. 'How do you . . . not see . . . what she's doing?' she demanded, ducking below Klaus's next attack and using his momentum to throw him to the ground. 'Is that delicate . . . flower . . . the Viv you fell in love with? She's manipulating you . . . idiot.'

'Don't you even say her name,' Klaus snarled, bounding back to his feet faster than Rebekah's eyes could follow. 'You tried to kill her.'

'I tried to make her talk,' Rebekah argued, her throat almost whole again. 'I don't want her . . . dead until we know what the hell she's doing here.'

'She's here for *me*,' he shouted, feinting for her head and then knocking her legs out from under her.

Rebekah landed hard on the sand, scrambling to get back up before Klaus reached her, his fangs extended again. For a moment, she remembered their fight in the mansion, before he had brought this evil down on their heads. She had been so angry, and he had been so unreasonable. That seemed so long ago. They had bickered like siblings then, but this time they fought like enemies.

Rebekah gouged at her brother's eyes, then bit back a scream when he snapped one of her thumbs. She threw sand in his face with her uninjured hand – a childish trick, but effective. She dislocated Klaus's shoulder with a deeply satisfying pop, then threw him as far as she could. As soon as he was airborne, she lunged for Vivianne, who threw up her hands in a futile gesture of self-defence. 'Tell him the truth,' she ordered, compulsion filling her voice. 'Tell Klaus what you are.'

Vivianne gulped in air, as if Rebekah held her under the water again. 'I'm Vivianne Lescheres Mikaelson,' she answered helplessly. 'That's all I know.'

Klaus barrelled into Rebekah's back, knocking the wind out of her as they crashed together onto the ground. Rebekah rolled just in time to see the flash of silver in his hand, and to realise her mistake. Of course Klaus had brought his daggers on his honeymoon.

The dagger burned as he buried it in the left side of her chest, and Rebekah felt tears building in her eyes. All Rebekah knew was that she had failed, and now whatever was hiding in Vivianne's body would be free to do its work unchecked. 'You're making a mistake,' she hissed at him, and he twisted the dagger deeper into her heart.

The blackness was coming, just the way she remembered it.

'You've lost your touch, dear sister,' he said. 'Perhaps some time away will help clear your head.'

Vivianne's face flickered in and out of focus. 'You deserve whatever comes your way,' Rebekah whispered with the last of her strength.

Their faces dimmed and disappeared. The beach was gone, along with the cabin and the roar of the ocean. All that was left was Rebekah. And then, in another moment, there was nothing.

EIGHTEEN

'I still think you should go in force,' Lisette said, resting one foot on the side of Elijah's desk. Her injuries from the battle had been even worse than he had originally thought. Like any vampire she had healed quickly, but Elijah still found himself watching her, checking on her, marvelling at her strength as if he hadn't seen the same kind of supernatural recovery thousands of times before.

'Bringing an army of vampires to meet an army of werewolves is more likely to start a war than an alliance,' Elijah disagreed.

Lisette laughed, tossing her strawberry-blonde hair back behind her shoulders. Elijah caught himself staring again. He could still see her lying lifeless in his arms, and he wanted to replace every shred of that memory with the sight of her now, vibrant and vivid and full of energy. 'Every vampire here follows your orders,' she assured him. 'No one would step out of line. They would just stand there. Looking . . . impressive.'

'They would look intimidating,' Elijah said. 'The werewolves don't want to be swallowed up by a stronger force. They'll want to know their voices will be heard.'

'Well then, if you feel so strongly about it, leave the army at home. But you should have at least one person there to watch your back. Me, for example.' She grinned, raising her pale eyebrows to make her face look especially innocent.

Elijah smiled in spite of himself. He would have loved to have Lisette's company during his visit to the wolves, but he wouldn't be able to concentrate with her there. When she was in harm's way, Elijah couldn't think about anything else.

He stood impulsively, then leaned down to kiss her on her forehead. When he stood again, she was staring up at him, her grey eyes looking larger than ever in her surprise.

'I will not risk you on this mission,' he told her firmly. 'And I need you here to keep an eye on things while I'm gone.' He didn't expect to Klaus and Vivianne to come home anytime soon, but he was concerned that there had been no word from Rebekah.

Lisette rocked her chair back down onto the floor and

stood. 'You can count on me,' she answered, as if she wished she were saying something else.

He stepped closer to her. 'I *do* count on you,' he said, then touched her chin lightly, tilting it up so that her mouth met his. She returned his kiss, reaching up to hold both sides of his face, keeping it close to her own.

He couldn't remember the last time a kiss had felt so natural and yet so thrilling. There was an ease in the constant friction between them that he couldn't begin to explain. The feel of her mouth on his was like coming home.

He rested his forehead against hers, feeling more at peace than he had since long before the *morts-vivants* came to the bayou. 'Stay here,' he repeated, but this time he was asking her rather than commanding her.

'Come home soon,' she replied, and *that* he recognised as an order.

'Yes, ma'am,' he agreed, and it was a promise he intended to keep.

Elijah's feet fell silently on the forest floor. He felt watched as he made his way through the woods, followed by dozens of yellow eyes. A twig snapped behind him and he spun, every sense alert. Elijah began to move even more cautiously, convinced that he was being trailed.

The werewolves had formed a little colony in the

shelter of the woods, as far in the opposite direction of the witches' compound as they could get while still remaining within striking distance of New Orleans. The reign of the Navarro wolves was over, and William Collado was their new leader. That was a bit of a sticking point for the Mikaelsons, since Rebekah was responsible for his father's untimely death. William Sr had picked a fight with Elijah at Vivianne's engagement party, then had the bad luck to be on hand when Rebekah needed a scapegoat for an unrelated murder. Rebekah had turned Collado over to Eric, the captain of the French army, who had tortured and killed the werewolf without ever learning his true nature.

His son was unlikely to forget that little piece of his family history, but Elijah was optimistic that they could overcome the bad blood between them. No personal vendetta would outweigh a chance to regain some of what had been taken from William's Pack.

Still, when the attack came, it blindsided him. Someone slammed into the centre of Elijah's back and knocked him down before he even heard the man. As the man's large, balled fist pummelled his face, he was grateful that the full moon was still another night away. He saw stars while the man twisted a rope around his hands, pinning him to the ground. Elijah exploded back up to his feet and looped the rope around the werewolf's thick neck, pulling hard enough to restrict his windpipe. The big werewolf's eyes widened in fear, and Elijah assumed he was starting to figure out that he'd caught some unusual prey. His meaty hands scratched at Elijah's forearms, but once an Original had the upper hand, the fight was as good as over.

The wolf began to gasp and then sag, and Elijah bound him with the rope. He paused to wipe the trickle of blood at the corner of his own mouth. Elijah resented being caught so off guard – for all his size, the creature had struck with unbelievable speed.

'What are you doing in this part of the woods?' the werewolf snarled. He didn't seem to care that one of the most powerful vampires in the world had tied him up. Elijah wondered what exactly the werewolves had been up to out there in the wilds of the bayou. It seemed that exile had made them bold.

'I have business here,' Elijah said, 'just not with you. Take me to William Collado,' he ordered. He didn't want the wolf to get any ideas about another surprise attack. It wouldn't do to have to kill one of them before asking the rest for their help.

Fortunately, the werewolf seemed to have had enough of tangling with Elijah, at least for the moment. He gave an annoyed grunt, but nodded. 'Have it your way, vampire. But werewolf business is everyone's business.'

Elijah paused for effect, then untied the werewolf. The man's thick lips were set with resentment, but he turned submissively enough to lead the way. When his back was fully turned, Elijah heard him mutter something under his breath.

'What was that?' he asked, steel underlying his light tone.

The werewolf kept moving forward across the carpet of undergrowth, but cast one spiteful glance over his shoulder. 'I said, "Be careful what you wish for",' he repeated.

More werewolves appeared as Elijah got closer to their hideout, slipping out from between the trees. They moved so silently through the undergrowth that Elijah was never quite sure how many there were. The scout was no longer content to lead the way in sullen silence.

'You'll need to go the rest of the way blindfolded,' he announced, planting his feet firmly on the ground and crossing his burly arms across his chest. No matter how much it annoyed him, Elijah had to let the werewolves pretend they were equals. If that was the ego stroke they needed, he would have to indulge them. But William Collado had better be more reasonable than his underlings, because Elijah's patience wasn't infinite.

He held himself still while a cotton rag was tied across his eyes, not risking any movement that might trigger a deadly misunderstanding. Rough hands shoved him forward, adjusting his direction along some path he couldn't see. But he could hear his destination, the sounds of werewolves ahead vastly outnumbering those who walked behind him.

Two werewolves grabbed his shoulders to stop his forward motion, and one of them had the nerve to push downward as if trying to get Elijah to kneel. He yanked the blindfold off his eyes, thoroughly sick of the charade. He stood at the centre of a ring of werewolves carrying torches so numerous that they washed out the stars.

There were more werewolves than there should have been – a lot more. They must have recruited new Packs since they'd left the city's borders. The man who stood in the centre of the circle was younger than Elijah had expected, and in his clenched jaw Elijah could tell that he still nursed his family's grudge.

'You found us, vampire,' the young leader acknowledged, his voice gruff. The moonlight glittered in his piercing-blue eyes. 'Now, what do you want?'

NINETEEN

*K*laus snapped a guard's neck and buried his fangs deep into another. He was hungry and angry. There were a few servants hurrying across the courtyard and he killed them, too.

Daggering Rebekah hadn't nearly satisfied his need to destroy . . . something. And anyway, Vivianne had forced him to let his sister go. He had fully intended to leave her lying on the beach with his silver dagger in her heart. With any luck the tide would have carried her body away. She might have drifted on the waves forever, powerless to bother anyone ever again except for the occasional passing ship that might need to steer around her.

But Vivianne had been overcome with compassion,

and she had pleaded with him to reconsider. It pained him that she could be so forgiving, but that was Vivianne's nature. Vivianne waited outside the iron gate of the palatial villa, her loose-fitting gown glowing under the nearly full moon. She seemed a bit thinner than he remembered, her delicate frame bordering on gaunt.

A guard ran across the courtyard brandishing a sword. Klaus snapped it out of his hand and used it to kill him, as well as two of his comrades, almost as an afterthought. Even as the guards collapsed onto the ground, Klaus noticed a footman stumbling towards the open gate. The man was probably just trying to escape, but the only way out of the villa happened to lead towards Vivianne, and for that he had to die. He flipped the sword up into a ruthless overhand throw, and a second later it was impaled in the footman's back.

The mansion's owner, the elderly Barón de Something-or-Other, was staying at his residence in Baton Rouge, so at least the villa was mostly empty, and not very well defended. Klaus owed Vivianne a honeymoon, and he intended to give her one. The first had been cut short rather dramatically by Rebekah's lunatic attack, but that was all behind them now. This would be even better: a palace deep in the countryside of Louisiana.

He tore both arms off someone he was too blind with fury to even see clearly, and then there was no one left to kill. There must be a few terrified servants left hiding inside the mansion, but compulsion would take care of the rest, and perhaps it was time for Klaus to regain a *little* self-control.

If he wasted his entire honeymoon venting this rage, Rebekah would have won.

He stepped casually across the corpses to rejoin Vivianne, and lifted her in his arms. 'My lady,' he said gallantly, 'our villa is ready for us.' He carried her across the threshold, and she nuzzled her face against his chest rather than look at the bodies. She definitely felt lighter than he remembered, and he hoped that a cook or two were left among the survivors. Vivianne needed rest and food and safety and love, and he intended to provide all of them in generous amounts. He set her down in the elaborately gilded foyer.

'Alone at last.' She smiled, although the expression didn't quite reach her eyes. 'For the moment, at least. Klaus, we will be hunted wherever we go.'

He should never have told her that it was she the *morts-vivants* were after – it weighed on her. 'I always admired this place,' Klaus told her, refusing to be drawn down that morbid line of thought. 'I never had a reason to take it over before, but for years now I have thought of it as somewhere I would love to bring you someday.'

She looked around finally, taking in the beautiful

mosaics and the graceful arches. Every inch of the mansion had been used to make the place even more stunning; the barón had plenty of money and no instinct towards restraint. His country home was hedonistic in its elegance, and Klaus looked forward to spending some very enjoyable days and nights under its frescoed ceilings.

'I've never seen a palace quite like this one,' Vivianne admitted. 'I had hoped to travel once I was married, but . . .' She trailed off, looking confused, as if her new life were overlapping with her former one in such a way that she couldn't tell which was which.

He hadn't given her onetime fiancé a second thought since the blast of gunpowder had gone off, taking Armand Navarro with it. It stung a bit that Vivianne still remembered him as the man she had once meant to marry. Armand had been too provincial to ever truly satisfy a woman like Vivianne. He had been a local boy through and through, already married to his family's pathetically small sphere of influence.

'Well,' Klaus replied, taking her hand and leading her down a column-lined hallway, 'you are married now, and we can go wherever you like. This villa was modelled after a particularly flashy palácio in the south of Mallorca, and we can go there next and compare the two.'

Vivianne laughed, the sound ringing musically along the length of the hall. 'Why stop there?' she teased. 'From what I saw just now, we could conquer the world.'

Klaus wrapped an arm around her thin shoulders and tucked her closer against his body, a loving gesture meant to conceal the worry on his face. Vivianne had never been bloodthirsty; if anything, violence repulsed her. Even he could admit he had got carried away in the courtyard, and yet she didn't seem troubled by it at all. She had only stood there, watching, and now she seemed willing to do it all again.

She drank blood, Rebekah claimed, *and she begged me to kill her.* Vivianne had hidden her face from the sight of the corpses outside, but once upon a time the mere thought of them would have continued to haunt her. She would have insisted on a burial, or at least a pyre, and she would have made Klaus swear that their next residence would be paid for in more traditional coin. What if she *hadn't* been blocking out the sight of the bodies from her own eyes? What if she had been concealing something from Klaus, instead?

It was ridiculous, and he silently cursed his sister for planting these doubts in his mind. 'If it's the world you want, Viv, just say the word and it's yours,' he told his bride, wondering whether this new, slightly unfamiliar Vivianne might take him up on the offer, where the old one never would have.

'As long as I have you, the world can take care of

itself,' she answered, and he felt muscles relax that he hadn't even realised he'd tensed. She had barely been back a month, after more than forty years on the Other Side. What more could anyone expect of her? If she had changed in death, who could blame her? It certainly didn't mean anything was *wrong*.

Klaus heard the soft click of a door closing somewhere along the hall, and knew that the servants were growing curious about the villa's new occupants. He should have been hunting them down one by one to lay his compulsion on them like a yoke, preventing anyone from trying to escape or send word to his siblings. But it didn't feel right leaving Vivianne alone.

'Come out,' he ordered. 'Show yourselves if you want to live.' After a minute, a handful of bedraggled humans emerged from behind the closed door.

One was injured, bleeding through a dirty bandage around his forearm. It couldn't have been from Klaus's attack on the courtyard, because all those people were dead. Maybe he had simply hurt himself by coincidence earlier in the day. Out of the corner of his eye he saw Vivianne staring at the spot of crimson blood as if it were the only thing she could see. She looked pale and drawn, almost as if she might faint.

Klaus shook it off, deliberately not looking at her. He needed to concentrate on compelling the servants to do his bidding, to bring his wife food and make up a bed for her. She needed to rest and recover, that was all. And if they didn't hurry up and help her do that, they could join their friends in the courtyard. In fact, Klaus decided it would be most efficient to leave the corpses there for the night. It would serve as a reminder to all that there were consequences for getting between him and anything – anything at all – that Vivianne Mikaelson desired.

TWENTY

*T*he first thing Rebekah did was feel around the bodice of her dress, searching for the dagger that had sent her away into the darkness. But that darkness was slowly receding – the dagger was gone. She didn't know who'd removed it or how much time had passed . . . seconds or centuries.

But she was still on the same beach and the moon looked almost full. Rebekah sat up and then winced as her head spun violently. She thought she might throw up. She could feel her blood starting to circulate again, sluggishly at first and then enough to warm her icy hands and feet. She rubbed her bare arms, trying to get a sense of the temperature of the air around her. Everything still felt cold, but she was pretty sure it was just her. As more sensations returned she could feel the pebbly sand beneath her, and the sound of the waves sliding across the sea.

The water was calmer than the night she had been daggered, and the tide was so high that it nearly lapped at her shoes. Forty-four years ago she had chosen this area because it was empty and isolated, and it hadn't changed much in all that time. She wondered how long she'd laid there before someone had noticed a girl with a dagger in her chest. But where was that person . . . and the dagger? Surely Klaus hadn't removed it before running off with his monster bride. He had looked deadly serious about taking Rebekah out of the fight, and remorse wasn't his style.

He would be far away by now, no matter how long she had been unconscious. His first priority would be to protect Vivianne from anyone who might force him to face the truth about the evil lurking in her. He had daggered his own sister for her. The thing inside Vivianne would never need another ally as long as she had Klaus . . . and maybe that was the whole point.

Rebekah's head was pounding, and she was starving. There was a fishing village not too far away, but the thought of dragging herself there seemed overwhelming. Even standing up was a challenge she didn't feel entirely ready for, but it wasn't as if waiting around would make her any less hungry. This was how it had felt to be human, she could dimly recall, weak and slow.

She forced herself to her feet, brushing off her hands and then shaking out her dress. It was hopeless – the fabric was stained with sand and salt, but there was no sign of rot or sun, nothing to suggest that more than a few years had passed, at the very most.

Rebekah sighed and trudged towards the cabin, which seemed like a good start. It looked deserted, but disrepair and decay hadn't set in. The longer she was awake the more certain Rebekah felt that only a few days had passed. Everything looked too close to the same, and it even *felt* the same. Klaus and Vivianne had left nothing behind when they fled, but Rebekah could still sense a lingering trace of them there, like the smell of dried oil paint or faded lilacs.

Besides, surely Elijah would have come looking for her if she had been gone much longer. He would have had a coffin built for her so that she could sleep beside Kol and Finn. Elijah was a loyal, caring brother, unlike some others she might mention.

Even after just a few days Rebekah knew that Klaus and Vivianne's trail would have gone cold. And there was no reason to think she would have more luck confronting them a second time than she had the first, especially since the silver dagger that had brought her down was nowhere to be found.

But Klaus wasn't the only one who could help her, she realised. There was someone else who would know exactly what was wrong with Vivianne and how to fix it. The witches – the witch – who had brought Viv back had a great deal to answer for, and Rebekah decided it was high time she paid a visit to Lily Leroux.

She left the little cottage, slamming the door behind her with a satisfying thud. It was time for a fresh start, a different direction.

Rebekah struck out in the general direction of New Orleans, meandering a bit to avoid the more thickly settled areas while still travelling along the main roads. She didn't feel like confronting a crowd in her weakened state, but one or two lone travellers would be just the kind of company she needed on such a journey.

She caught a man at a crossroads, warming his hands by a small fire. He had the sense to shrink back at the sight of her, although most humans weren't so wary. Remaining young and lovely forever had its perks, and Rebekah had grown accustomed to being welcomed just about anywhere she went. The man leaped up from his seat and held out a rough, handmade wooden cross in one trembling hand. The *morts-vivants* must have spread fear and distrust throughout the countryside. 'Stay back, demon!' the traveller shouted, and Rebekah smiled.

'You can put that away, good sir,' she called pleasantly.

'I'm not the kind of creature who fears such things.'

The man relaxed, and Rebekah was on him in the blink of an eye, her fangs extending towards his sunburned neck. His blood tasted like the sky, like wind blowing over an open field. The heat of it warmed her, and she could feel the strength returning to her body as it ebbed from his.

TWENTY-ONE

'William Collado,' Elijah greeted the werewolves' leader, keeping his voice polite. 'I am sorry that we have not met until now.'

'Stay away from us!' a wolf snarled from the crowd, but William silenced him with a stare.

'We haven't missed the attention of your kind,' William replied once quiet had fallen again. 'You might have stayed away longer, but I assume it suits you to come here now, just as it didn't before.'

'It suits us all,' Elijah corrected. 'A danger has arisen that threatens your kind just as much as mine. It will tear the city apart if we don't band together to stop it.'

William chuckled, a sound that sent shivers down Elijah's spine. 'Does it hurt your pride, Mikaelson? To know you aren't the only undead things roaming these woods any more?'

So they knew about the *morts-vivants*. But William didn't seem especially concerned about the danger stalking their lands. And neither did the rest of his kind, who smirked and rolled their eyes at the vampire.

'The witches have gone too far,' Elijah said, pitching his voice to carry over the whispers and laughs that rippled through the crowd. 'They have been led astray by a madwoman who would happily see everyone in this city dead.'

'As far as I know, her minions have only preyed on humans, although it seems they've managed to irritate your kind as well. Lily Leroux's plan doesn't seem to have anything to do with me and mine, so I'm not sure why it warrants your visit.'

Elijah ignored the implied threat, and met William's gaze. 'Lily is making a bid for control over New Orleans. She has raised the dead, set fire to the city and openly attacked my people in the town square. She has spun completely out of control, and it will take all of us working together to stop her.'

William smiled, a sinister expression that crept up to his blue eyes. The smile reminded him of Klaus when he was in one of his particularly dangerous moods.

'Have you stopped to wonder *why* they attacked you,

vampire?' William asked. 'Why they attacked you, and not us?'

'They haven't attacked you *yet*,' Elijah corrected. 'It's only a matter of time.' But he understood what William was driving at, and he had to concede that the werewolf had a point.

'It'll be a matter of a lot of time,' William disagreed, his smile vanishing as quickly as it had come. 'You said it yourself: Lily is after power. And that means your kind has left mine with nothing that she wants.'

Elijah inhaled steadily and then exhaled again, reminding himself to choose his words carefully. Nearly everyone in New Orleans could lay blame on the witches for the ruin they had suffered back in 1722, but the werewolves had more than one grievance. The witches had destroyed their home, but Elijah and Klaus had personally destroyed their Pack.

It would be harder for them to choose between the Mikaelsons and Lily than Elijah had assumed at first. They had no foundation upon which to base trust for either clan. Their histories were murky and complicated, and it had been naive to imagine that William Collado would set all of that aside now just because Elijah told him it was important.

The cluster of huts just beyond the circle of werewolves caught his eye: low with clay-tiled roofs. The contrast to the mansion Rebekah had built was inescapable. The vampires had prospered while the werewolves had huddled together in the night, hiding in the depths of the forest as they struggled to rebuild their decimated Pack. No wonder they couldn't see eye to eye with him now.

'They will not leave you alone forever,' he warned William, watching for the Pack's reaction. Just because the witches were starting at the head didn't mean they wouldn't eventually make their way down to the tail. 'Your kind has always been a formidable threat to the witches of this city,' he improvised, 'and they will not forget that.'

But he could tell at once that his speech had fallen on deaf ears. The werewolves were too prideful. They would rather take their chances against an army of witches than admit what Elijah could offer them.

William spread his hands in a mock show of helplessness. 'This is what you wanted, isn't it? To be king, to rule New Orleans? We had nothing to offer you back when you drove us out of the city we built out of untamed swampland, and I think it's best for us to carry on with that arrangement.'

'That's a mistake,' Elijah told him bluntly, losing all patience for diplomacy. 'Once we're out of the way Lily will roll over you like so many corpses, and it'll be too late to stop her.'

'Let's find out,' a pretty young werewolf suggested, appearing at Elijah's elbow with a sinister grin on her heart-shaped face. She caught one of Elijah's elbows, and he felt another werewolf grab his other arm. He could have fought them both off, but there were hundreds more behind them.

'Take him to the pit,' William ordered dismissively. 'I think the king of New Orleans could benefit from a night to think about the limits of his power.' His blue eyes found Elijah's. 'We'll see you tomorrow night, vampire, by the light of the full moon.'

TWENTY-TWO

*I*t was the same old dream again, but this time he knew that Vivianne was back where she belonged. How long would he remain haunted by the nights he had awoken alone? He just had to reach a little further, just find the silk of her skin . . .

Klaus woke up fully at last, sitting up and shoving the blankets away. The room was silent, and the longer he listened the clearer it became that the entire villa was just as still. Vivianne was gone. Again.

He slid from the bed and prowled from room to room, hunting for her. The villa was entirely deserted, and Klaus could feel his fear mounting. A thousand sinister scenarios flashed through his mind. He could almost see a vengeful Rebekah stalking Vivianne through the villa, and he moved faster, racing to find Vivianne.

There was an open garden in the centre of the villa, filled almost entirely with a lily-covered pond whose glossy, flat leaves and delicate fingerling petals seemed to mirror the stars overhead. It was the kind of place Vivianne loved, full of flowering vines and unexpected shadows. Klaus was so sure he would find her there that he paused long enough to search the place twice. At any moment he fully expected to see the edge of her nightdress or a lock of her hair disappearing around a corner. But the garden was as strangely hushed as the rest of the villa. He couldn't say exactly what finally turned his steps towards the front courtyard, where the evidence of his massacre still lay under the open sky.

He saw Vivianne before she saw him. She stood in the centre of the flagstones, her black hair settling around her shoulders like a shroud. In the brilliant light of the waxing moon he could see that her hands were coated with blood, and it ran down her forearms in streaks. The front of her nightgown was dark with it as well.

The source of the blood was easy enough to find. Vivianne raised a heart to her lips like a child with a stolen cake, and her white teeth tore into it again and again. When it was gone, she picked her way carefully over to another dead body, shoved her fist into the man's chest and removed his heart.

From the condition of the corpses around her, Klaus could see that she had been at it for some time. Everywhere he looked there were splintered ribs glowing white, half swallowed by the holes Vivianne had punched through dozens of chests.

When she saw him at last, he realised it was wet with more than just blood. Vivianne was crying as she devoured her gruesome meal, her tears turning from diamonds to rubies as they slid down towards her mouth.

Klaus wanted to hold her, to pull her close and tell her that everything would be all right. He found himself running at her instead, and knocked the heart from her hands. It was cold and tough, having sat too long in the chest of a dead man. It was revolting to touch, much less to think about eating.

The realisation that this stringy lump of dead flesh had called to Vivianne, pulling her from their warm bed and out into the night, made Klaus feel physically sick. She lunged after the heart, falling to her knees in her haste to recover it.

'Stop,' he demanded, finally finding his voice, however rough and broken it sounded in his own ears. He caught Vivianne by her shoulders, pulling her back to her feet and wrapping his arms around her. It was more to restrain her than to comfort her, but she bucked and squirmed. 'Viv, please! Stop, my love.'

She threw off his arms with a strength she could not possibly possess. She bared her teeth at him in a vicious snarl, and to his horror Klaus felt his own fangs extending in response. Vivianne turned to run for the wrought-iron gate that would lead her out into the countryside, freeing her to do things Klaus was afraid to imagine.

Desecrating the dead was bad enough, but whatever else she was, Vivianne's blood was still half werewolf. If she killed someone, even when she was not in her right mind, then she would change on the next night's full moon and be a thousand times more dangerous.

Klaus cursed himself as he pushed off the flagstones to catch her. He'd wanted Vivianne back so badly that he hadn't let himself think about what coming back might *do* to her. He'd struck a devil's bargain with a witch who couldn't be trusted, and he was responsible for whatever Vivianne was now. He had to find a way to make this right, but first he had to stop her.

She was faster than she should have been, but Klaus was faster still. He intercepted her at the gate, and she let out an inhuman howl of fury and frustration. 'Talk to me,' he pleaded, yanking her around by her arm. 'Viv, whatever this is, we can get through it together. You just need to—'

She struck his face, and Klaus's head snapped back from the force of her blow. It was far more than the strength of common madness. Vivianne was a changed woman, more than a witch or even a werewolf, and nearly a match for an Original. He wasn't even sure she could hear him right then, much less answer him.

Hating himself for it, he hit her back, hoping that he could simply knock her unconscious and then decide what to do. But she stayed on her feet, becoming even more violent in her agitation. She screamed and fought like a wild thing, and for a few horrible moments he began to wonder if he would be able to contain her.

But at last she collapsed against his chest, sobbing as if her own heart were breaking, and he felt his own cheeks wet with tears. He vowed that Lily would feel this same misery, as soon as he could make that happen.

'It isn't you,' he whispered, stroking Vivianne's hair with one hand while the other pinned her arms to her sides. 'This is something that is being done to you, and it's something we can fight.'

'I can't,' she moaned, burying her face against his chest. 'I've been trying, Klaus, but it's in me, clawing its way out. I can hear it all the time, and at night . . . at night . . .'

'It's going to be all right,' he told her, turning her gently to face him.

He saw the light of madness in the centre of her bottomless black eyes just a second too late, and she raked him across the cheek with her fingernails before he could even react. 'You don't own me,' she spat, elbowing him hard in the stomach and breaking away from his loosened grip again.

It killed him to chase her down, to knock her onto the ground and pin her down like a trapped butterfly. He felt as though he was betraying her somehow. The woman he had first fallen in love with was still in there somewhere, probably terrified and desperate to get out, and all Klaus could do was hurt her.

There was no doubt that she was a danger to herself, but Klaus still felt his stomach turn at the feel of her delicate wrists, her thin body being crushed beneath his own. Sensing his hesitation, Vivianne sank her teeth into his forearm so deeply that he could hear the grinding sound of bone against bone. He gritted his own teeth and struck her hard across the cheek with his other fist, ignoring the tearing feeling as her clenched jaw ripped flesh away from his arm.

Vivianne's eyes rolled upward, and her long lashes fluttered and then closed. He didn't know how long she would be out, and as much as he wanted to just cradle her in his arms forever, he knew he needed to move. He lifted her, startled all over again by how light her body was. No wonder she hadn't been eating enough, if she had been feeling these sinister cravings all along.

Klaus would find a way to make this right, but for now he needed to keep her safe from herself. In his search he'd found a wine cellar, a long, dusty vault with a sturdy door. He carried Vivianne into the house and down the wide stone steps, his ears alert for any sign that they were being observed.

The servants' fear served him well, and they were undisturbed on their way to the cellar. When he was halfway down the steps, he felt Vivianne begin to stir, and a faint moan escaped from between her ruby lips. Klaus sped up his descent, but by the time he reached the heavy door she was awake again.

Her furious wail echoed off the stone around them, and she began to struggle. Somehow she brought her knee crashing into the point of his chin, and he dropped her inelegantly at the foot of the stairs. She rolled into a crouch, teeth bared and eyes flashing, ready to do whatever it took to fight her way out.

But this time he didn't hesitate. What he had to do was awful, but it was for Vivianne, and he couldn't very well claim to love her if he put his own sensibilities above her safety. He used all of his strength to launch himself against her, knocking her backward into the shadows of the wine cellar.

She was on her feet again in a flash, charging back towards him with her bloody hands outstretched, but he slammed the door between them and drove the bars home into their sockets. He felt the wood shudder as Vivianne's body thrashed against it, and after a brief pause he felt the same thing again. His arm throbbed where she had bitten him. The flesh was already beginning to knit itself back together, but in the meantime it hurt like hell.

Vivianne hurled herself against the door over and over, at first screaming her fury and then in eerie, determined silence. Klaus placed his back against his side of the thick wood, then let himself slide heavily down to sit, still leaning against it.

There was still a lot of night left. He couldn't spend it with Vivianne, but he was hers as surely as she was his, and no matter what barriers lay between them, he wouldn't leave her.

TWENTY-THREE

A witch crossed the marshy expanse, and Rebekah parted the reeds to watch him. Elijah's previous descriptions had been detailed enough, but she still caught her breath at the sight of the witch simply winking out of sight. There was no question that this was the spot, and the answers Rebekah was seeking began exactly where the witch had vanished.

She carefully moved to where he had taken his last step, keeping low to the ground and using the scrubby trees for cover. But the last hundred yards offered no real concealment, and Rebekah threw caution to the wind and ran. Her speed carried her across the remainder of the distance in the blink of an eye.

When the palisade wall and the town behind it burst

into view the surprise nearly knocked the wind out of her. But Rebekah forced herself to relax and try to look as though she belonged. She wrapped herself more tightly in the dead traveller's cloak, trying to ignore the rich human stink imprinted on its wool. She walked evenly, not too fast, hoping that anyone who looked her way wouldn't bother with a second glance.

Rebekah headed towards the thatched roof of the meeting house, although she couldn't set foot inside it. Candlelight glowed through the windows, and she could hear the soft murmuring of voices inside. She paused beneath a window, but Lily and her witches only spoke of supplies and strategy. It might be hours before they happened to mention anything of use, and even longer before she was able to catch Lily Leroux alone.

Silently, she moved away from the meeting house, drifting among the dark wooden huts and letting a plan begin to form itself in her mind. One of these homes must belong to Lily, and home was where the hostages were. Lily had a daughter, after all. Her 'desperate mother' act was what had started this whole mess, and it might be the key to ending it. Rebekah was sure that Lily still had some normal human feelings left in her.

It was obvious which house belonged to the Leroux family. In spite of the swamp and the crude materials available, the queen of the witches had done her best to turn her hut into a palace. Ysabelle Dalliencourt had grown more relaxed and secure in her position as she had aged. Once opportunistic and power-hungry, she had developed into a mature and humble leader of her people, living simply among them and declining to make any kind of show of her status. But Ysabelle's only daughter had not yet achieved that kind of perspective, and staring at the eyesore that rose up out of the mud before her, Rebekah frankly doubted that Lily ever would.

It was twice the size of the structures around it, squatting gracelessly among them like a giant toad among tadpoles. Designs had been painted onto the wood, fantastical symbols in shimmering gold leaf.

Rebekah recognised some of them as mystical, but they were passive spells: glyphs for prosperity and strength with no sign of any protective magic. Rebekah pulled open a window and held her breath.

Nothing happened, and she lost count of her heartbeats while she waited. There was no attack or alert, only the ordinary rules that prevented a vampire from entering a home without an invitation . . . which would be easy enough to obtain. Lily's family must be asleep somewhere inside, and anyone as self-aggrandising as she was would have at least one servant living there as well. Servants could be useful in all kinds of ways.

Rebekah's window looked in on the house's kitchen, empty of any signs of life at that time of night. She began to slowly circle the foundation, inspecting one darkened room after another and always listening for the soft, promising sound of a pulse.

'Who are you?'

Rebekah flinched back, alarmed that she'd been seen. The voice was soft and female, and she guessed that the speaker was young. There was a rustling of fabric, and Rebekah saw the girl sitting upright in her narrow bed. She might barely have been eighteen, with wide brown eyes and a soft, sweet face.

'Never mind,' the girl told Rebekah, studying her sceptically. 'I know who you are, and I know you can't come in here.'

'I can't,' Rebekah agreed, charmed in spite of her annoyance. She didn't like to be surprised, but a thoughtful adolescent wasn't an especially threatening nemesis. Not even if she might be related to someone who was. 'Are you Lily's daughter?'

'Marguerite Leroux,' the girl confirmed, then bit her lower lip anxiously. Names could have power, and a witch should have known to be more cautious. Apparently, suspicion wasn't in Marguerite's nature.

Rebekah knew a thing or two about difficult relationships with one's parents, and she felt sorry for this girl. She could easily imagine what it might be like to be raised by Lily Leroux.

'I'm Rebekah,' she offered generously, resting her elbows on the windowsill. 'Your mother and I don't get along.'

Marguerite's mouth tightened, as if she wanted to smile but wouldn't give Rebekah the satisfaction. 'My mother does what she must to protect us from your kind,' she said, as if she was repeating something she had learned by rote. 'I wouldn't expect you to be friends.'

'Maybe not,' Rebekah agreed. 'But who will protect your kind from *her*?'

She could see her words hit home, and she saw Marguerite make a conscious decision to reject them. Her heart wasn't with her mother's lunatic actions, but her head certainly was. 'She's doing what she has to do,' Marguerite said, squaring her shoulders stubbornly. 'You conspired with the werewolves to drive us from our homes. If Mother has to resort to some darker magic to ensure nothing like that hurricane ever happens again, it's not too high a price.'

Rebekah blinked rapidly, trying to make the pieces of the strange speech fall into place. 'If she wants to make sure there's never another hurricane, all she has to do is not raise one,' she snapped, a little more sharply than she had meant to. Marguerite crossed her arms defiantly, but

Rebekah could see fear underlying the gesture.

'It's a lie that our kind had anything to do with the hurricane,' the adolescent replied. 'Grandmother wanted us to feel guilty because we couldn't stop it, but it is the vampires who are to blame for how we live now.'

Rebekah laughed. 'That's absurd. Witches called up the storm against the werewolves, then lost control of it. Many died on both sides, and plenty of humans, too. New Orleans was flattened to the ground. It was all thanks to a temper tantrum thrown by *your* coven.' The storm had killed Eric Moquet as well, and for a horrible moment Rebekah saw his lifeless body again, crushed beneath the mast of the ship that should have carried them away to their new life together. 'Your grandmother imposed a penance on all of you that may seem harsh these days, but it certainly was warranted at the time.' That and more, but Rebekah knew she was too biased to say so. No amount of rebuilding could ever truly make up for the fact that once upon a time, she had lost her entire future.

'That's not what . . .' Marguerite seemed to realise that she had already said too much, and stopped in confusion. The girl was thinking, and that was a start.

'She told my brother you were sick,' Rebekah said. 'Your mother told Klaus she needed his blood to cure you. She played on what little sympathy he has, claiming you were near death. She wanted that blood for something else, didn't she? It was a part of whatever black magic she worked. She rearranges the truth to suit herself.'

'She what?' Marguerite said, as if she really couldn't imagine that such a thing was possible. She had a lot to learn about mothers, although Rebekah suspected that the lessons were about to be flying thick and fast.

'You weren't close to your grandmother, were you?' Rebekah guessed. 'Your mother wouldn't allow it. She had her own version of how your people came to live here, and she sheltered you.'

'Grandmother was ill for most of my life,' Marguerite whispered. 'She was elderly and frail. She didn't need the stress of a child underfoot.'

Lily had indoctrinated Ysabelle's grandchild with her own resentment and bitterness, twisting the facts to suit her own feelings. Marguerite had believed it, the way any child would have, but she was no fool. Rebekah could see her reordering pieces of old memories and half-heard conversations, creating a new and darker picture of her world.

'I've lived a bit longer than you, Marguerite,' Rebekah reminded her, softening her tone into something as close to maternal as she could manage. 'But I've never forgotten the trust I placed in my own mother. I thought she was the most extraordinary woman, and in many ways she truly was. She was also flawed and fragile, for all the inhuman power she had at her command. She wasn't perfect, not even in her love for me. You're still very young, but I think you're old enough to understand that.'

Marguerite shoved her coverlet aside and set her bare feet on the polished wood of the floor. She was tall in an awkward teenaged way, with narrow hips and bony elbows. Rebekah could see unshed tears shining in her brown eyes, and she knew her words had hit home. Marguerite was barely past childhood, but she seemed to feel the weight of the responsibility that lay on her shoulders now. She studied Rebekah's face. 'You may come in,' she announced at last, and Rebekah lost no time in dropping into the bedroom.

'Thank you,' she said, straightening her skirt.

Marguerite's thin shoulders rose and fell in a huge sigh. 'Well, I suppose if you were going to kill me you already would have. It seems you're telling the truth.'

It was youthful recklessness at its finest, risking her neck – literally – to find out if the vampire at her window was also a liar.

'I lie when it suits me,' Rebekah admitted, 'but tonight I have no reason. The *morts-vivants* are dangerous, and your mother is out of control. And I think she's done something to a – a friend of mine. My sister-in-law, actually, except I don't think it's really her.' She knew she was rambling, but so much had happened in the last few weeks that it was becoming difficult to avoid. 'Look, Marguerite, I can't offer you proof or an unassailable reason you should trust me. So don't consider *me* at all. Think about what you know about your mother, and what you've seen and heard here recently. I suspect you already know things I could never convince you of, no matter how hard I tried.'

Marguerite twisted her long hands together, glancing at the window as if half expecting to see more vampires waiting outside. 'My mother doesn't tell me about things like the *morts-vivants* or their plans for them. Apparently, she doesn't tell me much of anything. But I do know where she does her spell-work, and I guess I could find out for myself.'

'We could really use your help,' Rebekah pressed, stepping forward. Marguerite took a simultaneous step backward, and Rebekah clasped her hands behind her back and tried to look as unthreatening as possible. 'And your help could go a long way towards righting the wrongs your people have committed – to redeeming your kind, the way your grandmother always hoped to do. I'll keep you safe from whatever comes next. I promise you that.'

Marguerite's spine straightened a little, and suddenly she looked more willowy than awkward. Rebekah could see the woman she might become if she could break free of the poisonous influence of her mother. 'I know you're not here because you want to help us,' she replied, with less softness in her voice than had been there before. 'But I also believe you're telling the truth.'

'And to expose all truths, I don't know if we're going to be able to save Lily,' Rebekah admitted. She knew it would be better to lie, to tell the girl that her family would come through this whole and happy, but she couldn't do it. It wasn't true, and it wasn't fair. If Klaus managed to break the link between himself and Lily Leroux, her life would be over. Marguerite was taking a huge risk by trusting a Mikaelson, and Rebekah wanted to deserve that trust.

Marguerite brushed her hair back and took another deep breath. 'I understand that.' She glanced at the window again, where the first traces of dawn were starting to turn the sky pink. 'My mother will be back soon,' she warned. 'She never sleeps any more, and she'll spend the day working. I'll find out what I can today, but you can't be here until she leaves again. Come back this afternoon. She rides out with the *morts-vivants* nearly every night now, and I'll be able to show you whatever you want then.'

'Thank you,' Rebekah told her sincerely. The warmth she felt towards the girl was so intense that it was almost unfamiliar, but Rebekah knew it had served her well. A spy was worth more than a hostage any day. 'I know this must be confusing, but you're doing the right thing.'

'It's nothing,' Marguerite mumbled, suddenly becoming a teenager again, letting her auburn hair fall across her face to hide the emotions on it. 'You're right that my mother has lost sight of what that is. She's in over her head, and she's trying to pull the entire clan down after her. I hope I can save her, but at the very least I have to save the rest of us.'

'You're a good girl,' Rebekah assured her, brushing the hair back. Marguerite had nothing to be ashamed of. 'Don't take any unnecessary risks, little witch. I'll be back this afternoon, and we'll find a way to end this nightmare together.'

TWENTY-FOUR

*T*he sun was still too newly risen for its rays to reach Elijah's prison, but he could see the sky lightening above him and knew morning had come. As if on cue, he heard the grating sound of the iron cover being removed from his pit, and one grinning werewolf's face after another came into view.

'I thought your leader intended to keep me down here until moonrise,' he reminded them as he climbed the ladder they let down. He had known William wouldn't be able to wait that long. His kind wasn't known for patience. 'It would be wiser.'

'Shut your mouth, vampire,' an older werewolf muttered, shoving him back towards the clearing.

William was already there, dressed like a common

human hunter in breeches and a long tunic that seemed to blend into the switchgrass. But his face set him apart, grim and hardened around the blue flares of his eyes.

'Last night we heard your proposal,' the werewolf leader told both Elijah and the assembled Pack. 'Today you will hear the crimes for which you have yet to answer.'

Killing his father must figure prominently on that list, but there were plenty of other items to choose from. 'I know my crimes,' Elijah told him, keeping his voice low enough that he might have been speaking to the other man alone. 'They are numerous and unforgivable.'

William raised an eyebrow, an expression of scepticism that somehow made him look even more menacing. Birds sang in the trees around them, greeting the new day, unaware of the standoff on the ground. 'In that case, I think we can skip right over the trial and go straight to the sentence.'

'You intend to try to kill me?' Elijah asked politely. 'I think we could all find better uses for our time.'

William stripped off his tunic. His torso was lean and strong, without an ounce of wasted space. His skin was crisscrossed with scars that looked like they had come from fangs and claws, and some still looked fresh. Elijah could feel the werewolves around him shifting eagerly, their taste for vampire blood mounting. 'My father raised me on stories of you,' William went on, as if he hadn't heard Elijah's interruption. 'We will be stronger under the light of the moon tonight, but so will you. As it is, only that ring on your middle finger keeps you from burning alive.'

Elijah glanced around at the crowd, ready for whichever of them would be the first to make a play for his daylight ring. The sun hadn't cleared the tops of the trees, but it was high enough for him to feel it, to remember how it would sear his skin. The werewolves would die by scores if fighting broke out now, but Elijah found that he had no taste for that kind of carnage. There was already more than enough violence to go around.

'Let us agree that I deserve to die,' he suggested, raising his voice now to include the entire bloodthirsty crowd. 'More deaths and more vengeance still won't get you what you want.'

'Unless vengeance *is* what I want,' William argued, but Elijah could see an amused turn to his lips. He might have spent his entire life preparing to kill vampires, but William had other instincts beyond that. 'What could you possibly offer me that's better than that?'

'I will restore your lands,' Elijah announced, and the silence that fell around the ring of werewolves was so sudden that even the birds hushed, suddenly afraid of the change that had come over the clearing. 'The old

Werewolf Quarter, a seat in the council and everything in this region that was held by the Navarros on the day before the hurricane struck in 1722. It would be the least I could do in recognition of your help against the new threat the witches have brought down on our city.'

It was a generous offer, but at least he had worded it to exclude the Mikaelsons' mansion. Rebekah would never have let him hear the end of it if he had traded that away.

A whisper ran through the werewolves as they absorbed his words. Elijah could pick out anger and distrust in their muttering voices, but he could also hear hope. Even William looked intrigued, although far from enthusiastic. 'An honourable man wouldn't have stolen it from us in the first place.'

'Your Pack was in no position to administer all that territory,' Elijah pointed out smoothly. 'So perhaps we can say that my siblings and I have been holding it on your behalf for all these years? And in exchange you will fight beside us in the coming war.'

'Beside you?' the older werewolf who had escorted him from the pit scoffed, so outraged that he didn't even wait for his leader to speak. 'You want us to pad the front lines so your precious vampire army doesn't have to get its hands bloody.'

That sounded like a good enough plan to Elijah, but

that wouldn't get him what he wanted. 'We will work together to take out Lily Leroux,' he promised. 'I ask only that none of your venom find its way into the veins of my people, and I can guarantee that mine will treat yours as equals.'

William's eyes narrowed as he considered the proposal. 'You'd say anything now, when you're surrounded, with the sun rising. Why should I believe your word will be worth anything once night falls again?'

'You're a leader, and you have led your Pack well,' he answered. 'Although my loyalty is to my family first and my kind second, I also bear responsibility for the innocent citizens of New Orleans, and I take that seriously. They need protection, not another war. If we forge a true alliance, it will put an end to the backstabbing and suspicion.'

'Nobility from a vampire,' William mused, his broad shoulders relaxing slightly. 'Now I've seen everything.'

'Do we have a deal, then?' Elijah stepped forward optimistically, one hand outstretched, but William held back.

'Not quite,' he countered. Dangerous yellow began to blossom in his eyes. 'I've waited a long time to fight you, monster, and I'd hate to let a petty alliance get in the way of my life's work. Let me make you a counter-offer: if I can best you in single combat, we win our lands back and you go on your way. If you can defeat me, I'll bring my army to your war.'

Elijah smiled, shaking his own shoulders loose . . . If that's what the werewolf wanted, Elijah wasn't one to turn down a fight. 'I accept your terms.'

William struck with stunning speed, and then was out of Elijah's reach as soon as his first blow had hit home. The werewolves roared their approval, but it was short-lived. The Pack leader was fast and well trained, but he couldn't hold his own for long against an Original vampire.

Elijah feinted at his adversary's head before landing a blow to his stomach. William was knocked off his feet, but he spun in the air and landed in a crouch, kicking off hard against the grass to drive his fist into Elijah's throat.

Elijah saw stars for a moment, but his other senses kept reporting William's movements back to him. He caught the werewolf's arm and threw him, hearing a thud and the breath knocked out of William.

Part of him was tempted to hesitate, to give the wolf a chance to take some measure of the revenge his family was owed. But to earn the Pack's respect Elijah needed to win. He spun and pounced, pinning the man to the ground and baring his fangs. He stopped less than an inch from his opponent's throat, watching the yellow in his eyes fade back to clear blue.

'My father is turning in his grave,' William grunted, resisting for a moment and then allowing his shoulders to sag back against the dirt.

Elijah stood and offered his hand, and this time, William didn't hesitate in taking it. The werewolves howled and cheered, every bit as enthusiastic as if their leader had won. In a way he had, Elijah supposed – he had faced off against a Mikaelson and lived to tell about it.

'Your father should be proud,' he assured him. 'I don't remember the last time a werewolf gave me so much trouble.' William was a superior fighter, and if he was anywhere near as capable a general, then Elijah was getting an even better ally than he had hoped for.

'No more, though.' William shrugged his tunic back on over his head. 'We'll save the real fighting for our enemies.' He raised his voice, shouting so loudly that the ground beneath their feet trembled. 'Tonight, when the moon rises, we take the witches down.'

TWENTY-FIVE

*K*laus couldn't remember a longer night in the past thousand years. The heavy wooden door seemed to have become a permanent part of his back, and the stone floor had grown icy cold as the hours crept on. But worst of all was the screaming.

Vivianne had howled like a woman possessed for most of the night. When her voice broke, she changed to softer appeals. For a few horrible minutes, she had attempted to seduce him, promising all sorts of lurid things. He hadn't imagined that she knew what all of those words *meant*, and it was a relief when she had returned to her hoarse screaming instead.

Klaus could still see Vivianne standing alone among the bodies she had desecrated in the courtyard and feel her inhuman strength as she fought to get away from him. He had been holding on to those memories all night, keeping himself strong against her pleas. But the more he listened, the surer he was that, at last, something had changed.

He stood up slowly, focusing on the sound. Vivianne's voice sounded drained and hollow, resigned to the idea that he wasn't really coming back for her. It was entirely different from her angry threats and unsettling promises. At last she was his Vivianne again. He could hear it, now that he had spent so many hours listening to the dark thing inside of her.

He slid the bars aside, then paused for a moment, fortifying himself against whatever was on the other side. But he still wasn't entirely prepared for the ruin.

Vivianne had splintered casks and shattered bottles in her rage, and the earthen floor was covered in shards of wood and glass. The stink of the wine assaulted his nostrils, and beneath it lurked the scent of old blood, and of things that had been dead for far too long.

Vivianne herself didn't look much better than the cellar she had torn apart. Her hair was matted with substances he didn't want to think about, and her nightgown was stained with so much blood and wine that no one could have guessed its original colour. She had torn at her own face and arms with her fingernails, and beneath the wounds she looked pale and gaunt.

'It's all right,' she told him, then swayed dangerously, her eyes rolling upward.

He caught her just before she fell, lifting her away from the debris that littered the floor. 'It will be,' he promised her, then kissed her on her forehead to show her that he meant it.

Klaus carried her up one set of stairs and then another before stripping off her ruined nightgown and setting her gratefully into a steaming bath. The villa's well-trained servants must have noticed their absence or even heard the disturbances, because while the brazier was piled with additional buckets, Klaus had never caught so much as a glimpse of whomever had placed them there. The water turned red at once, and he refilled it again and again until it finally stayed clear. Vivianne watched him as if he were her only anchor in this world.

'I'm so sorry,' she whispered, and he startled to hear the sound after they had spent so long in silence. 'The hunger comes over me, and I try so hard to control it. I just couldn't any more, and the more I ate the more lost I felt. I think . . .' She frowned, trying to remember. 'I think I tried to hurt you.'

'I'm not so easy to hurt,' he reminded her. Only his heart, which could still feel this devastating wound. 'Vivianne, how long has this been happening to you?'

She bit her lip and looked away from him for the first time since he had opened the cellar door. 'It wasn't so bad at first.'

Her evasiveness was every bit as revealing as if she had answered straightforwardly. Something had been wrong with his wife since the night she had come back from the dead, and it had taken him nearly a month to see it – love truly was blind. Even Rebekah had caught on more quickly than he had.

He knelt down beside the bathtub, caressing her shoulders. Her skin was flushed pink from the heat of the water, and there wasn't a trace of blood left on her. But he couldn't erase the stains it had left no matter how he wished they could just forget the whole thing. 'This isn't your fault, my love,' he assured her.

'I think your witch cast another spell on me, in addition to the one that brought me back.' Vivianne sank her shoulders back against his hands and closed her eyes. Even now, after all she had been through, her mind kept working. 'We already know that Lily took advantage of you in the deal you made, but there's no reason to think we know everything she did. At every turn we discover some new trap she's laid for us, and I think that whatever is happening to me is no exception.'

'I would have traded anything in exchange for you,' Klaus said, still bitter at the memory of how the witch had used him. He would do it all over again, but how long did Lily intend to make him pay?

'Lily knew that,' Vivianne reminded him. 'But she was still afraid there would come a time when you realised she was demanding too much. She knew you had limits, even if *you* didn't know it.'

'Not when it comes to you.' Klaus insisted, but he understood the point she was making. Lily had demanded Esther's opal pendant so that Klaus couldn't kill her when he learned what she was really up to. Why assume that she had finished with her schemes? Being linked to an immortal vampire could protect her from a whole lot of sins.

The bathwater sloshed as Vivianne pulled herself up onto her feet. Klaus reached for a thick, white towel and wrapped her in it, studying her face intently. There was no sign of anything but Vivianne, no mark of whatever curse haunted her.

'When it happens,' she whispered, not quite meeting his gaze, 'I feel like I'm becoming one of them. Of the . . . you know. Maybe Lily's trying to turn me into one of them, and that's why I . . . I—'

'Yes,' Klaus interrupted, to spare her the pain of saying it out loud. Bad enough that he couldn't stop reliving the bloody scene in his own mind. 'Perhaps the opal has more than one use. She could be using it to link you to the *morts-vivants*, the same way she linked herself to me. Maybe that's why you feel their hunger.'

He could only hope that Lily had felt the pain of Vivianne's attack. Lily would have healed just as fast as Klaus did, but at least the nasty bite on the forearm and the ringing blow to the chin would have hurt.

'If it weren't for that pendant, you could kill her and be done with it,' Vivianne pointed out, shrugging her way out of the towel and into a flimsy robe that lay over the back of a nearby chair. It was covered in images of peacock feathers, which shimmered and glowed in the morning light. 'Taking it back would do more than ending whatever spell she's been working on me. It could put an end to this entire nightmare, and we would finally be happy.'

She was right. Getting their hands on Esther's pendant would solve all of their problems at once. It was a shame it was guarded by an army of undead witches and hanging around the neck of a madwoman he couldn't attack without attacking himself. But Klaus had done the impossible more than once.

'So I'll go and get it,' he said, as if it were just that simple.

'And then what will you do?' She smiled, and he saw a hint of her old humour in the corners of her mouth. Some colour was finally returning to her face, and he was so transfixed by the cherry red of her lips that he struggled to register what they were saying. 'You're going to need to bring me along, Klaus.'

Klaus caught her by the shoulders, crushing her body against his chest. 'You need to stay away from Lily, love,' he insisted. 'You're the last person who should be anywhere near that witch.' Due to the linking spell, he knew he should stay away as well, but there was no one else he trusted to get the opal.

His mind was already racing, plotting out every angle of a possible attack. He could probably just charge in and make it up as he went along. That usually worked just fine.

'I think you're forgetting, darling, that I'm a witch, too.' Vivianne's smile had turned coy – she was definitely feeling better. 'I was a pretty decent one back in my day, you know. And I'd been reading your mother's grimoire back at the mansion, on nights when I couldn't sleep. I don't need to be able to ride into battle or even get close to her at all.'

As distracting as it would be to bring the most precious person in the world into the middle of a war, it would be even worse to leave her behind and wonder what might be happening to her.

'We'll go together,' he agreed. 'If we ride, we can be back in New Orleans by sunset. We'll find Lily and do whatever it takes to get the opal away from her, and if your magic can destroy hers, I will kill anyone who comes near you while you cast the spell.'

Vivianne stretched up onto her tiptoes and kissed him, and he could taste the fire his words had lit within her. 'Send word to the stables, and I'll be dressed by the time our horses are saddled.'

He pulled her hips against his and kissed her back, a slower and more lingering kiss than the first one had been. 'There's not *that* much of a hurry,' he suggested, and she shivered out of her robe.

His clothing followed the thin piece of silk to the floor, and their bodies came together before they could even reach the bed. They made love on the thick pile of the carpet while sunlight streamed in through the windows. Klaus held her tightly, claiming her through the touch of his hands, the searching trail of his mouth. It would have killed him to let her go, even for a second.

Eventually, they had to rest, and as he held her close he steeled himself for the wrenching, unbearable separation that was to come. It was only temporary, he told himself, but there was an insistent part of him that drove him to kiss Vivianne again, to breathe in the lilac scent of her hair, to memorise every inch of her skin.

Klaus couldn't rid himself of the fear that he was fighting fate, not just some witch. Nothing ever came for free, especially not when magic was involved. Klaus wanted to believe that he and Vivianne had paid enough already. But as he lay on the soft carpet, his legs entwined with Vivianne's and her face nuzzled against his shoulder, he couldn't shake the feeling that it was already too late for them.

TWENTY-SIX

*M*arguerite must have done much of her work right under her mother's nose. She had sifted through Lily's notes and spell books, even sorting the ingredients the witch stored in glass jars along the walls according to which she might have used. Rebekah was familiar with witchcraft, but without the girl's help she could never have made sense of the massive pile of information in Lily's private chamber.

Once they were able to begin their search in earnest, Marguerite was like a bloodhound on her mother's trail: tracking spells across scrolls and grimoires, testing them against the jarred ingredients and comparing notes with Rebekah about what Elijah had observed of the *morts-vivants* in action. It was impressive to watch, even if

Rebekah still chafed at each little setback and delay.

All in all, it didn't take long for Marguerite to form a pretty clear idea of what had been done to bring the *morts-vivants* back above ground. Rebekah could tell when the young witch had caught the right scent, even though Marguerite herself was maddeningly cautious about following it. She checked and rechecked her pages, letting promising bits of information slip so slowly that Rebekah thought she might scream. But the girl obviously knew what she was doing, and so Rebekah forced herself to be patient.

'They're still rising,' Marguerite murmured, holding a piece of parchment up to the sheltered flame of her lantern. 'The spell calls to them, but it takes time to work across distance. Our ancestors in New Orleans heard the call first, but it's still working its way outward.'

'Then every time we fight them, there will be more of them,' Rebekah interpreted grimly. The news was unwelcome, but not a complete surprise. The *morts-vivants* had started as a trickle and then become a flood.

Marguerite had been cagey about the clashes between their kind since Rebekah had left the wedding to find Klaus, but from what Rebekah had been able to gather, Elijah had fought the abominations again, and there were even more than before.

Rebekah hoped that he had been making new

vampires, but that was a short-term solution. Countless witches had died over the centuries, and they would have to turn the population of the entire world into vampires to stop the rising tide. And there was one in particular Rebekah would not look forward to meeting on the battlefield. She tried to imagine Esther tearing a heart out to eat it, and shuddered.

'There are mentions of *your* mother in here,' Marguerite marvelled. 'Esther, right? Grandmother used one of her spells.'

'Did she now?' Rebekah said. She could vividly recall the sight of Elijah bolting out of their hotel with their mother's grimoire under one arm. There were no actions without consequences, she reminded herself. Anyone who lived as long as an Original was bound to see the ripples of their choices extending across generations and continents, turning up when they least expected it.

They had been so quick to blame Klaus, but Elijah bore some real responsibility for this fiasco as well.

'It was something about contacting her ancestors,' Marguerite went on, rifling through the pages in front of her. 'Not to bring them back, but just to create a link between this world and the Other Side. The spell made the barrier permeable and located them behind it. Mother built on that, using the vulnerability that Esther's spell created to send her own magic through.'

Rebekah sometimes felt like she would never truly be finished with the past, no matter how hard she tried to focus on building a future. 'What we need to do, then, is to sever the link, and prevent this nightmare from spreading. So how is that done?'

She watched Marguerite for any shifting patterns in the young witch's loyalties.

'There's a beacon,' Marguerite said finally, pushing parchment into a pile and then tapping them to straighten their edges. 'The call is being sent out by something, and that same something provides the power that keeps the dead witches on their feet. It controls them and animates them, and if you destroy the signal the entire spell will end.'

Rebekah immediately thought of her mother's opal pendant. It had linked her to Klaus – who could say what else it might do? She imagined it pulsing with invisible light, sending out messages that only the dead could hear. Smashing it would free Klaus *and* send the *morts-vivants* back to their graves . . . a lot to rest on one fragile stone.

'I know what Lily used for the beacon,' Rebekah said. 'I may need your help in getting it away from her, though. Can you—'

'It's not an "it".' Marguerite frowned, her fingers tracing a complicated hieroglyph in a book that looked like it must weigh as much as she did. 'The beacon has to be alive. It has to have a heart. You don't destroy it; you *kill* it.'

'Alive?' Rebekah gaped. 'You mean it's a person?'

'A witch,' Marguerite clarified, turning a page and then flipping it back again. 'But it can't be my mother, because it needs to be a witch who's died before. They're the window the others crawl back through, and when there are no more left to come back, the first witch, the key to the magic, becomes one of them.'

That could only be one witch, and now Lily's plan made perfect sense. Returning Klaus's lover to the world wasn't *for* Klaus . . . it was for Lily.

She had worked her spell to raise the *morts-vivants* around the one dead witch whose safety was guaranteed. No one would be able to get near Vivianne, thanks to Klaus, so no one would be able to stop the spell. They made an unholy, unkillable triad: Klaus, Vivianne and Lily, each sustaining this evil in his or her own way.

'There has to be another way.' Klaus had nearly lost his mind the first time Vivianne had been taken from him. To lose her again, and to know this time that it had to be final . . . Rebekah couldn't imagine what that would do to her brother.

But Marguerite's face told her everything she needed to know. There was no hope for Vivianne, and no hope for the rest of them as long as she remained alive. 'You know who it is, then,' Marguerite guessed. 'I'm sorry if this is unwelcome news, but this is what the spell *is*. It's the fundamental architecture of the magic that brought the *morts-vivants* to life. You have to strike at the heart of their web if you want to bring the whole thing down.'

Rebekah had to remind herself that she was still grateful for the clever girl's help, even if the result hadn't been what she'd hoped for. Marguerite had betrayed everything she had ever known to serve the greater good, and Rebekah didn't intend to forget that. 'There's a place for you with us, if you want it,' she offered, although she knew the teenager wouldn't take her up on it.

'My place is here,' Marguerite answered, her round face solemn. 'These are my people, and they need me. Mother needs me, too, even if she doesn't realise it right now. I'm only doing this to help her. I'm no traitor, and I won't run like one.'

Rebekah embraced her, holding the girl's bony, awkward frame for a few moments longer than even she could have explained. 'I have to go,' she apologised, then hugged Marguerite again quickly, one last time. 'Thank you for all of this. You've done well, and I'll see that it wasn't in vain.'

Even if that meant the end of her own brother's happiness. Rebekah sped back towards her mansion, ordering her chaotic thoughts as she went. Elijah needed to know everything at once, and then they would need a plan.

To Rebekah's surprise, though, Elijah wasn't alone. His study was full to bursting in comparison to its customary silence. Without Rebekah or Klaus to rely on, Elijah had apparently turned to other confidants, and Rebekah dug her fingernails into her palms to control her automatic resentment.

She felt even pettier when Lisette jumped up from her chair, catapulting herself towards the door to fold Rebekah into a hug before she could even say hello. 'I'm so glad you're back!' the vampire whispered in her ear. 'Elijah needs you here.'

Rebekah gently removed her friend to arm's length, studying the changes that a few days and as many battles had wrought in Lisette. 'You look like you've been taking care of things well enough,' she decided at last, and Lisette beamed.

The other man in the study wasn't familiar, but the mere sight of him made the hairs on Rebekah's arms stand up. 'The moon will rise in less than an hour,' she told Elijah. 'Are you sure you want *that* in your office when it does?'

The man's brilliant-blue eyes flared yellow for a moment, but he looked just as amused as he was offended.

'This would be the sister,' he guessed, and Rebekah raked him from head to toe with her stare.

Plenty of men would have been shaking in their boots by the time she was done, but Elijah's new friend didn't so much as flinch. 'Strange bedfellows,' she muttered.

'We have more in common than not, tonight,' Elijah said to her, waiting for Lisette to stand aside before embracing his sister. He kissed her on the cheek and then looked her over, a brotherly habit he hadn't been able to shake after centuries of invulnerability. When he saw that she was unharmed, his shoulders relaxed.

'Brother,' she said, and gave him a quick hug, 'I have news.' She glanced at his two companions, not wanting the truth about Vivianne to slip outside of her family circle, especially to a werewolf.

But to her displeasure, Elijah didn't send them away. 'Whatever you have to say—'

'William,' Lisette interrupted, 'let's go and take a look at the ranks. I wanted to make sure your left flank wouldn't get tangled up with the scouts Julian's been leading through those hills to the east, and I think if you show me what you had in mind . . .' With a gentle but very firm hand on his back she steered the werewolf out of the study, leaving Rebekah and her brother alone.

Elijah watched her go for a long moment, and Rebekah could read his entire heart in the expression on his face. This was hardly the time to begin a new romance, but she had to admit that she approved of his choice. Elijah spent too much time alone, took on too much of the weight of running New Orleans. He deserved someone who made him happy. They all did.

'Killing Vivianne is the only way to stop the *morts-vivants*,' she told him in a rush. Elijah rocked back on his heels and set his mouth in a firm line.

'That's what I feared,' he answered. 'The moon will rise in less than an hour' – he rested his hands on her shoulders – 'and we will do what we must. As we always have to protect our brother and our family.' The daylight was fading and the witches were coming. They had a war to fight.

'So we will . . . Just tell me you didn't offer the wolves the whole city?' she asked, sliding her arm through his elbow.

'Certain arrangements have been made, but don't worry about that now. The night can still hold many surprises.'

'That sounds like something I should worry about, brother.'

'I'll explain on the way.' With a sly smile, he led her out of the house, towards the lawns where Elijah's motley armies had assembled. He outlined his deal with the werewolves as they walked, and Rebekah filled him in on the details of her encounters with Klaus and his dagger, Vivianne and Marguerite. For a couple of minutes, it was like old times: the two of them comparing notes and conspiring against their enemies. All that was missing was Klaus, but some things couldn't be helped.

They separated as they reached the others, moving among the ranks of vampires to pass along last-minute instructions, advice and encouragement. Rebekah could feel the excitement mounting in her blood as the first hints of moonrise began to lighten the edge of the horizon. She needed a good fight – something uncomplicated and violent.

Just then she heard shouting from the hills to the east, and the vampire scouts came racing back to the main group. They were ragged, and there weren't as many of them as there should be.

Rebekah vaulted up the side of the fountain in the centre of the lawn. She could see the advancing army, blackening the hills like a horde of insects. There were more of them than she had thought possible, more than they could possibly kill. 'The witches are coming!'

She heard hundreds of voices pick up the cry and pass it along, just as a mournful howl cut through it all, sending chills down her spine. One of the werewolves had changed into a shaggy brown beast with burning yellow eyes, and he howled again, calling to the rest of his kind.

The first rays of moonlight glittered on his bared fangs, and then the howling multiplied and drowned out everything else.

Elijah shouted orders, sending the vampires and wolves charging towards the witches, and Rebekah gamely jumped down to join them. It was going to be a bloodbath, and she wouldn't miss it for the world.

As her feet hit the ground, she was nearly bowled over by the hooves of a chestnut stallion, whose rider pulled up just before they collided. Klaus grinned down at her, and out of the corner of her eye Rebekah saw Vivianne stopping her own horse at a somewhat more reasonable distance. Klaus helped his wife down from her horse and then kissed her feverishly. Sharing a look of goodbye, Vivianne made for the open front door of the mansion, and Klaus turned back towards Rebekah. In the light of the rising moon, she could see that her brother's eyes were alight with the same battle lust that had already descended on her.

'Dear sister,' he greeted her with an irrepressible smile. 'You didn't intend to start without me, did you?'

'Never – ripping out hearts is your speciality.'

TWENTY-SEVEN

*E*lijah could feel an almost physical shock as the two sides collided, teeth and fists connecting in a thousand different ways. Werewolves' snarls filled the night as they tore into their prey with wild enthusiasm. Elijah could feel the decades of pent-up rage exploding within them as they sprang, tearing out throats left and right until a vampire arrived to neatly remove each *mort-vivant*'s heart.

His vampires attacked methodically, tearing out one bloody heart after another with grim efficiency. They had not forgotten the humiliating draw they had reached in the city a few nights back, and all around him, Elijah could see fighters who had no intention of reliving past mistakes.

Still, there were more *morts-vivants* than ever. Klaus's horse had become uncontrollable even before the battle was joined, and Elijah could see him surrounded on every side by the flesh-hungry creatures. Elijah fought his way towards his brother, feeling several spells and at least one pair of clutching, groping hands glance across his body.

But before he could reach Klaus, Elijah spotted a flash of coppery-blonde hair, and two of Klaus's attackers crumpled into a heap on the bloody grass. Lisette was there, watching out for his family. She looked stunningly fierce in the moonlight, her face streaked with drying blood. She could have been a Viking goddess, turning the tide of battle wherever she went.

Elijah turned to see Rebekah twisting a *mort-vivant*'s heart inside its ribcage, her mouth flattened into a grimace. Another one lunged at her back, but a wolf caught it by the ankle, dragging the dead woman to the ground. The witch wailed and sank her teeth into the wolf's shoulder, tearing at it even as the wolf shredded her torso with its claws.

Then Elijah was forced to concentrate on the knot of attackers coming his way. They seemed to creep in between the vampires, separating them by sheer numbers until they were isolated and vulnerable. Elijah tried to call to his troops to stay together, but every last one was fighting for his or her life.

Lisette reached his side, snapping a *mort-vivant*'s neck twice before finally killing her. 'They're splitting us up,' she warned him, and in spite of the violence around them he grabbed her around the waist and kissed her.

'Well, I didn't mean you and me, but I'll take it, Elijah Mikaelson.' She kissed him again. 'Just try to reorganise the troops before we're all cornered.'

'Are you now the one giving orders, Corporal?'

'Oh, just you wait,' she said, and then ripped out the heart of the nearest witch.

A wolf hurtled through the air, thrown by a *mort-vivant* whose hands were coated in blood all the way up to his shoulders. Its heavy body struck the ground in a heap, and Elijah could tell that it was already dead. The werewolves were paying a high price to regain their old lands, but they were certainly committed to the task.

Everywhere Elijah looked, wolves were cutting in and out of the ranks of the witches, slicing through them like knives. They linked the vampires together, creating pathways between them and opening up lines of sight. The bargain with William had been a good one, he decided.

He decapitated a *mort-vivant* and shoved the body towards Lisette. The headless man stayed on his feet, but he staggered and lurched, and she had no trouble finishing him off. They worked together, clearing space to reach little islands of isolated vampires, bringing their army back into a cohesive whole.

'Good fight, brother,' Klaus called, grinning while he broke the back of a *mort-vivant* who looked no older than sixteen.

'Glad you could make it,' Elijah answered, ducking below a werewolf so she could sink her jaws into the arm of a witch who had been casting a spell in Klaus's direction.

'Is Lily here?' Klaus asked urgently, turning his back towards Elijah so that they could fend off attacks from every side. 'I need to get to her.'

'Haven't seen her yet,' Elijah grunted, cracking open a tall blond man's chest to pluck his heart out of it like a piece of fruit. 'But she can't be far – she wouldn't miss this.'

Rebekah crossed in front of them, breathless, her honey-coloured hair swirling loose around her shoulders. A witch shot one spell after another at her, engulfing her in fire, then blood, then sickly-green mist before trying fire again. None of those trifles could bring down Rebekah Mikaelson, but they seemed to have her stunned, disoriented and unable to reach the woman.

Klaus broke away from Elijah, punching in the witch's head with one ferocious blow and pulling Rebekah towards the shelter of her siblings. Elijah could have sworn he heard his brother mutter an apology for Rebekah's daggering, which was surprising enough to make an impression even in the midst of a pitched battle.

'I'm sorry, too,' he heard Rebekah say, clearly enough to carry. 'I should never have . . .' Whatever else she said was lost under the scream of a werewolf, who rolled on its back with its entrails exposed.

The three of them were on the same side again. They dispatched one *mort-vivant* after another, working together smoothly, just like a family should.

But it was an illusion, Elijah knew. It would all explode again when Klaus found out about Rebekah's plan to end the spell. Klaus was determined to find Lily, and Elijah hoped against hope that he knew of a different way to end this.

'There she is,' Klaus said, flipping a witch through the air and throwing him into a pack of snarling werewolves.

Elijah looked up to see Lily standing just out of the fray. A tall, thin girl stood beside her, and even in the moonlight she looked familiar. Had Lily been so confident of victory that she had brought her teenaged daughter into a war with her? Elijah wouldn't have believed any other mother capable of such carelessness, but Marguerite Leroux was by her mother's side nonetheless. Lily's hubris must be boundless at this point, for her to think her invulnerability was enough to protect her daughter. Lily watched the fighting with a small smile on her face, as if it didn't bother her at all that her people were dying en masse.

Klaus moved off towards her, not caring that the path was blocked by dozens of witches. Elijah fell in beside him, and Rebekah did the same, keeping the worst of the fighting away from their brother. 'Slow down,' Elijah shouted, but Klaus was like a man possessed in his desperation to reach the witches' leader.

'I'm going to kill her,' Klaus announced through gritted teeth, spearing an undead woman with a long knife he had taken from some other unlucky witch along his way. He twisted the blade with determined precision, carving her heart out like a hunter cleaning a deer.

'You can't,' Elijah pointed out, wishing Klaus would use common sense for once in his endless life. 'She's linked to you.'

'Through the pendant she stole.' Klaus feinted at a dark-haired witch, who reacted too slowly and had his chest split open.

Klaus's talent for revising history was impressive under the circumstances – *he'd* brought this war upon them by trading away the pendant. Elijah knew he wouldn't get anywhere by arguing that point, and when Rebekah spun their way, her dark eyes flashing with outrage, he shot her a warning look.

'Taking the pendant back will let us kill Lily,' she snapped, 'but this is no time for petty revenge. We need to put an end to these monsters for good, not indulge every impulsive whim that comes your way.'

'All we need is that pendant,' Klaus insisted, scanning the field for the shortest path to his enemy. 'We can free Vivianne from her connection to the *morts-vivants* and let our armies put them back in the ground.'

Rebekah froze for a moment, her mouth open as if she wanted to speak but couldn't find the words. A ball of green fire hissed through the air and struck her squarely in the stomach. It sizzled as it hit home, and the force of it knocked her backward into the arms of a blood-soaked *mort-vivant*.

Rebekah turned to deal with her new assailant, the remnants of the spell still smoking in the fabric of her dress. In the meantime, another undead witch broke past her, leaping towards Klaus's unprotected back. Elijah moved to intercept the attack, and his boot smashed into the head of the *mort-vivant* in mid-air. The thing fell to the ground, stunned, and Klaus turned to engage him, his knife flashing brutally in the moonlight.

Too late, Elijah realised that Rebekah had shaken off her own attacker and had fought her way back to Klaus's side. 'The pendant won't free Vivianne,' he heard her say, leaning close to their brother's ear but keeping one cautious eye on the knife he held loosely in his left hand. 'Niklaus, I'm so sorry, but—'

'There's Lily,' Klaus interrupted, and Elijah honestly wasn't sure whether he had chosen to ignore Rebekah's words or simply not registered them at all. He shoved a werewolf out of the way and charged into the thick of the battle, leaving his siblings behind.

Rebekah shifted her weight as if she intended to follow him, but Elijah caught her by the shoulder, holding her back. 'We have enough to do here,' he warned her. 'Let Klaus fight in his own way, if you want there to be any chance of him coming around to yours.'

Rebekah's face was full of resentment, but she accepted Elijah's read of the situation. 'He's going to have to come around quickly,' she muttered darkly. 'I don't intend to spend the rest of eternity killing these *things*.'

'We'll end them well before then,' Elijah assured her, and then the current of the battle swept them up again.

TWENTY-EIGHT

*J*He was attacked from every side, but Klaus didn't care. Lily Leroux was within reach, and nothing so insignificant as a war was going to keep him away from her. Vivianne was watching the battle from the attic windows, preparing the spell that would destroy the opal's hold over her, and he intended to do her proud. He would get the opal from Lily one way or another, and if he had to take her head off to get it then so much the better.

A mangy werewolf, so thin Klaus could see its ribs through its rough grey coat, bounded in front of him, snarling. Klaus gave the beast one second to recognise him, ready to snap its neck if it didn't stand aside. The werewolf hesitated, its yellow eyes scanning Klaus from head to toe, and then it flinched away, seeming to realise its mistake. An arm shot out of the throng of witches, punching through the wolf's lean chest, and Klaus didn't wait around to see any more. He could win the war by destroying the enemy's leader, and casualties were going to be inevitable in the meantime.

There were only a few witches left between him and their general. They fought hard, and the *morts-vivants* were strong. But Klaus had been laying waste to armies for over a thousand years, and he had no intention of being deterred from his goal.

Lily was chanting something, her brown hair loose around her shoulders, partly concealing her face from view. She was so focused on her spell that she almost didn't see Klaus coming until it was too late. At the last minute her head snapped up, her skin thick with sweat from the strain of casting.

He could see the white opal that hung from her neck. It was full of flashes of orange and green fire, just how it had looked when he had handed it over to her. He couldn't wait to rip it off her treacherous, lying neck.

Klaus wasn't sure how his momentum reversed itself or when his reach for the pendant's chain shifted. The magic moved him seamlessly in the opposite direction, and his fingers closed on empty air instead of the ancient chain. He found himself facing a *mort-vivant* who grinned malevolently in spite of the fact that a werewolf had disembowelled her earlier in the night.

He twisted around, disorientation making his head spin. Lily blurred and then came into focus, looking enormously pleased with herself. 'Was it this you were after, vampire?' she asked, as casually as if the two of them were sharing tea. She touched the opal with a finger, and it glowed softly in the brilliant moonlight.

Klaus moved slowly this time, approaching her warily and trying to feel the edge of the spell before getting caught up in it again. 'You might as well hand it over,' he suggested. 'I know what you're using it for, and I'm not going to stop until I find a way to take it back.'

'The only way this chain comes off my neck is if I take it off myself,' she informed him, her voice dripping with disdain. 'And I can't be harmed as long as I wear it. What are you going to do, Niklaus – threaten me to death?'

'You grew up on stories of my family,' he reminded her. 'Is there anything in the long, ugly history between our kinds that makes you think I bother with idle threats?'

'You have no choice.' She shrugged. A howl rose up from the melee behind him, but he didn't take his eyes off the witch in front of him. 'We are linked for life, Klaus, whether you like it or not. And I suspect our life will be a rather long one, so you might as well get used to the idea now.'

He wanted to tear her smug face right off the front of her skull. 'If you think you have all the time in the world to turn Vivianne into one of your pet monsters, witch, you're sorely mistaken. You've put her through enough already, and I don't intend to rest until she's free of your curse.'

Lily laughed, throwing her head back so that her throat was exposed in the moonlight. He could just rip it out, just take her head off and pull the pendant over the bloody stump. If he could only get his hands on her, there was no limit to the ways he could destroy her.

'That curse is her entire life now,' she told him, still chuckling as she said it. 'Your blushing bride is far beyond your help, vampire. The spell is cast, and she is what she is. Killing me won't save her, and neither will this trinket of your mother's you so eagerly gave away.'

'You lie,' Klaus hissed, although he could hear the ring of sincerity in her voice. 'All you've done from the beginning is lie.'

Lily shrugged. 'I told you I could bring her back, and I did. Now I can take my city back, and you can watch her become like all the others.'

'I won't let that happen,' Klaus said through clenched teeth, wondering as he did how he would prevent it. Lily had laid her trap well, and he seemed to be blocked at every turn. Now, when the most precious thing he had ever encountered in his entire life was at stake, Klaus found himself running out of ideas.

'You can't stop it,' Lily said, as if she was enjoying a private joke. 'You, of all people, can't kill her. Why do you think I chose her for this spell? It was never about her – it was about *you*, and what you would do to keep Vivianne Lescheres alive.'

Klaus didn't care any more about the magic that linked them. He struck blindly, stabbing at the witch's face with the long knife he had taken from one of her minions. Lily didn't move or even flinch.

He heard voices shouting somewhere around them, and saw a flash of movement out of the corner of his eye. But he was so focused on his victim, her smug face. Her smile filled his vision, blocking out everything else, until it was too late.

His knife was buried in someone else, a slight girl who might have been barely eighteen. Her shout was cut off abruptly when the blade severed her throat, but another voice continued to scream. Lily went deathly pale, catching the girl beneath her arms to keep her from falling to the ground, and everything was wrong.

'What have you done?' Rebekah wailed, staring at the child as if she had been her own.

Lily sank down gently onto the grass, cradling her daughter against her chest. 'He couldn't touch me,' she whispered, so softly that Klaus could barely hear it. 'There was no need, Marguerite. Why did you interfere?'

The wound in Marguerite's throat bubbled and spurted with blood, and her brown eyes looked glassy. The rest of her life wouldn't last any longer than a few more breaths. She had tried to save Lily, but Klaus still regretted hurting her. She was too young to know better, and far too young to be brought to observe a battle. It was as much Lily's fault as his own that she would die, but that was little consolation.

'The opal pendant,' Rebekah said. She moved to kneel on the other side of the girl's shuddering body, but Klaus laid a cautionary hand on her arm, keeping his sister beside him. 'It links you to an immortal – if she wears it will it do the same for her?'

Lily touched the chain around her neck, closing her eyes for a moment as if the mere thought of it pained her. 'I can't transfer the spell,' she admitted, her voice breaking with tears. 'I'd do it in a heartbeat if I could. This was all for her – my life's work was to build her a future. I should have given her the opal to start with, but I never thought . . .' She wiped her tears away and, with a shuddering sob, composed herself just enough to finish. 'The pendant can't help her now.'

'It can,' Klaus disagreed. Both of the women stared at him, although Marguerite herself was too far gone to look his way. 'Give her the pendant, Lily. Take it off and put it around her neck, and I can guarantee that it will save her life.'

Rebekah's mouth gaped open in confusion, but Lily's tear-filled eyes narrowed in sudden understanding. It was the last bargain she would ever strike, but with time running out, she showed no interest in haggling.

'Save her, then,' Lily agreed. She bent to kiss her daughter's forehead, then slipped the opal's chain from her own neck onto Marguerite's.

'Give her your blood,' Klaus murmured to Rebekah, who wasted no time in opening her wrist and pressing it to the girl's parted lips. He could see her mouth working, just barely enough to drink a few drops, but it would be enough. The blood of an Original vampire would bring her back to life, as long as it was in her body when she died.

She would be a vampire, and she would be motherless, but Klaus thought that was a reasonable enough price to demand for a Mikaelson's blood. He had given the first vial away far too cheaply, but he was wiser now.

Lily wouldn't even look at him. She spent the last moments of her life staring at her daughter, searching the girl's pale face for any signs that life was returning to it. Marguerite's recovery would take much longer than Lily had left, though, and it was just as well. It was better for the girl to sleep through this ugliness, and she certainly didn't need to know just yet that her own actions had set her mother's death into motion.

Klaus made it quick, and far more merciful than the renegade witch deserved. He bent down and snapped her neck, and she slumped sideways, her war ended between one moment and the next. Rebekah caught Marguerite up in her arms, supporting her body while her mother's fell to the ground.

'She'll be all right in time,' he said to Rebekah, who still looked as though she was about to cry.

'She won't,' Rebekah muttered, but she spared him the indelicacy of his next request. She slipped the opal off over Marguerite's head and tossed it to Klaus, as if the trinket wasn't worth the blood that had been shed.

But he knew better. No matter what Lily had said, no matter what wild claims she had made in order to prevent Klaus from destroying her army, he knew the truth. Vivianne had been destined for him from the beginning, and nothing could keep them apart. Her magic could turn the opal into the cure they needed. He closed his fist around the chain so hard that it bit into his skin like a set of teeth.

All he had to do was get it to Vivianne, and they could finally set her free.

TWENTY-NINE

*M*arguerite's wounds were healing. Before long the skin would seal over them, and it would be as if Klaus's knife had never torn through her.

Rebekah watched her, waiting for any sign of life returning to her pale face, but she knew it would be hours before Marguerite began to revive. And even after she did, she would never be the same. Her life had ended forever on this night, even if she went on living for a thousand more years. Rebekah could have killed Klaus where he stood, gloating over his useless pendant.

'Look what you did to her,' she hissed, stroking Marguerite's hair back from her forehead. 'She's barely more than a *child*, Niklaus!'

'She'll live,' he replied, tucking the opal into an inner

pocket of his coat. 'She looks better already.'

'You know the opal is worthless, right?' Rebekah said. 'There's no way to—'

'It will save Vivianne,' Klaus interrupted, his voice rising over hers. 'It was worth any price.'

Even after centuries of betrayals and heartbreaks, he still believed there was such a thing as happily ever after. Rebekah didn't know whether to laugh or cry at his naivety.

'Marguerite found Lily's research and notes on the *mort-vivant* spell,' she tried. 'It's working *through* Vivianne. We can't save her from it, even with the pendant. Vivianne is becoming one of the *morts-vivants*, and the only way to stop it is to kill her like one of them.'

Klaus glanced contemptuously at the girl lying across Rebekah's lap. 'As you said, dear sister, she's basically a *child*. A child who nearly got herself killed trying to protect an invincible madwoman, so you'll have to forgive me if I don't consider her an authority on everything that is and is not possible in this world.'

Rebekah set Marguerite gently down on the cool grass, reluctant to let her go for even a moment. She could have been the little sister Rebekah never had, or even a younger version of herself. The self that Rebekah had been, anyway, before plagues and werewolves had chipped away at her family, and before her mother had cursed her and her father had hunted her. Before the prospect of an eternity full of more of the same had fully settled itself onto her shoulders.

Rebekah stood, trying not to look at the girl at her feet. 'Niklaus, enough is enough. I'm sorry for your pain, but open your eyes. Look at what your quest to drag Vivianne back into the world has cost us already, and think how much we still have left to lose. Our people are dying around us, and this stupidity of yours has torn our family apart.'

'Don't blame Vivianne for your own foolish choices,' Klaus scoffed. 'She didn't force you to poison our wedding feast or hunt us down on our honeymoon. You've done more than enough to tear our family apart, and all over your petty jealousy of a woman struggling under a horrible curse. If you had ever been on her side and, more important, on *my* side, we could have resolved this ages ago.'

'She shouldn't even be alive!' Rebekah shouted, losing her patience entirely. 'You did all of this for a dead woman! She had her chance at life, brother, and she threw it away. It was tragic and pointless and miserable, and I would have done whatever you needed if you had only had the decency to mourn her. Just grieve, like everyone else in the world has to do from time to time, and eventually learn to move on.'

Klaus's hands balled into fists, and Rebekah instinctively edged her body in front of Marguerite's, shielding her from whatever wrath her brother still had left in him. 'You have a lot of nerve, talking about who is supposed to live and die. Our whole existence is unnatural, Rebekah. The rules that people must live and die by don't apply to us, and my wife is waiting at home to prove it yet again. With this opal and her magic, she can have the same chance that you and I do, and you're crazy if you think that I don't intend to give it to her.'

It was hopeless. Klaus refused to accept that there were things in the world outside of his control, even while he was surrounded by the obvious. 'Of course you'll give it to her,' Rebekah agreed, changing tack and softening her tone. 'Niklaus, I'm not saying that you must keep the opal away from Vivianne, or that you shouldn't do everything in your power to help her. What I'm telling you is that it's *not* in your power. The opal won't help her, and neither will whatever spell she's cooking up in our attic right now. I'm not trying to talk you out of this. I'm trying to prepare you for the fact that it won't *work*.'

Something shifted in her peripheral vision, and Klaus saw it, too. For a brief, hopeful moment, she thought it might be Marguerite, healed from her horrible wound, but the girl still lay pale and motionless on the grass.

Instead, it was her mother who rose. Lily Leroux climbed to her feet, her neck snapping straight even as Rebekah watched in shock. There was a strange gleam in her brown eyes, a light that was also somehow a blankness.

Klaus stepped forward and snapped her neck again. The gesture was almost impatient, as if he were annoyed that killing her hadn't quite worked the first time. Rebekah realised that he didn't understand what had happened. He didn't know about the beacon – Vivianne would keep calling to the dead witches until they had all returned. Lily was now a *mort-vivant*.

Lily popped her neck back into place, lunging for Klaus almost faster than Rebekah's eyes could follow. Her hands were outstretched, her fingernails curving into talons. 'She's one of them,' Rebekah shouted, leaping on her back and gouging at her eyes.

It was just like Marguerite had warned them: dead witches would rise. It must be happening out in the main battlefield, too. The living witches were being reborn as the living dead. Rebekah wondered how Elijah and his armies were faring if the witch army kept growing in size.

Lily fought like a demon, whipping Rebekah round so hard that her skull cracked against Klaus's with a sickening sound. Rebekah caught Lily by her brown hair and twisted hard, pulling the witch off her brother and catapulting her through the air towards the open grass of the rolling hills.

'She's mine,' Klaus snarled, holding up one arm to block Rebekah from following after her, and Rebekah rolled her eyes.

'Abominations belong to everyone,' she snapped, shoving Klaus's arm down and chasing after Lily Leroux. Lily was just as responsible for Marguerite's condition as Klaus was – maybe even more. He may have struck the blow, but Lily had created this nightmare and forced them all to try to navigate it. Even dead she was more trouble than she was worth, and Rebekah's hands itched for the warm, slimy feel of her beating heart.

She caught the undead witch before Klaus could get there, but Lily swung wildly at her head and Rebekah ducked, giving him time to reach them. He twisted Lily's head all the way round, shattering her spinal column for the third time in five minutes, although by now Rebekah knew it was unlikely to do much good.

There was only one way to kill Lily, at least as long as Vivianne was still alive. Rebekah would have liked to do it herself, but just taking part in the death of Lily Leroux would still be a memory to cherish. Rebekah grabbed at the dead woman's arms, locking them behind her struggling body and generously offering her to Klaus.

He plunged his fist into her chest, and for a nauseating

moment Rebekah thought she could feel his searching fingers through the skin of Lily's back. Then he found what he was searching for and pulled, ripping the bloody organ out through the gaping hole in her rib cage. Rebekah could feel Lily's body go slack, slumping against her own before Rebekah dropped her unceremoniously to the ground.

'Well,' Klaus said in a conversational tone, squeezing the heart until it was misshapen and almost unrecognisable. 'We may have had our differences, dear sister. But if I have to spend the night tearing hearts from chests, I can't think of any better company than yours.'

The thought of having avenged Vivianne somehow had brought a sly smile to his face, an expression with which Rebekah was thoroughly familiar. Klaus thought he had won already, that nothing could stop him now from saving the love of his life from her grisly fate. Rebekah knew he was wrong with every fibre of her being, but the sight of him standing there, so jovial in the moonlight, softened her own heart until it was nearly unrecognisable as well.

There was no harm in letting him try, not really. A few more vampires might die, and probably an extra handful of werewolves. But the upside was that Klaus would finally realise what she had been trying to tell him all along: there was no magic spell that could repair all of the damage that Lily had done. Trying to rescue Vivianne from her fate – and failing one more time – might be just the bitter potion her brother needed to swallow in order to finally realise it was time to give up.

'Go home and try the opal,' she suggested. 'I'll take care of things here.'

Klaus discarded the heart, touched his coat pocket that held the pendant then turned and ran for the mansion. Watching him go, Rebekah hoped against hope that somehow she and Marguerite had been wrong. There was also something to be said for true love.

THIRTY

*E*lijah was doing his best to be everywhere at once, but he could feel the tide of the battle turning against them. The werewolves had seemed to bring them a substantial advantage at first, but over time it became clear that the full moon was as much a drawback as it was an asset. The wolves were strong, fast and ruthless, but in their current form they couldn't actually kill any of the *morts-vivants*. And there seemed to be more of those than ever, no matter how many of them Elijah and his vampires destroyed.

Even worse, the *morts-vivants* seemed to prefer the taste of vampire hearts to those they ripped from the werewolves. The losses were heavy all round, but even in the midst of battle Elijah could tell that his own kind were taking the worst of the hits.

For the first time since he had set out to recruit the werewolves the night before, Elijah was forced to consider the possibility that he had been too eager to secure the werewolves' help. He had given away a substantial chunk of the city – *his* city, which he had fought for, rebuilt and held together with his own two hands – and for what? So that William's wolves could harass the witches a bit, while his own vampires were crushed under the burden of winning the war?

If William had approached *him* with this bargain, Elijah would have been certain it had been a trick. But as things were, there was no one to blame except himself . . . and, of course, Lily Leroux.

Klaus's grief had been a dam waiting to burst. For forty-four years their enemies had refused to 'help' him, believing that the worst thing they could do to him was deny him what he wanted most. Only Lily had seen the real potential in Klaus's blind longing. She had given him the thing he most wished for in the form of a weapon – it truly was a brilliant kind of evil. Elijah sincerely hoped Klaus had found a way around their linking spell to repay her in the way she deserved.

He suspected his brother might have already killed the witch. There was no longer a sign of any central command. Spells were launched haphazardly, sometimes colliding in mid-air, and the *morts-vivants* clustered around every freshly captured heart, vying with one another for the first taste. It had been nearly an hour since Elijah had managed to catch a glimpse of their general, so maybe Klaus had managed to end her short, vicious reign.

Unfortunately, the witches' disorganisation only seemed to make them more brutal, and Elijah's forces were struggling to hold their ground. Even with Lily out of the way, it was beginning to seem unlikely that the vampires could overpower so many mindless, bloodthirsty attackers.

Elijah watched a werewolf spring through the air, perfect in its powerful forward motion. It landed squarely on the chest of a living witch, who saw it too late to turn his magic against the massive beast. The wolf tore out the witch's throat with murderous proficiency and then moved on, dragging at the leg of a *mort-vivant* who was close to overpowering two of Elijah's vampires.

He couldn't make sense of how badly they were outnumbered. The *morts-vivants* were hard to kill, no question, but their living comrades had been falling like flies before the combined might of the vampires and the werewolves. And yet their army seemed barely smaller than it had been when they had first been seen in the hills, as if more of the undead were somehow reinforcing their ranks without their approach being seen.

One of the monsters bit viciously into Elijah's shoulder, hanging on like a rabid dog when Elijah tried to shake her off. A werewolf appeared and tried to help, but the *mort-vivant* twisted like a snake, somehow maintaining the grip of her teeth while caving in the werewolf's sternum with one kick.

The creature fell, whimpering, to the grass, and the uselessness of its intervention made Elijah irrationally angry. He grabbed the *mort-vivant* by the nape of her neck and yanked her away, ignoring the feeling of his own flesh being torn out by her teeth that refused to let go. He held the monster away from him for a moment, watching the undead witch swallow her piece of Elijah's shoulder with revolting pleasure.

Still seething with anger, he reached out to seize her heart, but her attention shifted from her grisly feast just in time to see the movement. She caught his hand in both of hers, grinning to reveal blood-and-tissue-smeared teeth, and he felt like a human slamming his fist into a stone wall. Elijah had come to take his disproportionate strength for granted over the centuries – all of the Originals had – and the shock of impact was an unpleasant reminder of how heavily he relied on his own curse.

There shouldn't be anything walking the world with so much strength. Not the *morts-vivants*, and not the Mikaelsons, either. Elijah knew that to the ordinary, mortal population of New Orleans there might not be much difference between the two – he did, after all, survive by draining human blood. Maybe the two unnatural species should just wipe each other out and leave the world to those who would die on their own.

A clenched fist appeared in the centre of the *mortvivant*'s chest, holding her heart triumphantly out towards Elijah. The witch's body went slack, and he released his grip on her neck. Rebekah stood before him, still holding the gory organ, her porcelain skin streaked with the blood of a dozen more like it.

Elijah hadn't realised until then that the tide of battle had carried him to the westernmost edge of the hills, where he had briefly glimpsed Lily earlier. Her corpse was still there, he realised, along with the thin, tall body of a girl he didn't want to recognise. Rebekah stood over the girl, and Elijah understood that his sister had also been protecting Marguerite when she helped him. She was fighting tooth and nail to keep a clear space around the girl's limp form, although it didn't seem to bother her that, just a few yards away, Lily was being trampled.

'The bitch is dead,' Rebekah announced, then parried three of another dead witch's blows in rapid succession and drove her fist through his skull. He didn't die, but now his attacks were blind and unfocused. He swung wildly, connecting at random with friends and enemies alike but failing to get anywhere near Rebekah.

Elijah saw Lisette just moments before she put the *mort-vivant* down for good. She was alight with the thrill of battle, shining from within under the moonlight.

'We're outnumbered!' she said to him.

'We've been killing plenty of them,' Elijah assured Lisette, although he knew she was right. 'Where are they all coming from?'

'It's the spell,' Rebekah said, shoving a snarling werewolf out of the path of a nasty-looking witch before glancing back at the unmoving girl who lay behind her. 'It's what I've been trying to—'

Before she could finish, a cluster of *morts-vivants* broke through a ring of vampires who had been trying to contain them.

Elijah moved to help protect Marguerite, but before he had taken a step a stirring in the grass caught his attention. He whirled to face it, ready to put the *mort-vivant* back down, and out of the corner of his eye he saw Lisette preparing to do the same.

She started forward, eager to strike, but Elijah caught her arm and held her back. Something was nagging at him, a familiarity, a memory of having seen how that particular witch had come to lie in that particular spot.

Except it hadn't been dead then.

Elijah had seen that same witch savaged by a werewolf

just a few minutes before, and he was absolutely sure the man had been alive at the time. The wolf had torn his throat out and left him for dead – left him *dead* – but he had returned almost immediately as one of Lily's heart-eaters. There wasn't a scratch on him, no sign at all of the mauling he had just endured. He had fallen as one thing and risen up again as an entirely different one.

'The living ones are being resurrected as the undead ones,' Rebekah snapped, finally dispatching the last of her knot of *morts-vivants*. 'It happened to Lily, too.'

No wonder they were more and more outnumbered by the minute: each easy kill became a new, much more formidable, enemy. The witches were rebuilding their army even faster than the vampires were destroying it.

'That explains it,' Lisette agreed, slipping out of Elijah's grasp to engage the newest *mort-vivant*. He rushed to help her, and he thought the two of them made an effective team. But there seemed to be undead witches everywhere, attacking and interfering from all sides and making it impossible to pick them off one by one.

There was no telling how far the evil could spread, or what destruction it would wreak on cities that didn't have the protection of vampires. In her bid to take over New Orleans, Lily Leroux might yet take down the entire New World.

A vampire screamed, and no one was free to get to her

in time. More and more of them were dying, everywhere Elijah looked. He could still see plenty of bared fangs and yellow eyes, but they were like islands in an engulfing sea of *morts-vivants*. Vampires he had sired were being torn to pieces, and it seemed the next one was always in danger before he could even reach the last.

There was nothing to be done, though, but keep fighting. He had raised this army, and he had led them onto the field. Lily might have started this war, but it was Elijah's now, too, and he would keep defending his army until his army was gone.

THIRTY-ONE

Vivianne turned the opal over in her hands, staring at it as if its flashes of fire could reveal its mysteries. Klaus held every muscle in his body at the ready, waiting only for her word of what to do next.

'I'm going to need your blood,' Vivianne muttered, and Klaus had opened a vein before her words had fully died on the still, dusty air of the attic.

She held the stone out to catch the thick, dark liquid, and its smooth surface seemed to drink it in. He had seen the same thing, he remembered, when Lily had first done the linking spell, and he wondered how much of his blood the cursed stone could swallow.

Vivianne watched the opal for a moment longer, then held her own fragile wrist up to Klaus. 'Now mine,' she said.

He hesitated for just a moment before biting her skin, as gently as he possibly could while still breaking it. He knew she had been through much worse, but he couldn't escape the feeling that he had already hurt her enough – too much.

But Vivianne didn't even register the discomfort, intent as she was on the open grimoire by her feet. She set the pendant on the floorboards beside it and dipped one finger into the blood that welled up through her skin.

'The opal connects energies together,' she explained, tracing a design in chalk on the floor around the pendant. 'Yours to Lily's, mine to yours, hers to the *morts-vivants* so that they do her bidding. The connections serve different purposes, but they all run through this stone.'

'We don't need some necklace to bind us together, love.' Lily might have used magic to bring Vivianne back specifically to him, but if she had awoken on the other side of the world Klaus knew they still would have found each other.

'Exactly.' Vivianne stepped back to examine her design, then rubbed out one slightly crooked line and drew it again. 'None of the stone's connections are natural or necessary; they just suited Lily's purposes. This ritual will break them all, and then I'll be free of her and her monsters forever.'

The moonlight slid in sideways through the northern windows. It was hard to shake the impression of wrongness, even though Klaus knew that it was Vivianne working this magic and not the dark thing trying to take hold within her. The creature had only minutes left, and then she would banish it for good.

As soon as it was done he would take her away from all of this, somewhere with plenty of sun and no monsters. They would stay however long it took for her to heal, and to finally feel safe again.

'Does this look right to you?' she asked. 'Never mind, just stand right there where the lines cross, and let me concentrate.'

Her voice was brisker than usual. He could almost see the sense of urgency crackling around her, mixing with the invisible aura of her magic. Dark or light, Vivianne was powerful, someone to be reckoned with, and he suppressed a smile as he did what he was told.

Vivianne began to chant, and candles she had arranged around the outside of her symbol flared to sudden, brilliant life. The shadows they cast seemed to move in the corners of Klaus's vision, writhing and twisting until he turned to look at them directly. He could feel a strange tension building in the attic. Shadows danced and spun, coming completely unmoored from the objects that had cast them, not even pretending to belong to the mortal world any more. They swirled and flew around Klaus's head like bats, but he only had eyes for Vivianne.

He could almost see the battle of forces within her, the war she was waging for control of her own body and soul. She struggled to command her own magic while Lily's threatened to overwhelm her, and although she stood perfectly still, her slight form contained a raging ocean of power.

With a movement so swift that even Klaus's sharp eyes didn't see it coming, she brought the hilt of his dagger down on the opal, shattering it into a million splintered pieces. The shadows around them broke apart in the same instant, scattering and then slithering back into their corners. A sudden gale howled through the attic, gusting out of the broken stone or perhaps coming from Vivianne herself, but although Klaus could feel it tearing at his clothes, the flames of the many candles around him didn't so much as flicker.

They burned steadily until the wind died, then extinguished so suddenly it was as if the flames had somehow swallowed the tempest. There was no sign of any magic left, nothing but the faint smell of smoke that was already beginning to fade. It was over, and they were alone in the attic. Vivianne swayed a little on her feet, but

Klaus could see some colour creeping back into her face, and the ghost of a smile played on her lips. 'It worked,' she told him. 'I felt the spell work.'

He had certainly felt something, but he approached her slowly, trying to take in each subtle change in her at once. 'Do you feel . . . hungry?' he asked, searching the deep pools of her black eyes for anything sinister that might be lurking at the bottom.

'I don't know,' she admitted, pressing her hand to the bite on her wrist. The bleeding had already slowed to almost nothing, but Klaus lifted it to his lips and kissed it gently all the same. 'I feel dizzy.'

He was so concentrated on Vivianne that it took him a moment to register the strange hush that had fallen outside the house. There was no more screaming, no tearing or slashing of flesh to be heard.

He embraced her, holding her so close against his body that he could feel the beat of her pulse just as forcefully as his own. He could smell the soft lilac fragrance of her hair and feel the gentle curves of her hips against his. She was going to be all right; he would devote the rest of eternity to making sure of that.

He held her, inhaled her, tried not to hear the new shouts that rose up from the armies outside. Vivianne stirred, and Klaus knew that she must hear it, too. But he just pulled her close, wanting to share one last moment of hope with her, one last peaceful interlude.

'You need to back away from me now,' she whispered at last, and he could hear the hunger in her voice. 'Klaus, you can't imagine how hard I'm trying not to kill you where you stand.'

Klaus could feel it, though, in the way Vivianne's body trembled and by the tension in her muscles. The spell may have done what it was written to do, but nothing that mattered had changed. Rebekah had been right all along that magic didn't just come with any old price. What made magic so dangerous was that it came with a price worthy of the prize. There was nothing in the world worth as much to Klaus as Vivianne, and so the cost of getting her back could only be losing her all over again.

Klaus stepped back reluctantly, his eyes scanning up and down Vivianne's shaking body. 'Go and look,' she urged him through her clenched jaw, jerking her chin to indicate the nearest window. 'See for yourself how we failed.' Klaus hesitated for a moment, but she didn't move and so he crossed the creaking attic floor.

The scene outside was even more gruesome than he had imagined. *Morts-vivants* were everywhere, and they seemed to be killing everyone around them indiscriminately. One tore a live witch's head off while Klaus watched, and another seemed to be trying to tear the skin from a werewolf in one long skein.

Klaus turned back to Vivianne, searching for the words to describe what was happening. As he did, he saw the sudden shift, the almost imperceptible moment when Vivianne lost her battle for control. He jumped back just as she charged, but she was far too fast. Her fingernails raked across his throat, laying it open, and he felt his own blood pouring down the front of his shirt.

Klaus shoved her away hard, feeling sick as he watched her lick the blood from his jugular vein off her hands.

'The pendant was supposed to free you,' Klaus whispered. He hadn't let himself consider the possibility that it might not. He had never imagined failure, never prepared himself for the brutal, stabbing pain of this moment.

Vivianne screamed incoherently in response and tore out a few glossy handfuls of her raven hair. Klaus took advantage of her momentary distress to catch hold of her arms, pinning them to her sides. She struggled, and she was nearly as strong as he was, but he held on. She deserved to understand what was happening, even if he never truly would.

Finally, her muscles slackened, and her grating screams grew hoarse, eventually becoming hopeless sobs. She rested her dark head against his shoulder, and while he could not bring himself to relax his grip on her, she made no further move to attack him.

'There is no freedom for me,' she rasped, her voice a harsh ruin. 'I can feel that now. Klaus, my bond with the *morts-vivants* was never some frail linking spell, or any curse Lily worked after she raised me. It's born from the magic that keeps us all alive: them and me alike.'

'We'll keep looking,' Klaus promised, hearing that his own voice was nearly as rough as hers. 'There are other spells—'

'No,' she whispered. 'There's only one way to end this nightmare, and I think you know what it is. I think you've known for some time now.'

'Lily chose you because of me,' Klaus admitted, tasting bitterness in his words. 'She made you the keystone of her spell, because she knew that I could never – that I wouldn't—'

'Oh,' Vivianne breathed, and although there was sadness in her eyes, Klaus thought he could see relief there, as well. 'The spell survives as long as I do, then. And Lily believed you would never agree to let me die again.' She smiled and lifted a soft hand to touch his cheek. 'She didn't know you the way that I do, love.'

Klaus turned his face so that his lips brushed her fingers. 'You know that I'm yours, Viv.'

Vivianne looked up then and kissed him on the mouth, her full lips salty with her own tears. 'I love you,

Niklaus. I would give anything to share a life with you, but mine is already over. This thing I have now is no life, always waiting for the next time I start to sink. Sooner or later, I won't be able to come up for air at all, and I'll drown in this darkness forever.'

'I don't want to lose you again,' he murmured, kissing her lips, her tear-stained cheeks, her hair.

'It's still the first time,' she told him softly, closing her eyes. Her long lashes glittered wetly against her pale cheeks. 'We were fools to think there would be a second chance for us. There never was one . . . Pretend it never happened.'

He could never do that, and she must know it. There was nothing that could soothe this pain, no logic that could argue it away. The brutal finality of this second loss made it a thousand times worse than the first, and the first had already been unbearable. There was no way that Klaus could walk away from this night without being scarred by it forever, but there was also no other choice.

He had loved her enough to move mountains to bring her back, but he loved her too much to ask her to stay. Not like this, not caught halfway between her true self and some unspeakable monster. 'I would give anything not to do this,' he said, memorising every inch of her face over and over and over again.

'You wouldn't want anyone else to do it.' She smiled

through her tears. 'Neither would I. Say goodbye, Niklaus, and send me back to the Other Side so that I can dream about you again.'

She closed her eyes, and he kissed each lid tenderly. 'Goodbye, Vivianne,' he murmured. 'I'll never love another the way I love you.' Then he punched through her chest, feeling the scrape of her broken ribcage against his knuckles, and pulled her heart back out through the hole he had made. Vivianne Lescheres Mikaelson died with tears in her eyes and a smile on her ruby lips, falling into Klaus's waiting arms with a final sigh.

He held her and stared at the heart in his hand, feeling as if it were his own. Something was shifting within him, rearranging itself around the new, empty space in his chest before Vivianne's body even had the chance to grow cold.

He had told her the absolute truth at the end. It would never be possible for Klaus to love this way again. The suffering he felt now left no room for it, and that was a lesson Klaus would never forget. Losing Vivianne forced him to face eternity alone, because an eternity full of this kind of loss would be unbearable. The love of Klaus Mikaelson's life was gone, and there was nothing ahead of him now except for more life.

THIRTY-TWO

*I*t was all Rebekah could do to keep the violence away from Marguerite. There was no room to breathe or think, no opportunity to move the girl to a safer place. Elijah's armies had spent the night making new *morts-vivants*, and now they were everywhere. A werewolf's yellow eyes were extinguished right in front of her, and the monster who killed it bared his bloody teeth at Rebekah in turn – a pasty-skinned, short-haired man who stared hungrily at Marguerite as if he knew that her un-beating heart was still, somehow, miraculously alive.

His dead eyes flickered between the two women. He feinted left and then right, but Rebekah had been in more than a few fights in her time, and she wasn't willing to be drawn out. The *mort-vivant* lunged a little too far, shifting his weight just enough that he couldn't recover in time, and Rebekah struck. She rained down bone-crushing blows on his arms and head until he was forced to drop his guard, leaving his ribcage unprotected. She killed him quickly, because she could feel eyes on her back and knew that she had no time to spare.

A *mort-vivant*, a woman in her forties with a knot of white-blonde hair piled high on her head, had sneaked around Rebekah's guard and was poised over Marguerite's prone body. Rebekah caught her by her dingy white collar and threw her back as hard as she could, but the witch knocked her off her feet, and the two of them rolled, snarling and struggling for the upper hand.

Then the witch was lifted off her, and Rebekah caught a glimpse of red–gold hair and freckles as she sprang back onto her feet. The *mort-vivant* screamed incoherently and snapped Lisette's right arm, then plunged her hand into the young vampire's chest. Rebekah lurched forward to separate them just in time, then punched her own fist through the undead witch's spine and pulled her heart out through her back.

'Thanks,' Lisette gasped, her face even paler than usual in the moonlight. She cradled her hurt arm against her wounded chest, but Rebekah could see that both gashes were already beginning to heal. Soon Marguerite would be that unbreakable, but first Rebekah had to keep her corpse from being mauled by the vile cannibals the girl's own mother had raised.

'Have you seen Elijah?' Rebekah asked. 'Does he have a plan, or are we just fighting to the last one standing?'

'He was near the fountain last I saw,' Lisette said, rubbing at her healing arm with the opposite hand. 'A bunch of us were regrouping near the house, but he seemed worried you weren't there yet, so I came looking.'

'I'm fine out here,' Rebekah said, casting another look at Marguerite. Even with Lisette's help, she wasn't willing to risk carrying the body through a raging war. Rebekah would just have to hold her own until Klaus ended Lily's curse . . . one way or another.

'Look out!' Lisette shouted. Rebekah ducked instinctively. A *mort-vivant* broke through a cluster of werewolves, holding one of their severed hind legs like a trophy.

Then a shudder ran through the creature, and Rebekah could feel an echo pass through the battlefield. The *morts-vivants* – all of them – twitched and then crumpled to the ground, like clockwork that had finally wound down.

A strange hush fell over the field, and then Rebekah heard a handful of whistles and cheers. Their army was battered and exhausted, eager to claim this sudden stop as a victory. One moment they had been fighting for their lives, and in the next the horde of attackers had simply given up.

'Niklaus,' Rebekah whispered, wondering how he had done it. Had she and Marguerite been wrong after all? Could Vivianne's spell actually have worked? The alternative was almost impossible to imagine. If it hadn't been the spell . . . if Klaus had . . . Rebekah stared towards the mansion, wondering what might be happening within its walls.

Then there was another ripple, another indefinable disturbance that passed through the undead as quickly and silently as the first. Somewhere nearby she heard a scream, and then another.

Bodies wiggled across the field, torsos finding new arms, different heads – like rag dolls that had been ripped apart and then sewn back together with whatever pieces were available. Random hearts rolled back into random bodies, a nightmare of musical chairs. A witch rose before her, but as he staggered to his feet all Rebekah could do was stare. He stood on one of his own legs; a werewolf's haunch had replaced the other. The *mort-vivant* lurched unsteadily forward on one human foot and one ungainly paw.

'You don't see *that* every day,' Lisette remarked as the creature ambled towards them. 'Not even if you're us.'

'Go,' Rebekah snapped. 'Get back to Elijah – he'll

need everyone.' The *mort-vivant* reached her and swung viciously at her head, and Rebekah blocked the blow and then tore his arm off for good measure. She threw it as far away as she could, but out of the corner of her eye she saw it crawl towards an armless *mort-vivant*.

Before her monster could regroup enough to attack again, someone struck him from behind, punching through his back as if it were made of paper. As he fell away, Rebekah paused, intending to thank whoever had intervened, but she didn't recognise the owner of the hand that held the creature's bloody heart. Then, to her amazement, the man who had killed the *mort-vivant* raised the heart to his own mouth, tearing into it with red-stained teeth.

'He was one of yours!' she exclaimed, but she realised it didn't matter. Clearly, something had gone wrong with the magic that was holding the *morts-vivants* together and giving them purpose.

She had thought the battle was chaotic before, but now it was absolute madness. The *morts-vivants* that she and her allies had spent the whole night ripping apart were reassembling themselves at random, with the wrong heads on the wrong bodies and limbs attached backward. They were killing indiscriminately, and blood flowed and spurted everywhere she looked.

An undead witch lunged towards one of the few

remaining living ones, who cast a ball of unnatural fire at it. The *mort-vivant*, blazing like a torch, didn't even hesitate before tearing the witch apart and devouring her heart.

While Rebekah watched in increasing disbelief, the thing began to melt before her eyes. Still burning, incredibly, still eating, the *mort-vivant* began to bubble and collapse in on himself, his flesh sloughing off his bones into an unsightly mass on the ground.

Shouts went up across the battlefield, and she realised it was happening to all of them. Every single *mort-vivant* was disintegrating. Rebekah could still make out the outlines of faces, mouths frozen open in silent screams. Some reached their hands up, the skin flaking away, and she couldn't decide whether they were pleading for help or making one last, desperate grab for some unseen enemy's heart.

Rebekah waited with the rest of her army. Not one vampire or werewolf dared to believe this sudden victory, so hard on the heels of the false one. But the disgusting remains of the *morts-vivants* stayed as they were, and eventually, she knew, they were going to have to believe their eyes.

Rebekah could feel bile rising in her throat, and she skirted the battlefield, avoiding the outliers as best she could. In the centre, where the fighting had been the thickest, the sticky, deformed puddles oozed together, mingling the unnatural remains into a giant mass of indistinguishable vileness.

Rebekah slipped among the returning vampires to join Elijah. 'It's over,' he said when he saw her, as if that weren't the most obvious thing in the world that morning.

'Niklaus ended it,' she said, knowing in her bones that it was true. She had never admired Niklaus more than she did in that moment, knowing what he must have done and what it had cost him.

Elijah's square jaw clenched, betraying some emotion too deep for him to even put into words. 'We were losing,' he said finally. He glanced around at the remnants of his army, a few handfuls of vampires limping towards the mansion. The werewolves had already disappeared back into their woods, although Rebekah was sure they would be back to claim their reward before long. 'Niklaus will need us now.'

The eastern hills were already on fire with the promise of sunrise, and the wreckage of the battle at their feet had an almost beautiful glow. It was like a masterful oil painting of some long-ago disaster, misery turned into art. Rebekah took the arm Elijah offered her, and together the two of them strolled across the lawns towards their home and their brother.

In Rebekah's long experience, time changed

everything except people. She and her brothers had spent over a thousand years together, and they had been buffeted this way and that during their endless lives. But over time she had come to see that there was a core self in each of them that dated all the way back to their human days, and that couldn't really be touched by any of what had come later. They were who they were underneath, no matter what scars marred the surface.

Klaus might never quite be the man he'd been now that he had lost Vivianne for good. But he wouldn't be a stranger, either. He was her brother, as he always had been and always would be, and she could respect his grief enough not to fear it or try to ward it away. It would pass, just as everything else eventually did, and they would still be a family.

Once again it was time to rebuild.

THIRTY-THREE

*E*lijah rolled over, relaxing back onto his pillowcase. Lisette twisted to adapt, settling her head into the hollow of his shoulder as if the two parts had been made for each other.

'The sun is still up,' she murmured. 'We've got hours yet.'

'We have another hour at the most,' he disagreed, but he felt a smile tugging at the corners of his mouth nonetheless.

'An hour is *ages*,' she reminded him, running a nimble fingertip along his bare chest. He was nearly distracted by her offer, but as night fell it was becoming more and more difficult to block out all of the fresh irritations it would bring with it.

'The council will meet tonight, for the first time since I offered the werewolves a place on it,' he reminded her, as if anyone could have set foot in the Mikaelsons' mansion during the last two weeks without knowing that. In deference to William Collado's special circumstances, the city's shadow council had revived the old tradition of meeting at the new moon. It would keep the belligerence to a minimum, and considering Elijah's frame of mind about the entire affair, not much else would.

Lisette resumed the idle tracing of her fingernail. 'They should be grateful,' she said. 'They did little enough to earn that seat, and I would hope they will remember it.'

'Memory is a funny thing.' Elijah had seen it time and time again – grudges nursed for generations, and favours forgotten by the next day.

William would surely argue that this hadn't even *been* a favour. His wolves had, after all, fought as promised, and not a single vampire had been touched by the poison from their fangs. The fact that the werewolves hadn't turned the tide of the battle as expected, and had had nothing at all to do with their eventual victory, didn't change things in their eyes. William had kept his end of the bargain, and it wasn't his fault that Elijah regretted having to keep his own.

'You had to give them what you promised,' Lisette pointed out, 'and you have. Now that that's done, we can begin the business of taking it back.'

'We've done it before.' Elijah smiled, admitting to himself that she had a point. It had been enjoyable enough to ride high on his success in New Orleans since the hurricane, to think of himself as its shadow king. There was an energy in rebuilding a kingdom. 'I suppose I could be persuaded to do it again.'

Lisette laughed and snuggled closer, all length and surprising softness. 'I doubt you could be persuaded otherwise,' she chided. 'Even for an hour.'

There was already less time than that. They needed to dress and rejoin the rest of the world. But not immediately, and so he twisted his head to kiss her. She met the gesture with a tiny hum of approval, kissing him back enthusiastically.

Elijah rolled, pulling her beneath him in the centre of the bed so that he could take full advantage of the last few minutes of their time together. Lisette laughed and curled herself against him and drew his mouth down against her own. He lost himself in her, in the movement of her body and the mischievous glint of her grey eyes.

In the end, he just held her, sated and a little bit late. He would have liked to stay that way forever, but eventually Elijah couldn't justify letting his siblings wait.

He slid regretfully from the bed. Lisette stretched out along his sheets, well aware of how tempting her naked body was, and smirked when he hesitated one last time.

'Go,' she told him, snapping the bedspread playfully towards his legs. 'New Orleans isn't going to govern itself, no matter how many wolves find their way in.'

He did as she suggested, pulling on a cloak over his hastily donned clothes as he strode down the curved main staircase. Rebekah and Klaus waited for him at the bottom, looking ready to leave and more than a little impatient. 'Finally,' he heard Rebekah mutter, but no amount of glowering could dampen his spirits.

'The carriage is here,' Klaus observed, leading the way out of the front door. The coachmen jumped to the ground and hastily held the door of the carriage open for them. 'He's been here half an hour, although he's never minded waiting on our Rebekah.'

She made a face at Klaus as she climbed into the carriage, and Elijah sighed as he followed them onto the velvet-cushioned seat. No matter how many times their world was turned upside down, some things just couldn't change.

Klaus and Rebekah had been almost excruciatingly polite to each other in the aftermath of Vivianne's death and the end of the *morts-vivants*, but of course they hadn't been able to keep that up for long. Two weeks later they were back to their old selves, bickering and badgering and storming along the mansion's corridors shouting at each other like unruly children. Their brief détente had been enjoyable in its way, but Elijah found he was more comfortable with their old, familiar relationship. Family was what made a home, and without question his siblings were his.

'The old Werewolf Quarter is bustling again,' Rebekah mused as the carriage rattled down the drive. 'They haven't lost any time profiting from your little arrangement.'

'Why should they?' Klaus asked, apparently willing to shift the focus of his scorn away from his sister as long as Elijah was available to present a better target. 'It's not as if they stand to benefit from giving us time to reconsider.'

'What's done is done,' Elijah snapped. 'They held up their end, and so will we.'

'Nearly half our lands gone for nothing?' Rebekah scoffed. 'Their end of that bargain was a good deal easier than ours.'

'Niklaus was prepared to give away twice as much for love,' Elijah pointed out, irritated. 'And as I recall, dear sister, your main contribution to stopping him consisted of childish pranks.'

Rebekah looked struck, but Klaus didn't so much as blink. The blow had been too low, Elijah knew at once.

He couldn't imagine what Klaus felt now, having risked everything only to lose the love of his life a second time. He hesitated, torn between the impulse to apologise and the desire to simply ignore the barb the way his brother obviously had.

Maybe Klaus *couldn't* rise to Elijah's unfortunate bait – he'd had the same emotional non-response to everything relating to Vivianne. The wound seemed too deep for him to even feel it. He was a man so thoroughly changed by the loss of his true love that he seemed somehow not to have been affected at all.

It was troubling, and it put Elijah in the awkward position of constantly second-guessing himself around Klaus. Kindness was too forced; harshness was too brutal. Klaus might have resumed his old, familiar repartee with Rebekah, but Elijah still couldn't quite bring himself to join in the game. If Klaus would only grieve, Elijah would help however he could, but as it was he just couldn't fathom what his brother needed from him now.

'I'm sorry, Niklaus,' Elijah sighed at last. 'That was unfair of me.'

Rebekah looked smug, but Klaus smiled almost blandly. 'It's nothing,' he insisted, as he had been for two weeks now. As if losing Vivianne hadn't affected him in the slightest; as if they should all just go back to normal and find Klaus already there. 'I've actually been thinking about the opportunities this little snag presents for us,' Klaus went on, pulling back one of the curtains to gaze out into the streets of New Orleans.

'Opportunities?' Elijah repeated, uncertain he had heard the word correctly. Klaus had spent the forty-four years since Vivianne's first death painting aspects of her in his solitary attic. Had he begun scheming already? Barely a fortnight after her second death? The carriage struck an uneven patch of paving stones, jostling them all before continuing to run on smoothly in the night.

'We've seen how it goes when we hold the sole power in this city,' Klaus began, obviously eager to engage his siblings on the topic that had been consuming him, even to the exclusion of the grief he should have been enduring. 'Exiled, the werewolves grew strong and the witches went rogue.'

'Vermin are a constant concern in *any* city,' Rebekah agreed. 'Even if we managed to stomp them all out, more would trickle in from the countryside to take their place.'

'Exactly.' Klaus pounded his fist on the knee of his breeches as if Rebekah had made his own point for him. 'Control that excludes the werewolves is obviously no real control at all. But now they're back.'

'In some strength, though,' Elijah frowned. 'They aren't returning as our subjects. They hold land and a seat on the council. There are nearly as many of them as of us after the battle against Lily's witches, and they're hardly supplicants any longer.'

'No, not supplicants . . . tonight.' Klaus smirked. 'But life is long, dear brother. Now that the wolves are back, where we can watch over them and subvert them, we have all the time in the world to bring them to heel. Right here in the heart of the city, where they can never grow back into a threat without us noticing it.'

It was a clever observation, and Elijah had to admit that the idea had merit. Exiling the other clans had only hurt the vampires in the long run, and if there was anyone who should know to take the long view it was the Mikaelsons.

Elijah had made his mind up that he would keep his word, and he intended to do so. But as Lisette had pointed out earlier, the letter of his promise to William would be fulfilled that very night. After that, it was every family for itself. 'Keep talking,' Elijah urged, leaning back against the velvet-covered cushions behind him.

Klaus smiled, looking half like a wolf himself in the lantern light. 'This is our city,' he reminded Elijah and Rebekah both. 'It was from the beginning, and it will be in the end. The only question is how we govern it, what it takes to hold power against all pretenders. We will still be standing long after all of them have crumbled to dust, so I propose that we make sure we're standing on top.'

Even Rebekah looked intrigued in spite of herself, and Elijah found a smile that matched his brother's creeping onto his own lips. 'The werewolves have intelligent leadership,' he warned. 'They won't bow down easily.'

'I don't think "easy" is on Niklaus's list of requirements,' Rebekah said, but her deep-blue eyes were alight with her brother's words.

'A challenge would be welcome,' Klaus agreed, leaning his elbows on his knees and templing his fingers together. 'But I don't anticipate much of one. A few stray puppies should be easy enough to housebreak.'

The carriage rattled on, carrying them swiftly towards the next twist in their path. One war was over, and the next was stretched out before them like the waiting night.

The untold story of The Originals
has only just begun.

Read on for a sneak peek of
THE ORIGINALS: THE RESURRECTION

Coming soon from creator Julie Plec,
Alloy Entertainment and Hodder Children's Books . . .

PROLOGUE
1788

*T*he city was burning. From the east end to the church, New Orleans was lit up with flames, and Klaus Mikaelson was to blame. Sampson Collado, trapped in his wolf form, lifted his head and howled in fury at the full moon. Smoke rose from the city before him, billowing into dark, sooty clouds. The moon had been the most powerful force in Sampson's life for twenty-one years, and it glowed an ominous red as it hovered above the flames.

Sampson had been born into an unprecedented period of peace, but that was over now. The Mikaelsons just couldn't leave well enough alone. Any truce that involved the three Original vampires wasn't worth the paper it was written on, not in the long run. Sooner or later, one of them would get angry, jealous or just bored.

Nine times out of ten that 'one' would be Niklaus, the most volatile of the three siblings. Klaus Mikaelson had raised an army of vampires, violated the fragile peace between the clans and finally had set the city ablaze.

Thanks to the full moon, Sampson's Pack had all left their homes without so much as the clothes on their backs, and now those homes were burning. The fire had started near the bend of the river, sweeping north and west until the entire city was ablaze. By morning, there would be nothing for them to return to, and the wolves would be penniless exiles once again.

The smell of smoke burned in his snout. Even from the far side of the river, Sampson could feel the heat of the fire biting at his fur. The wind whipped along the water and launched a thousand embers from one wooden roof to the next.

Sampson growled low in his throat, wishing he could to do something – anything – to combat the spread of the flames. The Werewolf Quarter was the only home he had ever known. To watch it get razed to the ground was almost unthinkable, but in his wolf form there was nothing else he could do.

Still, Sampson couldn't bring himself to turn his back on New Orleans. As he stared into the flames he knew he was witnessing more than the death of a city – it was a resurrection. New Orleans would rise again from the ashes, just as she always did.

ONE

A few weeks earlier . . .

'**D**rink!'

Dozens of voices picked up the command, turning it into a chant. 'Drink,' they all shouted at the thief. Everyone else had already taken their turn, pledging their allegiance to Klaus's army by drinking his blood. Klaus let them think the gesture was symbolic; little did they know they'd all be vampires by the end of the night.

The energy in the room was at a steady thrum, and it felt as if the very blood in his veins vibrated with the cries of men. Klaus had outgrown the family mansion, shedding it in favour of a roomy four-storey garrison in the centre of town. It was a more fitting place for his new calling – a place of war.

There had to be a hundred of his new recruits carousing

in the large dining hall, banging their tankards on the long wooden tables and shouting encouragement. Klaus sat alone on a dais, where he had received each of them in turn. One was a whore from the Southern Spot, the oldest brothel in New Orleans, and by Klaus's estimation, still the best. She'd run afoul of the madam and been thrown out, showing some real fire and a surprisingly creative vocabulary. Another group of bandits had been rounded up by Spanish patrol in the countryside, and Klaus had found a fresh crop of young runaways near the harbour.

The last recruit to drink was a thief named José. He'd been caught with one hand in the safe of the Southern Spot. The manager – a hothead Klaus suspected might be doing some skimming of his own – had wanted to just kill the man and dump his body in the river. But Klaus had an eye for potential; he could spot those who were loyal. All Klaus needed to give him was a new life, a new family and a new mission. That might have seemed an impossibly high price to most people, but not for an Original vampire.

Drinking blood – human blood, they believed – was a gruesome way to pledge, but the high entry price was a sure way to have volunteers clamouring to join up. Everyone in the hall understood that being a part of Klaus's army would require dangerous things of them, and that was part of the appeal. Once this last lowlife thief drank his share, all they would ask of Klaus was to lead.

That was what Klaus was good at, what he was destined for. Everything else was just a distraction, and Klaus was done with those. His past self would have traded the entire city for a life with Vivianne Lescheres Mikaelson, but he understood now that it was never meant to be. If he couldn't have her, he would rule New Orleans, and the werewolves could consider themselves lucky if he stopped there.

As if their role in Vivianne's two deaths wasn't enough of an insult, New Orleans's wolves had grown bold in recent weeks. There had been daytime raids on Klaus's businesses, an ever-mounting pattern of attacks on his warehouses and ships. Now Guillaume, one of the humans whose eyes and ears Klaus relied on, informed him that the werewolves were poised to strike at the vampires themselves.

Elijah had generously given the Collado Pack a foothold in the city even after they had failed to save Vivianne. And yet, instead of showing gratitude, the werewolves had spent the last twenty-two years grasping for more. There was no reasoning with them, no dealing with them. The only solution was to wipe them out, as Klaus had wanted to do from the night he first arrived on these shores.

He stared down at the thief who knelt before him, ready to use compulsion if he tried to bolt. José had sharp, ratlike features, with a long pointed nose and rheumy blue eyes. He didn't look like much, but he didn't need to be. Klaus had more than enough power to go round.

'Drink!' his soldiers shouted, and Klaus could see the thief's pulse beat in his throat.

He lifted his glass and drained it in one swallow, the blood leaving an unsightly stain on his narrow lips. He gagged a little as he tried to control his disgust at the taste of the thick, warm blood. Klaus could dimly remember once feeling the same way, but centuries upon centuries as a vampire had cured him of that distaste.

Becoming a vampire was a cure for any number of life's ills.

The thief looked around uncertainly, cowed by the thundering roar of approval that seemed to shake the house from its foundations. The army was in a merry mood that night, and it was only going to get better. Klaus studied the trembling man before him for a long moment. With a welcoming smile, he stepped forward and snapped the man's neck, feeling the vertebrae pop under his fingers.

The hall went silent, a hundred faces staring, mouths gaping open in shock. The dead man collapsed to the floor in an awkward heap, but Klaus didn't bother to watch him fall. Instead, he leaped forward, moving faster than human eyes could follow, reaching for the neck of the nearest human, and then the next.

There was barely time for the last man to scream, a thin, strangled sound that choked off when Klaus's hand closed around his windpipe. He killed the last man slowly, watching him struggle for air as surrounding bodies thumped to the ground.

The whole ordeal was over in seconds. He walked among his men and women, down along the narrow aisle that ran between the tables. They had all been criminals and deserters, lost until he had come along. Now they were an army of the dead.

Klaus was the only one who seemed to realise that true safety lay in power. A better network, a bigger army, more resources, more weapons – there was no position too strong, in Klaus's opinion. The fact that Mikael hadn't come for them yet didn't mean he had ended his hunt. His children – and Klaus, his hated stepson – needed to be in the strongest position possible when he did.

Elijah had had his turn at trying to run the city. The vampires had only subsisted for the last twenty-two years, and as long as they were forced to share and negotiate, true power would never be theirs. Without love, power was the only prize left worth fighting for . . . and, as it happened, Elijah himself was distracted by love at that very moment. If he couldn't fully dedicate himself to controlling their city, then Klaus would do it. And he would do it in his own way, as he should have from the start. The werewolves were coming, and Klaus was determined to strike first and in force.

The last of the brisk winter air swept through the open courtyard and struck him in the face. The night was already promising; he could feel it. Klaus's blood was working, breaking and changing and re-forming the men and women, dragging them back towards an entirely new kind of life. By the following night, he would have a hundred new vampires in his army, all of them fanatically loyal to him and him alone.

TWO

Rebekah inhaled the smell of damp earth as her horse cantered through the countryside. It felt good to be out of the city, free of the confining walls of the mansion and away from the oppressive eyes of her brothers. She had once promised them that they would remain together for eternity, but back then she had had no idea just how long eternity could really be.

'What a shame to let the horses have all the fun,' Luc called to her. 'We could just run ourselves.'

Rebekah couldn't match his lightness of spirit, not with the sight that had driven her from New Orleans still so fresh in her mind. She longed to, though. It was the ease of Luc's joy that had inspired her to invite him along, in the hope that some of it might pierce the gloom that had shrouded her ever since she had found Marguerite Leroux's dead body in her bed.

'We're in no hurry,' she countered, and Luc's blue eyes twinkled wickedly. In spite of everything that weighed on her, Rebekah couldn't even seem to look at him without either laughing or lusting . . . often both at once. She had definitely made the right choice of travelling companion. 'The horses may be a bit slower than we are, but they serve their purpose.' There was no need to risk unnecessary attention, after all, not even in the dark of night. Elijah had intended to keep Klaus out of trouble by placing him in charge of New Orleans's booming shipping business, but all that had done was give Klaus eyes and ears everywhere.

Luc urged his horse on as they crested a low hill, and she kicked her own forward to keep pace. An emerald valley spread out below them, carpeted with lush grasses. A little village huddled near its far end, near a stream.

'We should stop here for daybreak,' Rebekah suggested, feeling the stress of New Orleans, her family and even poor Marguerite begin to fade just a little bit. 'I'm sure there's an inn.'

'I think I see one,' Luc agreed, swinging down from his saddle. She did the same, falling in beside him as if they had walked together for decades. 'Should I be expecting your brothers to drop in on us at any point, or will we be alone?'

Luc Benoit had been born in the New World, and, to Rebekah's eyes, it showed. He had all the restless curiosity of an explorer, and the casual confidence of a boy who had been raised to believe he could tackle any challenge that came his way. Wolves, bears and whip-fast alligators had prowled the bayou around him, so he had never bothered with learning to fear the unknown.

That swaggering recklessness had eventually been his undoing, although Rebekah could tell it had taught him nothing whatsoever. Luc had fallen in with a gang of privateers, bullying the British along the northern coasts, and when that work was done he had simply kept on tormenting others for profit. He had become exactly the kind of shiftless troublemaker that Klaus was rounding up now to form his ludicrous 'army', and in fact Klaus had already recruited him when Rebekah had first met him.

She'd had no choice but to make Luc a vampire herself, saving him from a fate tied to Klaus's endless, futile attempts at self-destruction. Her troubled brother had only ever managed to destroy everyone around him, emerging unscathed again and again, and Luc was far too handsome to end up dead. She deserved a good distraction. Then Klaus had killed Marguerite, and everything had changed.

'I have lived and travelled with my brothers for centuries,' she told Luc. 'But this is a trip I intend for us to make alone.' She couldn't promise that Klaus or Elijah wouldn't pursue them, as neither would be pleased with Rebekah's decision. But she and her loyal new lover had a good head start, and Rebekah knew how to disappear when she needed to.

She was done answering to her family. That had all been over the moment she had laid eyes on the bloody stake broken off in the centre of Marguerite Leroux's thin chest. The awkward, lanky girl should have finished growing into a woman years ago, and she would have if Klaus hadn't accidentally killed her during the madness that had followed his foolhardy resurrection of Vivianne. Rebekah had saved her, freezing her as a teenager forever . . . or at least until Klaus got it into his head to make good on some of his wild threats.

Klaus had always enjoyed using the vampires closest to his siblings as a means to try to control them. It hadn't taken him long to see that Rebekah felt a genuine bond with Marguerite, and he seemed to take particular pleasure in reminding Rebekah that he could destroy that bond permanently in a single, violent moment. She hadn't ever really believed he would do it, though – not until she had seen the proof with her own eyes.

It was too cruel, too unfeeling even for Klaus. But

apparently Klaus had no shred of decency or family feeling left in him, and so as Rebekah held Marguerite's cold body against her own, she vowed that she would put an end to Klaus's misery once and for all.

'Your brothers would not approve of this journey,' Luc guessed, watching her intently. His full lips pressed together thoughtfully in a way that made her want to bite one. 'You can't trust me to keep our destination a secret.'

He started to speak again, but Rebekah caught him by the shoulders to kiss him – and quiet him. Too many questions were never a good thing. He glared at her with mock ferocity before kissing her back.

'My family was whole once,' she began, linking her arm through his and resuming their stroll towards the first houses of the little village. The sun wouldn't rise for at least another hour. 'But a plague took my oldest sister, and after she died my father wanted to take my mother and my older siblings to a place where they would be safe. I was born in the New World, not far from here.'

Luc glanced sidelong at her. 'There are plenty of other dangers here,' he pointed out.

'Exactly.' One of the horses whickered softly behind them, and Rebekah felt the sudden burst of its warm, wet breath against the small of her back. 'We discovered werewolves in what is now Virginia, and I lost another brother. My parents realised then that nowhere was truly safe. They could run forever, but they would keep losing children everywhere they went.'

'And yet here you are today,' Luc reminded her. 'Whole and living and, if I may say so, in *extremely* good health.'

Rebekah smiled ruefully, unable to deny it. In his usual, direct way, Luc had struck on the same bottom line that once motivated her mother to change her children into vampires in the first place. Esther had believed – at the time, at least – that strength and life were all that mattered, even if they cost her family everything else.

'My mother was a witch,' Rebekah explained. 'She was an exceptionally powerful one, and she cast an immortality curse on us.'

'I've heard you call it a curse before,' Luc interrupted. 'But I don't understand.'

'It's a *curse*.' Her voice was flat and forceful, like a slap to the face. She saw Marguerite's glassy brown eyes, her auburn hair spread out like a fan across Rebekah's pillows. Leaving her there had been an extra little twist of the dagger from Klaus, a reminder that nothing was safe from his reach. 'I was there when the spell was cast. My mother made us as strong as she knew how to do, but the price of that strength was terrible. The hunger – you've felt that, and you know how it tears at us. She imagined us running through the hills, free again from fear, but every touch of the sun scorched our skin. We were confined to the night, and our neighbors grew distrustful of our new, strange habits. Soon they wanted nothing to do with us, and we quickly learned it was within their power to bar us from their homes. We couldn't enter without their invitation, and none were willing to offer it any more.'

'People fear what they don't know.' Luc shrugged, as if the total isolation the Mikaelsons had been faced with were just some trivial faux pas. 'But the benefits, surely, outweighed those minor concerns.'

'Our mother thought so at first,' Rebekah admitted. 'She thought that our safety was worth anything, until she saw what life she had condemned us to with her own two eyes. She regretted her choice, and my father went even further than that. He vowed to use his own immortality to destroy ours, to kill the children he had once demanded that his wife save.'

'But you cannot be killed.' Luc frowned. The serious expression suited his handsome face: all squared angles and broad planes.

The Originals certainly didn't go broadcasting their mortal flaw, but every strength came with a weakness. Their mother had called upon the power of the white oak tree to grant her children immortality, and the wood of that same tree could take it away again. Rebekah had heard rumours that it still stood in Mystic Falls.

'My family is complicated,' she compromised.

'Then it's just as well to have some time away from them,' he said mischievously. Luc was a straightforward man with simple tastes – the intrigue of the Originals must seem impossibly foreign to him. That was yet another thing that made him the perfect partner for a voyage like this one, and Rebekah felt the unhappy fog she had been carrying with her begin to dissipate and drift away.

Between thoughts of her past and thoughts of Luc, she was so distracted that she was startled to realise that they had reached the inn. A bleary-eyed woman peered out of the door, suspicious of the couple arriving on her doorstep before the sky was even light.

'Our horses need tending,' Rebekah announced, continuing to advance so that the woman had no real choice but to move aside and let her pass. Luc waited outside until a groom arrived to lead the horses away, and to her surprise Rebekah noticed that he followed the man at a bit of a distance, trailing after him as he led the beasts towards the stable. 'We'll need a room just for the day,' she went on, curious what Luc was up to.

The innkeeper fished around for a key, still eyeing Rebekah doubtfully. 'These parts aren't always safe at night,' she ventured. 'It's lucky you and that handsome fellow made it here unharmed, but wouldn't you rather stay over until the next morning to travel on by day? There's a lovely room with a view over the valley, much nicer for a young couple like yourselves than those treacherous roads after dark.'

'Consider it, darling.' Luc appeared again at her elbow, looking unnaturally flushed. Rebekah thought she could spot a tiny fleck of blood in the corner of his mouth. 'I would hate to risk our safety, no matter how much of a hurry you're in.'

She glanced up at him, trying to read his bland, polite smile. His blond hair was tied back away from his face with a strip of leather, and she was struck by a sudden impulse to let it down and run her fingers through it. 'Let us see the room,' she agreed. 'It might be nice to rest awhile.'

Seemingly reassured, the innkeeper turned towards the wooden staircase. Luc fell on her as soon as her back was turned, wrapping a hand around her mouth and sinking his teeth into her neck. His skin still looked tanned against the woman's sallow flesh, even though it had been weeks since he had seen the sun.

He punctured the innkeeper's jugular vein and then passed her to Rebekah, his blue eyes glittering eagerly. She needed no more urging than that: she drank deeply, savoring the feel of the woman's heart fluttering and then finally stopping. Her kind had been made to hunt humans, not for all of this backstabbing and infighting. This was what the Mikaelsons should have been doing all along, rather than scheming and manoeuvring and betraying one another. Klaus had lost touch with his own nature, and for a while he had managed to drag Rebekah into the darkness with him.

'I thought you could use a bit of a diversion,' Luc suggested when the innkeeper fell to the floor. 'Perhaps an inn full of them will take your mind off whatever troubles have driven you from New Orleans.'

Just then there was a noise on the staircase: a patron with the bad judgement to be an early riser. Rebekah smiled and positioned herself out of sight at the foot of the stairs, lying in wait as the man descended. She could have simply rushed at him, but Luc was right: after the night she had had, a little fun was in order. Playing with their food would be much more enjoyable, and Rebekah found herself growing excited at the thought of picking them off one by one.

By noon the body count included all of the guests of the inn, as well as the keeper's husband, a milkman and an exceptionally pretty young chambermaid. Rebekah felt nearly drunk on all of the blood she had consumed, and its heat radiated out from her skin.

She slipped out of her dusty travelling gown and then

the shift she wore beneath it, letting her golden hair down for good measure. She could feel every tiny stirring in the currents of the air she could hear earthworms pushing through the dirt two floors beneath her bare feet. She felt almost human again . . . only better.

The bedroom where they had ended their merry hunt was by far the best of the lot, although the windows were carefully shuttered against the view. But even in the semi-darkness, Rebekah could feel the heat of the sun overhead as if its light were streaming out through her own skin. She raised her arms and Luc stepped into them, his lips crushing down on hers with even more passion than usual.

Rebekah helped him out of his clothes, not caring that his tunic landed on an ice-cold, bloodless corpse. They barely made it to the four-poster bed before they began to make love, their bodies moving together to the beat of their racing pulses. Luc invented a hundred new ways to worship her, reminding her over and over again of the urgency of his desire for her.

She had chosen well indeed. He was exactly the man to fill all of the idle hours between here and Mystic Falls.

THREE

*E*lijah was not usually a man to hide in darkness. No alleyway held any real threat to him – by his very nature he struck fear into others. He never needed to think about commonplace dangers, especially not in the city that he had called his own for so long. New Orleans had been his home for the better part of a century, and yet tonight he found himself hiding in its shadows, like any ordinary criminal.

Elijah had suspected for some time that Klaus was up to no good. The unconvincing reasons his brother had offered for moving out of the family mansion were proof on their own that he was hatching some troublesome plot. And then the vampires had appeared in the streets. Overnight there were more of them than the three

Originals combined had made in the last twenty years, and there was only one plausible explanation: Klaus was raising an army and getting ready to make his play.

A man who had almost certainly been a dock worker the night before accosted a prostitute in the alley across from Elijah's place of concealment. It would likely be her last night in her current job as well. By the next she would either be dead or a vampire herself.

Elijah waited until the pair was engaged to the point of distraction, then moved on. Vampires were unnaturally observant, with the heightened instincts of true predators. It wasn't easy to pass near one unnoticed. But while Elijah had little enough experience with thinking like prey, he *had* recently learned a great deal about avoiding detection by other vampires.

He had been forced to practise that skill earlier that very night, slipping out of the mansion without being seen by Lisette. She seemed to be everywhere, waiting around every corner and behind every door like a lovely, flame-haired reproach. She had every right to her anger, but Elijah wasn't prepared to bear the brunt of it every time he stepped out of his bedroom or study, and so he had taken to avoiding her.

Elijah had adored Lisette, and his time with her had restored more of his faith in the world than he had even realised he'd lost. But the Mikaelsons had enemies everywhere, including some exceptionally dangerous ones within their own family. Ultimately, their romance had simply been too public.

No matter how brash or capable she was, Lisette could never be more than a second-generation vampire. She was a hair slower and a shade weaker than Klaus and Rebekah, and worst of all she could be killed by a simple wooden stake through the heart.

She made Elijah vulnerable. Any danger to Lisette was a threat to him, and her own bravery, which bordered on recklessness, didn't help matters. She refused to be careful, and she accused him of wanting to keep her locked up and away from the world.

She wasn't wrong, but Elijah felt like his hands were tied. And when Klaus had threatened to decapitate her – for the hundredth time – over some minor dispute about using a werewolf-owned vendor at his precious whorehouse, Elijah had finally understood that he had no choice.

He knew Lisette would never forgive him for his weakness in ending their relationship, no matter how pure his intentions had been. It was easier to avoid her than to face the constant, silent accusation on her face, the reminder that he had given her up in order not to lose her.

Elijah had spotted her just outside the front door of

the mansion that very night. At least she only put herself in his way – she had far too much pride to follow him. Elijah wondered what she would do if she happened to stumble across one of his meetings with Alejandra. Would knowledge of her free Lisette from her need to haunt him? Or would she decide to burn down his house – perhaps with him still inside it?

A pair of vampires burst out of a tavern in front of him. Momentarily caught almost out in the open, Elijah darted sideways into the slim cover of a doorway. That wouldn't have been enough to keep a more experienced hunter's eyes off him, but these two were newly made, and drunk on both blood and ale. Elijah held every muscle in his body perfectly still until they had passed, their raucous singing echoing along the cobblestoned street in both directions.

When the way was clear again, Elijah moved on, all of his senses alert, but his mind elsewhere. He had first seen Alejandra Vargas at the Southern Spot, of all places, when he had gone there to warn his brother that his raids on werewolf holdings weren't as discreet as Klaus believed them to be. The wolves were starting to retaliate, disrupting the imports and exports Elijah had delegated to Klaus, and at this rate it wouldn't be long before war broke out once again. Elijah had been prepared to bully Klaus back into line, but the sight of the brothel's new fortune-teller had knocked the fight right out of his body.

He could tell at a glance that Alejandra was far too well bred to make a living reading the palms of Klaus's usual clientele. She was tall – nearly as tall as he was – with curling black hair and startling green eyes that seemed to pin him to the door the moment he walked through it. The purring accent Elijah heard when she spoke wouldn't have been out of place in the court of King Fernando VII.

'Please sit,' she told him, an order masquerading as a request.

Elijah suspected that Klaus was in one of the back rooms with two or three of his more buxom employees. Ever since he'd won the brothel back for the fourth time, Klaus seemed dedicated to enjoying his ownership to the fullest. Elijah sat in the chair she indicated, and she settled herself across from him. Women moved in and out of the main room, mingling with customers and occasionally peeling off to more private areas. But Elijah only had eyes for Alejandra, and from the moment she took his hand in hers he would have sworn they were completely alone.

'You have interesting hands,' she informed him, brushing one fingertip along the lines that cut across his palm.

'I might say the same,' he replied. Her fingers were decorated with precious stones set into heavy, intricate rings. Each of them must have cost more than she could make in a year telling fortunes, and he wondered what had prompted her to seek out such work.

'Then perhaps you should tell me *my* future,' she teased, catching his wrist more firmly and holding his palm towards the light of the nearest candle.

'You can't read your own?' Elijah asked, twisting his hand so that he could study hers more closely. Her skin was warm and supple. 'What kind of a gift is that?'

'I'm not so arrogant as to want to know my own future,' Alejandra said, 'so whatever you see you may keep to yourself. But you, señor, have pride to spare. I can see it here' – she touched the base of his thumb, sending thrills up his entire arm – 'and here as well.' Her fingernail rested in a second spot on his palm, and he stared at it, fascinated.

'You may have me confused with my brother,' Elijah murmured. 'I simply prefer to be prepared for whatever might come my way.'

'Your brother?' Alejandra asked, adjusting the angle of his hand again. 'You have more than just the one. Your family is closer-knit than most.'

Elijah chuckled at the understatement. 'We can't seem to escape one another,' he confirmed. Even Kol and Finn, staked by Klaus centuries before, had remained with their siblings. They slept deeply in coffins that the

Originals had carried back and forth across the world. 'Family is forever.'

Alejandra smiled as if he had reminded her of some private joke between them, as if they were old friends who each knew the other's secrets. He wanted it to be true, to know her and be known, and he had to remind himself to be cautious. She was a stranger, however appealing she might be.

'I hope you like them, then,' she told him, her voice brimming with laughter. 'This line here is your life line, and it is . . . *exceptionally* long.'

The words might have been innocent enough: surely it was good for business to assure her customers of long and healthy lives. But there was no doubt in Elijah's mind that she knew exactly what he really was, and that she had known it before he'd walked through the door.

He was thoroughly charmed, but forced himself to proceed cautiously. The last woman Elijah had found so intriguing had been used against him. Lisette was lost to him because he had pursued a life with her too eagerly.

There was a stirring in the darkness in front of him, and Elijah tensed, ready to fight. But it was Alejandra who stepped out into the starlight, her tall body swathed in a hooded black cloak. She had kept up her work at the Southern Spot to avoid raising Klaus's suspicions, and she smelled of smoke, whisky and lust.

Beneath the hood he could just make out her sharp, strong chin, her high forehead, and the midnight curls of her hair. Elijah longed to push the hood back and kiss her right there, but he could hear more than one set of footsteps nearby, and he couldn't risk being caught with her in the open.

He wrapped an arm around her instead, guiding her wordlessly towards the house he had prepared for their rendezvous. The previous occupant had been a politician who leaned a bit too far towards the werewolves' interests for Elijah's taste, so his death had served a variety of purposes all at once. 'Here,' he said, opening the door and then stepping back to let Alejandra enter first.

He caught her in the hallway, spinning her back into his arms before the door had fully closed behind him and kissing her deep, red lips.

Julie Plec skilfully juggles work in film and television as both a producer and a writer. She is the co-creator and executive producer of *The Vampire Diaries* and the creator of *The Vampire Diaries* spin-off, *The Originals*, which tells the story of history's first vampire family.

Plec got her start as a television writer on the ABC Family series *Kyle XY*, which she also produced for its three-year run. She also collaborated with Greg Berlanti and Phil Klemmer on the CW drama *The Tomorrow People*, the story of a small group of people gifted with extraordinary paranormal abilities.

Julie wrote a screenplay adaptation of *The Tiger's Curse*, which has Ineffable Pictures and Lotus Entertainment attached to produce, with Shekhar Kapur directing. She will also produce the feature *@emma* with Darko Entertainment. Past feature production credits include *Scream 2* and *Scream 3*, Greg Berlanti's *Broken Hearts Club*, Wes Craven's *Cursed* and *The Breed*.

NIGHT WORLD

Welcome to the Night World -
a secret world of vampires, werewolves,
witches, shapeshifters, and ancient souls
where humans are prey and relationships
with them forbidden. But we all know,
there's nothing like forbidden fruit ...

bookswithbite.co.uk
Lose yourself in fantastical fiction, join up now

f bookswithbite **🐦** BookswithbiteUK

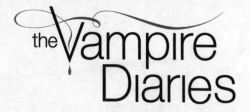
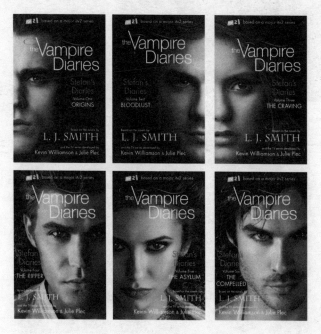

FATHOMLESS

A dark retelling of
The Little Mermaid

Lo was human once. Now, she is almost entirely a creature of the sea - an ocean girl, a mermaid - terms too pretty for the soul-less monster she's becoming.

When a handsome boy named Jude falls into the ocean, Lo and human girl Celia work together to rescue him from the waves. But Lo has an ulterior motive.

To become human again, she must persuade a mortal to love her... then kill him and steal his soul.

978 1 444 91555 6 pbk   978 1 444 91556 3 eBook

www.hodderchildrens.co.uk

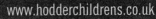